ABOVE AND BEYOND

ABOVE AND BEYOND

By Jim Morris

Copyright © 2004 by Jim Morris

Cover copyright © 2004 by Max Crace
Cover artwork by Max Crace of Max Crace Studio
www.maxcrace.com. All rights reserved

ISBN: 0-9743618-4-4

All rights reserved. Except for use in a review, no portion of this book may be reproduced in any form without written permission from the publisher.

Published by Real War Stories. For more information on our books please visit our web site at:
www.realwarstories.com

DEDICATION

This book is dedicated to my mother, the late Elizabeth Morris. Her example of courage and professionalism was my greatest asset in Special Forces, and in life.

ACKNOWLEDGEMENTS

There are many people to thank for helping me with this book. First, of course, are the U.S. Army Special Forces, which provided the background, and the parameters of the characterizations.

Thanks to Paul Williams for editorial help, as well as the members of the Zoetrope Magazine short story workshop. I dare not list them by name for fear of leaving someone out.

And finally I must thank Dennis Cummings for publishing the E-Book version of Above and Beyond.

The spirit of a warrior is geared only to struggle, and every struggle is a warrior's last battle on earth. Thus the outcome matters very little to him. In his last battle on earth a warrior lets his spirit flow free and clear. And as he wages his battle, knowing that his will is impeccable, a warrior laughs and laughs.

--Carlos Castaneda
Journey to Ixtlan

PROLOGUE

Lauren hated the shoes; she hated the dress. She liked being out of school. It was even kind of cool to meet the President. She wished, though, that if she had to dress up in this humiliating stiff pink garment, that she could at least meet a President who looked less like Rocky the Flying Squirrel. That's who he reminded her of, and she liked Bullwinkle better.

"Lauren, stop it!" said her mother, seated beside her in the back of the government sedan.

"Huh?" She looked up.

Her mother pulled her hand away from where it had been unconsciously picking at a scab on her knee. It was a brown scab about the size of a dime, healing around the edges except where she had picked it. On that side it was bent back, with just a little blood showing.

"Don't pick. Do you want blood running down your leg when you meet the President?"

Lauren said nothing. For all she cared it could run down her leg, soak her socks, fill her shoes, and run all over the carpet. She was missing an important game for this, and the lack of the two or three runs she could be depended on to bring in might keep her team out of the playoffs.

When she had protested her mom told her that the President of the United States couldn't run his schedule to suit hers. What could he have to do that was more important than her championship?

Lauren's grandmother on her dad's side, Rep. Thalia Crane (D. Tenn.) had sent this car to pick them up at the airport yesterday when they flew in from Indiana, Pennsylvania--where her mother taught at the confusingly named Indiana University of Pennsylvania, and Lauren went to Sixth Grade and played shortstop. She had worn jeans and sneaks on the plane, gotten unlimited Cokes and extra peanuts, and watched the cloud banks below for the first time.

Now they were back in the same car, with her grandmother, whom she knew mostly from telephone conversations and one Christmas when she was six, twisting in the front seat so she could talk to Lauren's mother.

"What I want to know," she said, "is how this could happen now, ten years after…the incident. I certainly haven't pushed it."

"McLeod," said Lauren's mother, Juliana. "He's been on the phone to the Pentagon once or twice a month for years. He made the initial recommendation, and he's stayed on it all this time."

Her grandmother frowned. "For God's sake, why?"

"Neil's not the only one. He's pushing on a couple of other medals, and to get several disabilities increased."

"How nice," Thalia replied coldly.

Lauren's mother returned the frown. "McLeod's done a lot," she said. "He keeps in touch with his men, or their families. He even helped with the research on my dissertation. He loved Neil."

Her grandmother started to speak, but said nothing. She turned and readjusted herself in her seat, silent for the rest of the drive.

Her mother was also silent, lost in thought. Lauren was suffused in the emotions of these thoughts. All of a sudden it had gotten heavy in the car. She inspected her mother's face and saw nobility and tragedy, love and deep suffering, traits for which she had no words, but felt all the same. She quit picking at her leg and looked at the broad streets of Washington, and the buildings that looked like they ought to be in Rome, only they weren't crumbling yet.

A street sign said Pennsylvania Avenue, and then they pulled up at an ornate entrance. A guard came out of a little shack by the gate. Their driver's window hummed down, and he muttered, "Thompson. Medal of Honor presentation."

The gate buzzed open and they drove inside.

When they parked they were met by a guy in uniform, sort of like a modern version of those old cavalry uniforms that you see on TV, same colors, same kind of shoulderboards. He said he was Major Somebody-or-other, and led them into the building, into a room where they could sit and wait. The room looked like a museum. She sat on a couch and her mother and grandmother sat on chairs facing sort of three-quarters front at opposite ends of the couch, actually more of a love seat. Lauren looked around at her surroundings. The furniture was old style, but bright and shiny. When you saw it on TV the men wore knee breeches and the women long gowns. And everybody wore powdered wigs. "Fanceeee!" she said.

"Lauren!" her mother snapped. It was time to shut up. She kicked her foot a little bit, like two inches. Actually this arrangement of furniture looked like something she'd seen on the news, with the Flying Squirrel talking to the President of Botswana or Upper Volta or someplace. He had grinned like Rocky through the whole thing.

The major was still hovering. "A Colonel Schmidt will escort you in to see the President shortly," he said. "Would you care for coffee while you wait. Perhaps a coke or some cookies and milk for the young lady?"

Lauren lowered her voice into her Walter Brennen imitation. "Gimme a shot o' red eye," she growled.

Lauren's mother shot her an evil glance.

The major grinned, contorted his face into a broad scowl, and growled, "Ain't got no red eye. How about a root beer?"

"That would be fine, thank you," Lauren said in her most ladylike voice, which was also an imitation.

The major disappeared and soon a black man in a white coat brought a coffee service and china cups with the presidential seal embossed on them, and a frosted mug of root beer, also with the presidential seal. Before the coffee was poured and properly creamed and sugared Lauren had gulped half her root beer.

"Moustache," he mother said.

"Mmmmm," Lauren replied, and licked her upper lip, then wiped it with a napkin.

They were left alone in silence. After awhile her mother asked her grandmother a question about politics, but Lauren wasn't interested. She was lost in unfamiliar thoughts. Her mother had told her that they were to be presented with a medal that her father had died earning a long time ago when she was just a baby. She had seen pictures of her father, a coldly handsome man in glasses, and in a camouflage suit with a dinky little hat. There had been another guy in the picture, who looked like a crazy redneck, and four little brown men.

She had spent a lot of time when she was five or six, going over old photo albums; her mom in high school, her mom when she was a hippie in New York, her mom in Vietnam where she had met her dad, wedding pictures; her mom in that '60's get-up, her dad in a uniform with a lot of medals, and boots, her grandmother and the Congressman, whom she had married, and who had died, and the little colonel on the walker.

She'd gone through her dad's old high school yearbooks too, when he'd been a cadet at the Tennessee Military Institute, where, according to the yearbook, his nickname had been "Slick."

But she always came back to the Vietnam photo, black and white, six guys in front of a helicopter. You could barely see their faces, they were so caked with crud, and they weren't smiling. They weren't frowning either; they just wore these quiet forceful expressions. On the back, in her dad's writing, it said, "SSG Royce "Shoogie" Swift, KIA 23 Jan 1968, Ksor Drot, KIA 13 Jan 1968, Y Buhn, KIA 23 Jan 1968, Nay Thai, KIA 23 Jan 1968. Underneath that in her mom's writing it said, in red ink, "Captain Neil Thompson, KIA Sept. 21, 1970."

The inscription hadn't identified which was who, so one of the little brown guys might still be alive, but she didn't know which one.

She wondered what her father had been like, but all her mother had said was, "He was terribly determined." She hadn't acted like she wanted to talk about it, so Lauren dropped it.

And now, ten years later, he was getting the Medal of Honor. Why? What good would it do him? He would never know. Maybe it was for the family; but her mom and grandmother didn't want it. Yet that little colonel had pushed it through, just like her mom said. And he *knew* her mom and grandmother would have been happier if he'd just let it die. And then she knew. He had done it for her. Or rather he had done it because he knew that her dad would want her to know who he was, and what he had done. Her mom would get the medal, but it was really hers. It wasn't like having a real dad, but it was more than a black and white photograph.

An older guy in a bellhop suit--she wasn't sure, but he was maybe like a Marine colonel--came in and said, "Mrs. Crane, Mrs. Thompson, Miss Thompson, if you will come with me."

They got up and followed him into another, smaller room, where they were met by an old guy in a civilian suit. But it wasn't the Squirrel. A secretary set behind a desk, frowning over her glasses. She looked kind of like Lauren's grandmother.

The guy introduced himself, but Lauren didn't catch the name. He said, "In a moment we'll go into the Oval Office. You'll meet the President, and Colonel Schmidt will read the citation. The President will present the award. Are there any questions?"

There weren't.

They followed him down the hall and through a door into a fancy office with curved walls, and a window with something wrong with the glass. Maybe it was thicker or something. Whatever it was it didn't look right.

There was a little, smiling old guy standing there. She recognized him as Rocky immediately, but he looked like a different person than he had on TV, more intelligent, more real, and not squirrelly at all. She decided that anybody would look stupid with about three thousand photographers following him around, waiting to see him slip.

He came forward and took her grandmother's hand. "Thalia, it's been too long."

"Good to see you, Mr. President."

He shook her mother's hand also. "Dr. Kos, it's an honor to meet you. This isn't a happy occasion, but it is a proud one."

Lauren half expected her mom to tell him to jam it, but all she said was, "Thank you Mr. President." Lauren was really surprised that the Prez knew her mom was a Ph.D., and that she didn't use her Dad's name. The soldier hadn't known that, and neither had the old guy in civilian clothes. She decided to quit thinking of him as a Flying Squirrel.

The old guy in civilian clothes stood off to the side, and the two soldiers, the colonel and the major, stood next to each other. A guy in a suit softshoed around them, his camera whirring and clicking.

The colonel held some paper, and the major held a flat box. The President nodded and the colonel began to read aloud. Lauren didn't catch it all, because the words sounded stiff and strange. Then she realized it was a badly written description of what the medal was for, what her father had done. She listened carefully.

The colonel intoned, "On 21 September, 1970, Captain Neil S. Thompson, OF407187, while leading a raid on an enemy installation in a classified area, directed his own helicopter to land in order to lead a rescue force to a subordinate unit of his command which had come under intense hostile fire...complete disregard for his own safety...continued to fight while seriously wounded...successfully supervised evacuation of his command..."

Even though Lauren was astonished at the horribleness of the prose--at eleven she could write better than that--she read between the lines to see what a fiasco the thing had been. She also caught the bloody awful magnificence of it. Whatever her father had done, and once her mom had said it was futile and stupid, it was also epic and tragically beautiful. She did not use those words, but the feelings came through strongly. It was real; it wasn't a movie and it wasn't bullshit. It seemed to her the most real thing she had ever encountered.

"...called close air support to within fifty meters of his own exposed position...carried SFC Ackerman on his back, while seriously wounded himself, to the LZ, killing six enemy en route. Captain Thompson's actions are above and beyond the call of duty, and in the finest traditions of the military service. Signed, R.L. Fouquet, the Adjutant General, U.S. Army."

The major stepped forward and handed the President the flat box, which, on closer inspection, contained the medal in a frame.

Lauren had heard of the medal before, of course, but never seen one. She felt shy around it. She knew it was an object of great power. And she knew it was for her.

"Dr. Kos, it gives me great pride to present this medal to you, and to the family."

"Thank you, Mr. President," her mother said. She took the framed medal from him.

Lauren longed to touch it. She plucked her mother's sleeve. "May I see it please," she said.

They looked at her, startled, but when she saw the intensity of Lauren's gaze her mother handed it to her immediately.

She held it in her hand and looked raptly at the blue silk ribbon, the crest of white stars on a blue field, the eagle over the bar with the word "VALOR" on it, and the wreathed five-pointed gold star with the center point down. It was as though a spirit had entered her body.

"Thank you," she said, and handed the framed medal back to her mother.

ABOVE AND BEYOND

Chapter One

In the five days they had been out none had spoken; they communicated only by gesture. Ahead of him Neil glimpsed a small wizened man named Nay Thai, his angular camouflaged shoulders hunched under a light pack. The man ahead of Nay Thai was visible only as a flicker of brush against the jungle. They moved in almost perfect silence, the only sound an occasional scrape of brush against a pack.

Nay Thai stopped. Neil stopped too, looking slowly around through the smudged lenses of his glasses. The jungle enclosed them; thick brown trunks of ancient hardwood trees four to six feet thick rose into the dripping canopy above, closing off all direct light. The color of this everdripping jungle blended perfectly with the green, brown, and black stripes of his tigersuit, as it did with the green camouflage greasepaint smeared and caked on his hands and face, and the filthy green tape on the outer edges of his glasses.

It was quiet. Because an abrupt move might reveal his position Neil took a slow look at his watch. It was three-thirty. Another half-hour and they would start looking for a place to crawl in for the night.

But at noon chow the loose smile on Shoogie's face, the bright eyes behind his green-crud-caked face, had told Neil he had a plan.

Somewhere back there Shoogie had gotten hooked on adrenaline. A patrol did not please him unless he made contact, and he had formed the habit of thinking of his little six-man reconnaissance team as a raiding party. Still, Shoogie had been with the Project since Day One, while dozens of his more cautious colleagues had gone home maimed or in bags. To Neil he seemed to exist on a plane of special grace reserved for those who simply do not give a fuck.

Their situation was scary to start with; six men, two of them Americans, the rest Montagnards, snooping around in the middle of a North Vietnamese Army troop concentration. Worse, their primary mission was to capture a prisoner. Prisoners offer the best kind of intelligence, but they are difficult and dangerous to get. Other teams tried when they could, but Shoogie took the POW snatch as a holy calling.

The rest of the guys in the Project thought Shoogie was useful, and very good at his job, but, truth be known, not wrapped too tight. He was their living legend, and welcome to it.

By turns Neil felt as though he was about to go to sleep, and like someone had placed a quick-frozen lead ball in his stomach. His throat went dry and he gulped air in great compulsive swallows. He'd be all right once it started, but right now, Jesus, he was scared.

The brush ahead flickered and Nay Thai started forward. He lifted a limb and swung it over his head, not letting go until Neil grabbed it. In this way they moved forward quietly and almost invisibly. But to Neil, even though he knew better, they looked and sounded like the circus come to town.

Moving like this all day they had covered about two hundred meters.

Twenty minutes later they stopped again. There was a rustle ahead and Nay Thai locked eyes with Neil, then jerked his head toward the front. Shoogie wanted to see him. He crouched low over his CAR-15, the short-barreled, collapsible stock version of the M-16, and moved forward.

Shoogie was waiting; squatting flatfooted, Montagnard fashion, as Neil came through the wet brush. He rose, the faintest suggestion of a smile on his camouflaged face.

Shoogie was average height, skinny but strong. His lips were thin. He was twenty-four years old and there were no backs to his eyes.

He led Neil forward to a small trail about two feet wide, winding through the thick growth. Y Buhn, the point man, sat invisibly beside the trail. He looked up and winked. Shoogie pointed down at the trail. There were bicycle tracks. He made a grabbing motion with his hands.

Neil nodded and went back to get his two tribesmen. He brought Nay Thai and Frenchy up, pointed out the bicycle tracks and made the same snatching motions Shoogie had made. They nodded. Adrenaline roared in his veins and he felt infinitely powerful. He put Nay Thai and Frenchy in beside the trail ten meters apart and got between them, kneeling on the jungle floor. Shoogie put Y Buhn and Ksor Drot on the other side of the trail and got down also. They remained motionless. After awhile Neil could see them only by remembering where they were.

He anticipated a long wait and threw his mind into neutral. His CAR-15 had a fresh mag and was set on full auto, and directly across the trail Shoogie had a morphine syrette ready.

Fifteen or twenty minutes went by and he heard some rustling down the trail to the right. A few seconds later an NVA soldier appeared, peddling stolidly. His floppy blue hat hung over his eyes, and his tire sandals flapped on the pedals. He looked totally complacent, with his AK-47 slung across his shoulders where he'd never get it in time. He wore a blank, preoccupied look, like he was thinking of home. Go on, motherfucker, Neil thought, think of home. This is home to us; we are the *yang* of the forest.

The bicycle drew abreast and Neil jammed the barrel of his CAR-15 between the spokes of the front wheel. He rose, pushing. The bicycle jerked to a stop and tumbled; the rider's eyes went wide as he flailed his arms and legs, trying to regain his balance.

He started to yell. Shoogie rose, clamped a hand across his mouth, and threw his left hand across his chest, jamming the needle into his right shoulder.

Y Buhn sprayed an entire twenty-round magazine down the trail and Neil wheeled at the sound, just in time to see another startled Gook on a bicycle jerk backwards as his face broke apart in chunks. Behind him two more were trying to fall off their bicycles and get their weapons free, all at the same time.

Y Buhn ran through the middle of the team. Nay Thai sprang up and sprayed out his entire magazine. He ran also. "LZ X-ray!" Shoogie shrieked the designation of their helicopter landing zone, and rally point, and took off after him, their prisoner in a fireman's carry across his shoulders. Ksor Drot fired up a magazine and took off, and Frenchy followed. They had spent days practicing this drill.

As Frenchy moved out Neil snatched a frag grenade off his belt and pulled the pin. He rocketarmed it directly into the bloody mass of squirming Cong, then ran, fumbling at his belt for a teargas grenade. He pulled the pin and dropped it, holding on to a nylon cord wrapped around the grenade. The cord unwound as he ran through the slapping, grabbing, sticking jungle, leaving a cloud of gas clinging to leaves in his wake.

Rapid movement was impossible in the jungle and soon he jammed up against Ksor Drot. The gas ran out and he flipped the empty grenade off into the bushes. They moved single file down one long hill and across a crashing, rockfilled stream. Shoogie stopped them for a moment at the top of the next hill and muttered into the radio, "Gray

Ghost Six, this is Crazy Horse One-Zero. Lemonade. I say again, Lemonade. Out!" They had perhaps forty-five minutes to get to the landing zone.

Neil's adrenaline high was over, replaced by barely suppressed panic. His mind functioned very fast, independent of his fear, and he was slick with sweat. He knew he would move swiftly and make no mistakes. But the other guys might not make any mistakes either.

They ran on and on, wet branches slapping and clawing at them, their prisoner long since nodded out.

During a pause they chopped down a small tree and tied a poncho to it to make a one-pole litter. Neil got out his map and compass. Half a kilometer to go to the LZ. About twenty minutes in this stuff.

A signal shot sounded behind them and Neil started. Nothing particularly unusual about that. Shoogie said the time to get worried was when the signal shots started coming from the front.

The closer they got to the LZ the slower they seemed to be moving, until finally each moment seemed to take forever. Neil shut off his time sense, so there was no past and no future, only the perpetual wetslapping, up-climbing, down-sliding present.

Moving without time sense it was both an eternity and an instant until they came to the small clearing in the trees that was their LZ. It was dusk, late dusk.

They formed a small hasty perimeter, with Shoogie and their prize in the center. Neil lay facing the way they had come, CAR-15 ready to fire, face pressed in the damp, gamy earth. He loved that smell and the drip of this jungle; he loved the loneliness and the quiet. But right now, with the prisoner snatched and Charles on their trail, his soul was clawing its way through his body to get out of there.

Shoogie whispered into the mouthpiece of the radio, "We are at X-ray. Clyde is right behind. Be ready to use the hook. Out."

There was another signal shot from their backtrail. Neil figured they were about fifteen minutes behind and hoped the choppers would be here before that. He lifted the black leather lid that snapped over the face of his watch. An hour and a half later he did it again. Three minutes had passed.

Another hour and a half and another signal shot later he heard the whop-whop of approaching helicopters.

Neil got up and took the small signaling strobe out of its pouch on his harness. He pointed it at the sound of the approaching choppers. It blinked a blinding light. Shoogie talked them in on the radio. The ragged clatter and downdraft of helicopters passed over the clearing fifty feet above.

Shoogie nodded.

Three gunships circled in tight while the slick recovery ship, a passenger ship with no rocket pods, jockeyed over the hole in the trees.

Their little clearing became a wind tunnel as the recovery ship eased down between the towering trees rising over a hundred feet on all sides. The LZ lay in a little mountain valley, steep hills rising around them. The chopper maneuvered its way in between the trees with what seemed only inches of clearance on either side of the tail and main rotor. Shoogie talked constantly on the radio and Neil could see Stan "the Man" McAnn, their Sergeant Major, in the door, giving the pilot hand and arm signals. Seeming to move only inches at a time the chopper eased into the hole until it loomed over them, etched black against the fading sky. In the terrific downdraft grass and bits of dirt battered Neil's face.

When the chopper was thirty feet up it stopped, hovering, and the cable, with its horsecollar seat, descended.

Frenchy and Ksor Drot, who had been carrying the still unconscious Charlie, took him out of the litter and tied him into the swaying cable rig. Shoog gave the thumbs up and he was winched into the chopper.

It took what felt like an endless time for the crew to get the Cong out of the sling. Then the chopper started inching its way in again. The gunships still orbited, throwing bursts of machinegun fire into the surrounding hillsides.

Finally the chopper dropped to about fifteen feet off the ground and a wide ladder, three steel cables with six-foot long aluminum pipe rungs, was rolled out of each door. The recon team went for the rungs and started climbing, Neil and Shoog last.

Neil's pack dragged him down and his feet swung up as he started up the ladder. He didn't get much push from his feet it was mostly a hand-over-hand pull into the chopper.

When he got his arms on the corrugated aluminum floor of the Huey Nay Thai and Frenchy grabbed his shoulders and pulled him in, just as a burst of AK-47 fire chopped away at the brush underneath. The door gunners opened up and slowly, majestically, the chopper lifted out of the hole.

Chapter Two

The chopper landed in the dark and two men from the Intelligence Section picked up the prisoner. Intelligence gave Neil and Shoogie two hours before debriefing.

They released the Montagnards, washed their hands and went to the empty mess hall. The Project was a priority operation with a huge budget. In the field its men were highly disciplined and effective, but in garrison they did exactly as they goddam pleased, with absolute license, and money no object. There was a massive bureaucracy in Saigon, existing solely to evaluate the intelligence produced by Theta and her sister projects. The young sergeants who produced that intelligence were stars.

After reading the menu Neil and Shoogie gave their order to a Vietnamese waitress in a white uniform. Neil ordered a medium pepperoni pizza washed down with a San Miguel beer and Shoogie had three cheeseburgers and a mountain of fries with three or four Kirins. Neil ate half-reclining in his chair; relaxing obscure muscles he hadn't known were tense. Bearded and gamy, they wore wary grins; they had gotten away with it again.

After supper they walked through a doorway of colored plastic strips that separated the mess hall from the bar and had a couple more beers; then properly lubricated, they walked to the Tactical Operations Center, a bunker under the headquarters, heads thrown back, arms and legs swinging loosely, as though a greater weight than their packs had been lifted from them.

It was a long complicated debriefing, with many congratulations and a couple of belts courtesy of Colonel McLeod. By the time they were through the sun was up.

* * *

Neil was shaken violently, and awakened looking into the kindly grizzled face of Sergeant Major McAnn. "Huh? Whattaya want?" Neil growled, pulling the sheet back up over his face. "Sleep, sleep, for Chrissake!"

McAnn shook him again. "Get up, Thompson! It's thirteen-thirty. The Old Man wants you at the TOC at fourteen hundred. He says it's a VIP briefing, and he wants you shining like a diamond up a goat's ass."

Neil sat up naked on the edge of the foam mattress. He was a little hung over, but mostly he just wanted to sleep for another day or two. "Oh God!" he said. "Oh mother fucker." He put his head in his hands.

"You gonna make it?" the Sergeant Major asked.

"Yeah!" Neil replied, peering bleakly through heavily lidded eyes. "Once I get my feet on the floor I'm okay." He got up and turned on his portable record player, which started in the middle of the Beatles' *Got to Get You Into My Life*. The jangling of all those overdubbed guitars drove him into grudging consciousness. He looked around, blinking at the shambles of his room the two stacks of paperback books climbing toward the ceiling from his desk, the filthy tiger suit flung in the corner for the maid.

His books were adventure tales, books on guerrilla warfare, and revolutionary warfare, books on Vietnam and Indochina, some science fiction, and a copy of the *Tao Te Ching* that McLeod had given him when Neil hit him up about a direct commission. Neil hadn't been able to get into it.

Beside the books lay a letter from his mother, received just before the patrol. He eyed it fearfully. He hadn't read it last night because he'd been too tired. And he wouldn't get to read it now because he had to head for the TOC. He'd have to read it later today. It would wait. He could do without the guilt for another few hours.

He remembered their final dreadful meeting before leaving for Vietnam, and the interview with his commanding officer which had preceded it.

* * *

Neil knocked on the door. A gravelly voice snarled, "Come in!" Neil opened and entered, advanced to two paces from his new C.O.'s desk, slammed his right heel into place, and saluted. "Sergeant Thompson reports as ordered, sir."

The captain, a skinny, jug-eared geek with moist eyes and a sneering mouth, lazily returned his salute and said, "At ease, Sergeant." He stared at Neil's glasses with open hostility.

Neil assumed a relaxed parade rest posture, hands loosely draped behind his back. He kept his eyes to the front.

The captain examined his records for a long time, long enough to establish that he had the power and could be as rude as he pleased.

Neil almost smiled. In the almost three years preceding his dismissal from West Point he had encountered many officers who were dangerously egocentric, or who placed career over country, but he had encountered few who were crude or stupid.

"Good scores, know how to type. I'd say we got just the job for you, soldier."

"Sir?"

"Personnel clerk, Center Headquarters."

Neil's spirits fell, then rose again. He wouldn't be a personnel clerk long. "Sir," he said, "I am a school-trained Special Forces demolitionist, crosstrained in weapons and commo, and with a modicum of French. I would like to be of service to my country, and I feel I can best do that in Vietnam. I would like to volunteer."

The captain looked at him under an arched eyebrow. "Well," he said, "I can understand that. Everybody on this hill would like to go to Vietnam. Or go back. But we got the rest of the army to run. I been back from the Nam for six months, and in six or eight months I'll be gone again. But my prediction for you, *Sergeant* Thompson, is that you'll be here behind a typewriter for the three years you owe Sam."

Neil felt a rising chill in his gut. Crude and stupid or not, this fool knew something he didn't. He wouldn't make such a threat idly. In the normal course of events Neil would expect to be in Vietnam in a year at the latest. For his purposes he needed to be there a lot sooner than that. He wanted a commission before his class graduated from West Point. The only way life in the army would be bearable would be if he outranked them, and was more highly decorated.

"Sir," he said, "I can see why you would want a man with my superb intellect and typing skills in your personnel section, but three years? Why do you say that? We need guys in Vietnam."

The captain gave him a quizzical look. "You jivin' me, Sergeant?" You know what this "P" here on your record jacket means?"

Neil shook his head. "No sir, I don't" There were so many arcane symbols on a set of military orders that he had never given the matter any thought.

The captain nodded sagely, condescending, pleased to be one up on this ex-West Point puke. "Well, sergeant, it stands for 'political influence', and it means your lily-white ass has about as much chance of getting shot at as mine does of avoiding it."

"Sir," said Neil, "my mother is an administrative aide to a congressman, but I hardly think that constitutes political influence."

The captain riveted Neil with what was intended to be a piercing glare, but came off as more of an angry glower. "Well, in your case it does, Sonnyboy. You're going to be a rear echelon motherfucker, the most rear echelon motherfucker in the whole U.S. Army. You're going to be a personnel clerk at Fort Bragg, North Carolina." He handed Neil his records. "Get your barracks area squared away and report to the Personnel Sergeant Major."

* * *

Neil was stuck at Bragg for three weeks before he could get a three day pass to go to Washington about this "political influence" business. He called his mom and made a date for dinner.

Aside from his G.I. haircut Neil looked every bit the young congressional aide, although leaner and tougher. As the maitre d' led them to their table Neil spotted older men here and there throughout the restaurant wearing the same white sidewall crewcut, field grade officers stationed at the Pentagon. Neil pitied them; they looked so sad, trapped in offices under florescent lights for ten-twelve-sixteen hour days, six and seven days a week, losing their hard-won physical fitness at an age when it was much more difficult to regain.

The rest of the diners were soft, complacent civilians.

Neil followed his mother, who followed the maitre d', who prissed along in a faultlessly tailored dinner jacket, carrying himself as a prince among peasants. Neil's mother wore a beautifully tailored lime suit that set off her flame-colored curls, and she carried her tiny body with the authority of a queen.

Neil marched behind. He tried to saunter and be cool, but somewhere in his head a little corporal went *hawn-tup-thrip-fawp* and he wished the goddam maitre d' would pick up the step.

He felt suddenly awkward in his college clothes that his mother had picked so carefully for him long years before, for his one wretched semester at Vanderbilt. Now the waist on the pants was loose, but he had to wear his jacket unbuttoned because it was tight in the chest and shoulders.

Hobart, the only one in the procession with any claim to real power, trudged in the rear, in a jacket and tie similar to Neil's, since his mother had chosen them also, blinking owlishly at the world through hornrimmed glasses that he didn't really need. He thought they made him look intelligent.

They reached their table and the maitre d' seated Thalia. Then the men sat down and a waiter hustled over and gave them their menus.

Neil opened his quickly, before the awkward conversation could start again. As Hobart ordered a bottle of wine to begin, a cabernet, Neil and his mother carefully examined their menus. Neil finally chose steak *au poivre*, since it was the closest thing to a cheeseburger on the menu, and, that business taken care of, squirmed to find a comfortable position on the dinky French chair. He wondered how Hobart did it. He was two inches shorter than Neil, and twenty pounds heavier, but he seemed to flow into the chair like Louis XIV. Just looking at him you'd never know he'd sold used cars in Knoxville.

Neil's mother sat perfectly in her chair; in fact her back did not touch the back of the chair. It seemed to Neil that these places had been made for people like his mother. He could not imagine a man voluntarily entering one.

"Well, young man," said Hobart, "how are you enjoying Fort Bragg?"

Neil shrugged. "I'm working as a personnel clerk," he replied. "So I don't see much of the post. I get out for a jump now and then, and that's about it."

His mother winced slightly at the word "jump", and said primly, "And what are your plans for after the service?"

He could feel the resentful glare on his face. Since puberty he had regarded his mother's slightest interest in his welfare as unwarranted interference. He knew he was overreacting, but in the absence of a father her influence on him had been so overwhelming he had to fight to break away from it. "I have no plans for after the army," he said. "I plan to get my commission and make the military my career, just as I always have."

Hobart arched an eyebrow with a look that was both quizzical and exasperated. But his mother looked as though she had been shot. "Don't you think," Hobart said, in the thoughtful, measured drawl that had made him one of the most effective orators in the House, "that your leaving West Point is going to louse that up?"

Neil colored. It was hard for him to think of the incident, much less speak of it.

The wish to follow his father and grandfather through West Point and into the army had consumed his every waking thought since early childhood, as had the doubt that he was good enough to do so.

Neil had never known his father. So he created an imaginary father from the known facts of his father's life; that he was a West Pointer who had been a platoon leader in the 82d Airborne Division during the Normandy Invasion, and had died when his planeload of jumpers was parachuted at night into the English Channel by a green and terrified aircrew. The rest he filled in with the myth of Sir Galahad.

He was determined to live up to that myth.

"Yes," he said, "but it won't kill me if I can get to Vietnam and cover myself with glory. West Point was bad, but the thing that's going to ruin me is that "P" on my records jacket."

Hobart looked puzzled for a second, then he understood. The terminology eluded him, but he grasped Neil's meaning quickly enough.

"It stands for 'political influence'," Neil all but snarled, "and if I don't get it taken off, I'm dead."

Hobart smiled blandly. "I did mention to a friend over at the Pentagon that if you went to Vietnam it would upset your mother, and the efficiency of my office would suffer."

Neil shook his head. "No good," he said. "My problem at West Point was a conflict between my personal code and the Academy's. But for a soldier to evade combat in wartime is wrong by anybody's standards."

Again, Hobart smiled his oily smile. "You aren't evading it. Your administrative talents are being used and you have nothing to say about the assignment. You even volunteered to go."

"Right," Neil nodded. "But my C.O. thinks that's just camouflage. It's caused me some trouble."

"What kind of trouble?" his mother demanded, determined to defend him against hurt of any kind.

"Nothing I can't handle, Neil said. "That's not the point. I want that "P" off my records jacket, and I *will* go to Vietnam."

Hobart fixed Neil with the harsh glare of a man used to power. "You'd better forget that one, m'boy," he said. "You've played soldier long enough." He swung a quick glance at Neil's mother, as though seeking support. Neil looked at her too, and her eyes were icy.

To her credit, even though she had not helped, she had not thrown obstacles in his path until now. But he could see that she had lost a husband in one war, and was determined not to lose a son in another. He, for his part, was equally determined to lead his own life as he saw fit, just as she had. That was the single most important lesson he had learned from her.

Sometimes in the midst of the conflict between them he forgot how much he loved her, how much he admired what she had accomplished, and what an example of courage and determination she had been to him. Sometimes too he could schmooze her back to memories of times when she was a girl, and a giggle would break through her businesslike façade. At those times Neil would fall in love with her all over again, with the qualities she had sacrificed to raise him, and to achieve her goals.

Hobart was in the middle. But he was the guy with the power, and he was in Thalia's pocket.

"Look," Neil said, "this is terribly unfair. Untrained kids are dying over there, and I'm a good soldier. You gotta let me go."

"Young man," said Hobart, "I don't gotta do nothin'. I pulled in a lot of favors getting you out of Vietnam. I'm not going to pull in any more getting you into it. It's stupid for you to be in this thing anyway. You know how many congressmen have sons in Vietnam? Zero, that's how many. Anybody with half a brain can beat the draft, and you're trying to sign up."

Neil was truly shocked at the statistic he had just heard. "Well, sir," he replied, "what that says to me is that this country's run by people who think they're too good to fight for it."

Neil's eyes blazed as he dismissed Hobart with contempt. He held his tongue, but he wanted to say that he would get to Vietnam with or without Hobart, around him, over him, or through him. You're playing on my turf now, buddy, he thought. I know ways to get by in the army that you will never know or imagine.

It was at that point that the soup arrived.

* * *

Monday morning he spun into his office chair and started typing a set of orders with over a hundred names on it, a levy for Vietnam. Only he deleted Thomas, Robert A. and inserted Thompson, Neil S. and his own service number. No one would notice until he was gone. And when they did, what were they going to do, send him to Vietnam?

But his mother's letters on the subject were agonizing.

* * *

His eyes refocused on the objects in his room. His CAR-15, cleaned and oiled before he went to bed, hung by the sling from a nail on the wall. Stacked under it was a pile of loaded magazines and three or four grenades. Two or three other grenades lay on his desk among the paperbacks, some upright, and some on their sides. He'd tried to use them for bookends but they were too light.

His patrol harness hung beside the CAR-15, mud-caked and held together by filthy green tape, hung with a hundred and fifty rounds of ammunition, two smoke grenades, two frag grenades (he'd have to get a new tear gas grenade and a couple of frags), a strobe light, a signal mirror, a compass, two pressure bandages, a box of morphine syrettes, and a Randall #14 survival knife.

His pack lay under the harness, and beside that lay his bright orange signal panels and all the stuff he'd carefully wrapped in plastic bags. The sky shone blue through little square windows, small to keep out blowing dust in the dry season, and the woven rattan outside walls of his room ballooned, quivering slightly in the breeze. His big poster of W.C. Fields in a top hat squinted over a poker hand.

He wrapped a towel around his waist, picked up his toilet kit and headed through the door.

The latrine was two doors down the hall. For Vietnam it was a fine latrine, with porcelain bowls and stools, but short Vietnamese workman had put the basins and mirrors six inches too low. He spread his legs wide and hung his head to get in front of the mirror, rubbing his beard.

He heard a piercing feminine giggle and the towel disappeared from his waist. He looked around to see a tiny Vietnamese woman in a leopard-print mini and tight tank top waving his towel teasingly. Although only four-foot-eight, and with one gold front tooth, she was a lush little wench. But he was in no mood, and had no time.

"Ohhhh, beaucoup!" she said, and giggled again, behind her free hand.

"I'll give you beaucoup," he grinned, and grabbed the towel, flipping it at her behind as she scampered from the latrine.

"We oughtta run these whores off," he muttered without conviction.

Chapter Three

It was almost 1400 by the time Neil got into a clean uniform and spitshined boots. He cocked his beret over his right ear and stepped off across the courtyard, trying to keep the dust off his good boots. The flag in front of the headquarters hung limply in the midday heat.

Colonel McLeod, his operations officer, and the sergeant major waited out front of the headquarters, beside three jeeps, with GI drivers. McLeod leaned on a jeep hood, a Vietnamese Ruby Queen cigarette between the first joint of the first and second fingers of his right hand. He was below medium height, had a little pot belly, powder blue eyes and a wispy mustache. He had seen too much and he drank too much. But he had enough style to be a topic of conversation in officers and NCO clubs worldwide. He also had the balls to set his helicopter down in the middle of a firefight to haul Neil and Shoogie out. For Shoogie he'd done it more than once.

Neil saluted the little clump of people leaning against the jeeps. "Mornin' sir," he said.

"Morning, Mr. Thompson," McLeod nodded, smiling slightly. It was a joke between them. Cadets are addressed as "Mister" and when McLeod so addressed Neil it told him that as far as McLeod was concerned he was still training to be an officer.

The sergeant major scowled. "You almost didn't make it."

"I always make it," Neil grinned.

"You always almost don't make it. Where's Swift?"

Neil shrugged. "Who's the VIP?" he asked. But what he wanted to know was, why was he, almost the junior man in recon, here to greet him?

The little colonel took a drag, put out his cigarette and cocked an eyebrow. "It's our old chum from West Point, Shaky Jake Frenier. Only it's General Frenier now. The Project is doing his recons for the duration of Operation Whitewall. He's our new daddy."

Frenier! He felt the uniform collar tight around his neck, his high and tight haircut when he and Colonel Frenier had their little chat, Neil stood at a rigid *achtung* in front of the colonel's desk. You couldn't say the colonel hadn't been fair. Neil could have been facing an honor court, for not turning his roommate in for cheating. And, as the colonel had tactlessly pointed out, there was the matter of his math grades. Mister Thompson, N.S., might have the stuff to make an officer, but he would never be a civil engineer, and therefore never a West Point graduate. So really, he had a free choice, resign or be thrown out.

Neil frowned resentfully. "Putting Frenier in charge of a special operation, that's a tree surgeon runnin' a heart transplant."

Sergeant Major McAnn snickered, dipped his head, cupped his hands around the end of a filtertip cigarette, and fired it with a zippo lighter. He took a deep overhand drag and expelled the smoke through his nostrils. "This shit do get old," he muttered.

"How's that?" McLeod inquired, without looking up.

The sergeant major contemplated the helipad through slitted eyes. “We got the casualty rate down to fifty percent a year…"

"Fifty-three," McLeod amended.

The sergeant major nodded. "Fifty-three. But that's only because Group lets us run our own ops. This fuckin' leg general's gonna get us all killed."

McLeod sighed and said, "No, Stan, not all of us. He'll come in here snortin' and rarin' and try to make a lot of changes. He's a straight-line thinker, but he's not stupid. What he'll probably do, unless I can convince him otherwise, is get one or two of my teams wiped out for no reason, and then he'll let us go back to doing it our way.

"I'll have to write some letters to mothers, and we'll go to a Montagnard funeral or two and get three-day hangovers."

A chill shot through Neil as he realized whose mother was the leading contender for one of those letters. "I'd think I'd be the last person you'd want him to see," he said to McLeod.

The colonel grinned wanly. "He specifically wants to meet the legendary Sergeant Swift and his assistant patrol leader. Actually you're the second to last person I'd want him to see. Shoogie is last."

McLeod glanced at his watch. "The man sets down in six minutes," he said.

In the distance they heard helicopters. Then they appeared on the horizon, a formation of three slick passenger ships in trail, flanked by two gunships. Even in the sky it looked like an entourage. As they passed over the chopper pad the gunships broke off and set up an orbit over the jungle surrounding the Project Theta camp.

McLeod carefully fieldstripped his cigarette and scattered the tobacco, then looked up irritably. "Sergeant Major, tell those people that any troops they see moving out there belong to me. I want no casualties from friendly fire."

The sergeant major muttered into a radio on the back of McLeod's jeep.

Colonel McLeod stood up and watched the three slicks wheel majestically over the compound. He sighed, then snapped, "Let's go."

They got in the jeeps and drove to the LZ, just as the three slicks landed in line, showering dust all over them.

McLeod got out of the jeep, moving lazily and totally without snap. Neil smiled at this. McLeod was built on the British officer model, in that, while he accomplished a great deal, he tried to give the impression that he did no work.

Shakey Jake, hopping down from his helicopter, was of the opposite style; even standing stock still by his helicopter he seemed to hum with activity. His brow furrowed his eyes darted nervously. His staff officers arranged themselves around him, quivering like whippets at the starting gate.

McLeod and his bunch sauntered forward and stopped. He reported formally. His moustache bristled. The general's eyes narrowed. He glared. McLeod returned his gaze coolly. The general beat his thigh with his swagger stick.

Although clean, cleanshaven and shined up, the men from the Project were a Bohemian contrast to the crewcut, freshly-starched staff in front of them. The general's aide peered at them, bug-eyed. The others were stonefaced.

They did not appear to be in the same army. The brigade staff wore monochromatic green jungle fatigues and billed baseball caps, which sat lumpily on their heads. The Project Theta staff wore tiger-stripe camouflage, with their sleeves chopped off and rolled up, green berets mashed to cocky angles.

And since the beret did not shade their eyes, they wore sunglasses. Neil and the colonel wore simple army aviator shades, but the sergeant major wore mirrored wraparound Saigon pimp glasses and the operations officer wore yellow shooter's glasses. Neil and McLeod wore brass Montagnard bracelets on their right arms, but the operations officer wore six, and Stan the Man wore fourteen, which tumbled clinking down their arms as they saluted.

The contrast in values they represented was clearly shown in their stances. The brigade staff were Americans, by God, and their purpose in life was to get the next promotion and buy a new station wagon. McLeod and his people were in their glory *now*. They sauntered; they swaggered. They were obviously happy men. In an army of unwilling cannon fodder the only elite volunteers were the paratroops; in the airborne the most elite were the highly-trained, independent men of Special Forces, and within the Forces the absolute crazies inevitably gravitated to the reconnaissance projects.

These guys had gone so far out on the edge they had flaked off. Their very existence was a challenge to the values the general and all people like him treasured.

Neil had a theory that Special Forces men fell into two broad categories; the Robin Hood's Merry Men model, and the Waffen SS model, and within each model they fell into two types; the type to whom this work came naturally, and those with something to prove. As far as he could tell McLeod was a Model A, type one, although, in Neil's view, marred by an excessive fondness for alcohol, and by the fact that he was so cool in a crisis he tended to lecture on the battle at hand.

The sergeant major was a model B, and he had been playing the role for so long that Neil couldn't tell what type he was.

Neil considered himself a model A, type two, since he liked McLeod's easygoing ways, but he definitely had something to prove. He'd count his tour a failure if he came home with only his stripes.

As for his comrades, he had a variation on his theory, that the two types were in reality only one, those with something to prove, and sub-type IIa, those with a real good front.

The introductions were brief and brisk until the general came to Neil. His eyes narrowed, the left one almost shut, as he gave Neil an icepick glance; his head set down more squarely on his shoulders.

Maybe it's the haircut, Neil through wryly. His grin was just this side of insolence.

Frenier whirled on McLeod, an angry question on his face, then stopped, and his eyes glazed over. "Let's continue with the briefing, shall we?"

They mounted their jeeps and rode to the headquarters, then dismounted and went downstairs to the Tactical Operations Center.

For the first time Frenier seemed impressed. The room was paneled, curtained, and air-conditioned. Each person being briefed had desk space, with ample room to take notes. The charts were well-done, in color. Being always on the move, the general's brigade had no such facilities. The Theta Operations Officer, who, in addition to being competent, was an absolutely beautiful staff captain, handsome and sharply uniformed, led off with the mission and organization of the project. He had been three classes ahead of Neil at the Academy.

Their mission was strategic and tactical reconnaissance. The Theta organization consisted of twelve recon teams of two Theta personnel and four Montagnard tribesmen, three mobile strike force companies of Montagnards with six American advisors apiece, a U.S. Army helicopter company attached in direct support, and a three aircraft Air Force forward air control team, also in direct support.

Neil had heard it all before. He fingered the little place card on the table in front of him that read "SGT Thompson". He looked at Frenier, who was totally absorbed in the briefing. It was easy to see how he'd become a general. He sucked up information like a vacuum cleaner. Occasionally he interrupted to ask an incisive question. In spite of himself Neil was impressed.

The operations officer finished and the intelligence officer mounted the podium. He drew a framed map and overlay down in front of the operations officer's beautiful organization chart, took what looked like a stainless steel ballpoint pen from his jacket pocket and extended it into three sections of pointer, rather like an automobile antenna, then flipped a switch and a tiny light came on at the point.

The intelligence officer, dark, Latin, overweight, but like all Theta's officers, sharp, spoke, tapping his pointer along the map. "NVA infiltration routes run generally along the lines indicated on this overlay. Our recon teams locate their units moving through, but our Mike Force is not able to take them on now that they are moving in battalion strength. In the past Military Assistance Command, Vietnam, has not been able to get a fast enough reaction from conventional units when we relay the intel through our next highest headquarters. Therefore we have been assigned to the operational control of your brigade, so that your heavier firepower will fill that gap."

As the intelligence officer neared the end of his briefing McLeod leaned back and whispered, "Where the hell is Swift?"

Neil shrugged. "Haven't seen him since last night, sir."

McLeod pursed his lips. "Well, we can't stall forever. You'll have to brief him on your patrol.

"Me?"

"I've seen you in class, Thompson. Bullshit you've got."

"All right, sir. If that's what you want, I can do it."

When the intelligence officer finally ran down, just before he was about to announce McLeod's conclusion, McLeod interrupted, "Sir, Sergeant Thompson will now brief you on Recon Team Crazy Horse's patrol, from which he only returned last night."

Neil stood and strode briskly to the podium. In an army in which the ability to explain away failure was as highly prized as the ability to succeed--in some quarters even more so, since it didn't make one's contemporaries look bad--skill on the briefing platform is a great asset. Neil liked to think of himself as a field soldier, and tended to regard this particular talent with contempt, but there was no denying that he had it.

Once on the platform he picked up the pointer the intel officer had collapsed and left behind him. Neil casually flicked it open, squared his shoulders, set his jaw in the MacArthur manner, and began speaking in the approved duckspeak. "Sir, on two January, at approximately 1930 hours, three reconnaissance teams of Project Theta were inserted by helicopter into operational area golf-niner." With his little illuminated pointer he outlined the area on a one-over-fifty thousand map. "RT Geronimo here at Bravo Quebec three-niner-seven-four-zero-niner, Cochise at Bravo Romeo…"

Glancing briefly at the general Neil could tell he was impressed. This crap just rolled out of Neil without an "ahem" or "harrumph." Neil didn't care if Frenier was impressed or not; he wished the bastard would go suck on a rock.

He kept it up for fifteen minutes, but there was just so far he could run it. Your ball, colonel.

"If you have no further questions, sir, Colonel McLeod will close."

As McLeod advanced to the platform General Frenier said, "Before we continue, Colonel, I have been asked to present awards to one of your reconnaissance team leaders and his assistant. I see Sergeant Thompson is here." He favored Neil with a glare. "Perhaps if you might send for the other man." He glanced at a paper in his hand, "a Staff Sergeant Royce S. Swift, it might save us a wait later."

Neil smiled. The general's glance was intended to make McLeod feel like frozen dogshit for having failed to have him here already.

Apparently unruffled, McLeod stepped to the platform and said, "Right, sir. Sergeant Major, go get Shoogie."

The general started slightly at the nickname.

The sergeant major eased silently out of the room as McLeod launched his closing spiel. "Sir, this briefing has given you an idea of some of our capabilities and how our services might be of benefit to your brigade. Do you have any further questions?"

"Well, McLeod," said Frenier, his voice a half sneer, "J-2 MACV tells me you people can do me some good. Can you?"

From the podium McLeod smiled. "Well, sir, I was going to save this for last, but the prisoner RT Crazy Horse brought in last night says there is an NVA division gathering to overrun your Firebase Debbie Sue. That might prove useful information."

The general pursed his lips and nodded sagely. "Yes, if confirmed, it would."

The side door to the briefing room slammed open, throwing a long rectangle of lemon-colored light across the floor. The rectangle filled with the elongated shadow of a man. Shoogie entered, blinking against the darkness, muttering, "Get a man out of a sound sleep, Jesus Christ!" He wore black VC pajamas and flip-flops. He had not shaved and his shaggy brown crewcut was long overdue for a haircut. Perched on his shoulder was a large, somnolent parrot.

Shoogie looked at the colonel with guarded respect.

McLeod walked to him, put a hand on his shoulder, and said, "Sergeant Swift, General Frenier is here to present you with an award."

Shoogie nodded, smiling. He liked awards.

The general arose and approached, stonefaced, but somewhat warily. He shot a stern glance at McLeod, who smiled back.

Shoogie stuck out his hand, grabbed the general's and pumped vigorously, saying, "Howdy, General! My name's Shoogie and that rhymes with boogie. Recon is my middle name."

The general cleared his throat. Even Mcleod looked embarrassed for a second. Neil almost laughed. No one else in the room showed any expression at all. It was as though the temperature had dropped fifteen degrees. Their eyes darted toward neutral objects.

Frenier flung a fierce glance toward his aide and snarled, "Read the award!"

Neil fell in beside Shoogie. The lieutenant came to attention and started reading. Shoogie proudly came to an exaggerated attention, as did everyone else, automatically.

The citation, as intoned by the lieutenant, was a highly stylized and not particularly accurate account of the occasion on which Shoog had put the team on line and assaulted an NVA company to get a prisoner. Neil remembered they had bugged out, throwing tear gas left and right, firing furiously, while Shoogie dragged a Charlie away, trying to knock him out by beating him on the base of the skull with the silencer on his Swedish "K".

As the general pinned the Silver Star on Shoogie's pajamas, the parrot spoke the only phrase it knew, "Awwwk, holy shit. Holy shit! Awwk, holy shit!"

This time the general didn’t blink. He took one step to the right and pinned a Bronze Star on Neil's uniform.

A few minutes later they emerged into bright sunlight on beaten dirt, in front of the headquarters. The general grabbed Colonel McLeod firmly by the shoulder and looked down six inches into his eyes. "McLeod," he said, "I don't know what kind of off-the-wall outfit you're running here, but when I get back..."

He was interrupted by what sounded like a concerto for garbage can lids, and looked up to see three companies of Montagnard troops saluting in front of the flagpole. A small band of tribesmen stood to the side of the formation in camouflage fatigues, berets, and white leggins. They played a tune of their own devising on copper gongs.

Automatically the assemblage came to attention and joined the tribesmen in saluting as the flag came down. The general looked at the flag, blanched, and said, "Oh my God!"

Neil knew there was no use explaining that advisory units, such as the Project, were forbidden by treaty to fly the American flag, the Montagnards flatly refused to work if the Vietnamese flag was flown, and, of course, the Montagnard revolutionary flag was illegal. Even then the general would have preferred something more sedate than the Theta flag.

It flew proudly from the halyard as the guard detail lowered it, fluttering, clearly revealing every detail of its design, a black field with a huge red Greek letter theta, with an embossed skull, blood dripping from it's teeth, over crossed commando daggers, green beret mashed down over the skull's head. At the top, in red, were the words PROJECT THETA (B-54). At the bottom, also in red, was the motto "FUCK COMMUNISM!"

When the flag was down they dropped their salutes. The general blinked several times. "Would you show me to my helicopter, please?" He marched off, stern, proud, rising above his surroundings.

Chapter Four

Shoogie drove, so the accelerator on the jeep was floorboarded. In this particular jeep that meant they were going sixty miles an hour instead of the forty-five for which the vehicle was rated. The road was fairly open, but what traffic there was still seemed strange to Neil; three-wheel open Lambretta mini-vans, army trucks jammed with Vietnamese soldiers, laughing and gawking like students on a high school band bus, ox carts, little kids walking alongside the road.

Shoogie had the back end of the jeep jammed with kids. He swerved out around a Lambretta and cut back in again, just in time to avoid a head-on with a Vietnamese two-and-a-half ton truck. The kids in back didn't seem to notice; they continued laughing, jabbering, pointing, and wiping their noses. Neil supposed he shouldn't pay attention either. He sighed and slid down in the seat. Beside the road on the left was a row of Vietnamese houses, and on the right were the straight tree rows of a French rubber plantation. To the front the trees seemed densely grouped, their slender, evenly-spaced trunks rising to a low canopy as their foliage seemed to merge, but to the right he could see straight down the twelve feet between rows, spaces swinging like gates into view and out again as they drove past. It looked so cool in there. The Viet Cong hid there sometimes.

They broke past the rubber plantation, passed the Lions and Rotary Club signs, a road directory billboard and an Esso station. They were on the outskirts of town.

Neil held out his hand to Shoogie. "Gimme the list!" he said.

Shoogie handed him the list. Even though he was all business on a recon, he was utterly hopeless on anything like this shopping expedition. All they had to do was take it by the Chao brothers' and haggle a bit. Neil looked at the handwritten list the sergeant major had gotten from their Chinese cook:

4 Caisse Tiger beer
4 Caisse Biere' La Rue
4 Caisse San Miguel beer
2 Kilo shrimp
2 Kilo Cheese
2 Caisse czaz
1/2 Kilo California dip
2 Caisse potato chips, fritos, etc.

"Look at this!" Neil shouted, pointing at the list. Shoogie did, almost sideswiping a bus with double the maximum passenger load, top jammed with bicycles and chickens in wicker baskets. "Czaz?" Neil demanded. "What the fuck is czaz?"

"You got me, Ace," Shoogie admitted. "But we better figure it out or McAnn's gonna have a severely chapped ass."

They were in city traffic and Shoogie breezed around the traffic circle next to a Montagnard village of perhaps fifty thatch-roofed longhouses, high up on logs like telephone poles. Just past that was a police checkpoint, Vietnamese cops in white uniforms going through the back end of a long line of Lambrettas and ox carts.

When the Cong came to town in Lambrettas the drivers let the ones who didn't have good ID cards out a block and a half before the roadblock, and by the time the Lambretta was searched they had walked a block and a half past it, which was a good safe distance to get on the Lambretta again.

They let the kids off in front of the crumbling old cathedral, grass growing up around a statue of the Virgin.

Shoogie looked at his watch on its two-inch black leather cuff. "It's only nine o'clock," he said. "Let's get a beer before we go to the Chao's."

Neil nodded assent.

Shoogie gunned the Project's old solid black jeep around the corner and down a block. CIA funded the Project, so their jeep had no army markings. He pulled over down the street from the Imperial Hotel and they got out, towering over the Vietnamese even though neither was much above average height. They moved through the crowd, being carefully polite to old ladies, careful not to step on kids who zipped through, between, and around. But their height and natural swagger, the green berets over their eyes, the jungle fatigues, sleeves carefully rolled, the Swedish "K", with the silencer removed, draped over Shoogie's shoulder, the Browning 9mm pistol in Neil's shoulder holster, assured that they had little trouble moving easily through the crowd.

They walked catlike, shoulders hunched, loose and silent. They cut across the street and rattled the anti-grenade cage in front of the Imperial. A grinning Viet in a sport shirt, striped boxer shorts and flip-flops opened the cage; they stepped into the cool interior, walked past a white-haired wisp of an old lady in black silk bell-bottom pants and gray cotton blouse. She squatted in the doorway on gnarled feet, her dark darting eyes taking in everything. She smiled at them, her betel-stained teeth a shade between purple and black. Neil nodded and smiled back. He and Shoogie climbed the concrete stairs to the club.

Upstairs it was dark and they groped their way between low narrow padded seats and rickety two-foot-high wooden tables. The bar was lighted, the rows of whiskey bottles lit by spots.

"Hey!" Neil bellowed, pounding the bar. "Little service here!"

"How about a drink?" Shoogie yelled.

Mama-san came out of the back. She wore pink checkered pajamas and a goldtoothed smile.

"Mama-san, my love," Neil called. "Tiger beer."

"Seven-seven," Shoogie growled.

* * *

An hour and a half later they stood outside the Imperial, berets over their noses, hands deep in their pockets. "They sure gotta nerve throwing us out like that," Neil muttered darkly.

Shoogie's expression was innocence itself. "All I done," he said, "was stir m'drink with m'dick."

It was a two-block walk to the Chao brothers' store, and when they arrived an ancient Chinese gentleman in a sleeveless undershirt and a pearl gray homburg informed them that the brothers were at the Chinese school across the street.

The school had a high yellow-plastered cement wall around a central courtyard. Neil pushed open the heavy wooden gate and they stepped inside. Just inside the gate was a cement basketball court.

Four young Chinese men were playing. Quite well too, Neil noted. George Chao had the ball and drove past a short man wearing round goggle glasses, rather like Neil's. He took his shot, which sailed through the hoop with a smooth solid *whunk*. Then they stopped playing. George and Bernard Chao came over and said hello, introducing the other two Chinese as teachers at the school.

"Sahjong Swif' and Sahjong Thom'son," George said, then went into singsong Chinese, presumably a flattering description of the Americans.

The Chao brothers were both in their mid-twenties, although their draft registration said otherwise. George was medium height for a Chinese, had regular features, and a serious manner. Bernard was taller, skinnier, had buck teeth and was inclined to giggle and roll his eyes. They both usually wore pleated slacks and polo shirts, but now, playing basketball, George was barechested and Bernard wore a sleeveless undershirt.

"Game over," George said. "You guys want play one game? Twenty-one points."

Shoogie listed a little to starboard. He swung, hands in pockets, back over to port. "Sure," he said. "Why not?"

The two teachers went over and sat on some benches against the yellow plaster wall. Neil and Bernard were the taller, so they centered the ball. George flipped the ball in the air and Neil, wondering how he'd ever gotten into this, easily jumped over the shorter Chinese and clumsily batted the ball into Shoogie's waiting hands.

Even drunk and in combat boots Shoogie wasn't bad. He took the ball, slid by George and drilled in hard to sink the first basket. By the time the basket was in Shoogie was covered with sweat. He pulled his shirt off without unbuttoning it, like a sweater, and flung it over by their weapons on the bench. His body was almost fish white where the shirt had been, with long ropy muscles under the white skin, big pockmarks where a grenade had caught him in the back.

Neil watched all this through a haze. He was so uncoordinated that games of this sort were normally an agony of embarrassment to him. But drunk he didn't much care.

George flipped the ball to Bernard. Neil crowded in to cover him and Shoogie charged in, the solid gold dogtags he'd brought back from Bangkok bouncing on his chest, great shining beads of sweat sliding down his face. He snagged the ball and dribbled back to the Chaos, very low to the ground, while Neil strolled in a leisurely fashion down to the basket. Shoog flipped him the ball and Neil sort of lobbed it over into the hoop.

No matter how good the Chaos were they had no chance. The drunken Americans played the game a foot over the Chinese reach. In twenty minutes Neil and Shoogie had their twenty-one points against twelve for the Chinese.

"You guys played good though," Shoogie said, shaking hands with George after scoring the last basket. He was panting, dripping, the folds of his trousers dark with sweat.

Neil smiled sheepishly. "You just can't beat the height in this game," he said, feeling foolish. Both Chaos were better players than he was.

"Yes," replied Bernard, grinning gaily. "Fortunate for Chinese all games, not have to be tall." He slapped Neil on the back, somewhat diffidently, and giggled.

George shot him a reproachful glance and said, "Let's go to house for drink."

They gathered up their stuff and went out the gate, threading their way across the street through cyclos and jeeps, people walking and riding bicycles.

Downstairs at the Chaos the old gentleman in the homburg sat behind the counter, eating soup from a tin bowl. The storeroom was almost bare except for some stacks of tires in the corner and a Japanese calendar on the wall with a picture of a young oriental woman in western dress drinking a Coca-Cola. The Chao brothers led them upstairs and into their Chinese Moderne living room.

They sat down on a low green couch behind a flimsy blond coffee table. George put a Connie Francis album on the record player, under the mistaken impression that Neil and Shoogie would like it, then turned it up too loud. Bernard brought their drinks, a Tiger beer for Neil and an enormous seven-seven for Shoogie. The Chao's drank scotch and orange juice.

Neil smiled. "We're having a party to celebrate the end of this last operation in a couple of days," he said. "The sergeant major wants to order a few things."

He handed the list to George who studied it intently and passed it to Bernard, who studied it equally intently and passed it back to George, who studied it some more.

While they studied the order Neil rose, beer in hand, and wandered over to the window, looking out into the street below; the narrow streets, the French design of the buildings, the billowing black trousers of the older ladies, their hair tied in buns at the back of their necks, the young girls in tight jeans or mini-skirts, the boys with Beatle haircuts over zipper eyes, riding their little red Hondas.

"What this czaz?" George asked finally, from behind him.

Neil turned to see George standing, holding the list. Bernard and Shoogie were slouched down, drinking, each with a beatific smile on his face.

"I was sorta hoping you could tell us," Neil replied. He turned and looked back out the window. "If you guys can't read it either, maybe we better just forget it."

He wondered what Utrillo could have done with the Asian street scene. The essential quality of it would be lost in a photograph, but some of Utrillo's paintings had it. He wondered if Utrillo had ever been to Asia.

"Okay," George said, "we figure it without czaz." He named a figure.

Neil sucked air through his teeth, exhaled theatrically through flared nostrils and uttered a disapproving

"Hmmmmmm!" Then he mentioned a figure one-half the one George had named.

George giggled and sucked in his breath, eyes darting wildly about the room in feigned embarrassed amazement. They inched toward each other's price for a few minutes and finally arrived at a figure that was acceptable to both.

"Can you guys deliver?" Neil asked.

"Sure," George replied. "We bring out in Toyota pick-up tomorrow afternoon."

Neil and Shoogie finished their drinks and chatted awkwardly with the Chaos for awhile. Both liked the Chinese brothers, but conversation was not comfortable. They excused themselves and went out into the street again.

"That it?" Shoogie asked.

Neil grimaced. "Yeah," he said. "Listen, I've got an album on order at the PX. Let's swing by the Mac-Vee Compound and I'll see if it's in yet. Then we can get some lunch before we go back to the Project, okay?"

Shoogie shrugged. "Okay by me."

* * *

The Military Assistance Command, Vietnam Compound was a series of low concrete structures surrounded by a high storm fence. It had a small sentry box at the entrance, occupied by a sleepy Vietnamese guard, who gave them not so much as a glance as they drove through.

They parked in front of the little PX building and went inside. Shoogie headed for the paperback rack and Neil went to the customer service counter to see if his record had arrived. A Vietnamese woman, young and pretty, demure in a dark dress, and with none of the brassy quality of the whores, checked through a mound of orders, then went back to the storeroom. Neil was elated. He had waited over two months for the album. It was the first RCA album by a group he'd loved during his San Francisco days, the Jefferson Airplane.

The Vietnamese girl came back to the counter, held her hand over her mouth and tittered. "Record come in, but no can find. Maybe in rack." She nodded toward the record display.

His heart sank. What if some straightleg soldier, some non-paratrooping fucking leg, had bought the album he'd waited months for? He barged over to the rack and almost shouldered the American girl going through the J-K-L section out of the way.

The *American girl*?

He did a fast doubletake. He hadn't seen a Caucasian woman of any description in three months, and this one made little electrical tingles race all over his body.

Huckleberry Finn's big sister in hiking boots, jeans, and a green work shirt; carrot-colored hair, one long braid erupting out of the middle of that mass as though in an idle moment she had reached up and doodled it. She was longlegged and high breasted, with the ass that jeans are made for, and she moved like a dancer. Just as he moved up to the rack she gasped and pulled out an album with a black and white photo of a strange group of young people on the cover, under a pink band at the top; *Surrealistic Pillow*, Jefferson Airplane.

"Oh, wow! This is wonderful!" Her voice was soft and husky, curling around the words like cigarette smoke.

"That's mine!" Neil announced. She was lovely, but he was still a little drunk, hadn't had lunch yet, and had almost been killed the day before yesterday. He was not in a mood to surrender his album.

She whirled to face him, hugging the album, thick random braid swinging wide. Her face was heart-shaped and freckled. Her big eyes narrowed angrily, not in the least intimidated. "The only name on this album is Jefferson Airplane," she snapped. "Is your name Jefferson Airplane?"

"Practically," he insisted. "I ordered the album. They weren't even supposed to put it on the racks." He flipped through the rack. "Look at this shit! Mantovani, The Kingston Trio! The hippest thing they have here is Sonny and Cher. These people never heard of the Airplane. Come on, I'll show you the order form."

She hugged the album to her chest, but her eyes softened. She knew he wasn't lying. "But it *was* on the shelves," she insisted. "I got it first." There was an expression of real anguish on her face, which he understood perfectly.

He laughed. He wanted her a whole lot more than he wanted the album. "All right, you can have it on one condition...two conditions."

"What are they?" she demanded, still hugging the album, but smiling."

"You have to let me tape it, and you have to have lunch with me and my buddy. Our jeep is right outside."

She smiled slowly back. He felt as though he was on an elevator that had suddenly started down. "Okay," she said. "That seems harmless enough."

"What the hell are you doing here?" he demanded. "Vietnam, I mean. I thought the only American women here were army nurses and newspaper reporters."

"IVS," she replied.

"What's that?"

"We're a sort of poor man's Peace Corps. I'll tell you about it at lunch."

She had her own transportation, and they agreed to meet at a small French sidewalk café about six blocks from the MACV compound.

* * *

Neil and Shoogie arrived first.

The White Rat was in a crummy-looking wooden building under a huge spreading flame tree, covered with fire-colored, gardenia-shaped blossoms, which also littered the ground. There was a chipped and fading sign over the door, a drawing of the café's animal namesake and a handlettered sign, "*Le Souris Blanc.*"

The proprietor, a slender, dour Frenchman in a stained apron stood in animated conversation with another Frenchman, a dumpy little guy in a blue beret. He had a dusty old Citroen, with a baggage rack on top, drawn up in front of the restaurant.

Neil hadn't told Shoogie they were meeting anyone. He wanted to watch his surprise when the round-eye girl joined them.

As Neil and Shoogie strolled into the place the two Frenchmen stopped waving their arms, bussed each other on both cheeks and muttered, "*Au 'voir, mon ami.*" The one in the Citroen left.

The front of the little restaurant was all doors, drawn back to create a sidewalk café, absent the sidewalk. Wax from many candles had built up on empty Algerian wine bottles. The menus were handwritten in French and English, but not Vietnamese. The tablecloth was red and white checkered plastic and the salt and pepper sat in a little two-bowled glass dish. Neil wondered if this was a French custom, or was due to the Southeast Asian climate.

The proprietor came in his stained apron and took their order. Neil ordered a steak sandwich and a San Miguel beer; Shoogie wanted a small pepperoni pizza and a coke. The proprietor made a face as they gave their order, and left. Neil picked at a spot of coagulated gravy on their tablecloth. He heard the sound of a light motorcycle engine stop across the street, and sneaked a peek out of the corner of his eye. It was his redhead.

"Hoooeee!" Shoogie exclaimed. "Look at the jaws on that!"

She dismounted from a yellow 250 Yamaha. Neil followed the lovely curve of her ass as she swung a leg over the saddle. "Over here," he called.

She looked their way and blinked dimly into the sun.

"It's that fuckin' hippy English teacher," Shoogie muttered as she started walking their way.

Neil was lost in memories and hopes. "Babe," he muttered, "after West Point I lived two months in Golden Gate Park. I watched the grass melt and listened to my hair grow. I love those people." He grinned. Modigliani eyes, he thought.

Shoogie slid low in his seat, his face screwed up in a truculent pout.

She walked over with a longlegged dancer's shashay that Neil found almost unbearably arousing. She gave Shoogie a soft hesitant look.

"Sit down and have some lunch," Neil insisted. "I never did even ask your name. "I'm Neil Thompson and this is my friend, Shoogie Swift."

Shoogie gave her a malevolent wolfish grin. "What's a foxy little honey like you doin' in a shithole like this?"

"She's with IVS," Neil volunteered, perhaps too eagerly. "She works with the Montagnards at the province school."

Shoogie nodded. "Do-gooder. Whataya do, teach 'em English?"

She burned him a hard look. "Among other things; English, sanitation, baby and child care…the Twentieth Century. I'm learning too, the Rhadc' language, tribal customs."

"Name?" Neil insisted. "You have one of those, like everybody else?"

"Juliana Kos."

"Kos?" Shoogie asked. "Ukrainian?"

"Uh huh, you?"

Shoogie bared his teeth in something which might be taken for a smile. "Used to know an SFC Kos in the Tenth. He was just waitin' around for World War Three so he could go liberate the Ukraine."

She frowned.

"You like the Rhade'?" Neil asked, hoping to bring the conversation back around to something he knew about. He felt much less confident than he had on the briefing platform.

"Oh, yeah," she smiled again and looked at him. "Even in the middle of this war the Montagnards are happier than anybody back in the States."

Shoogie's eyes glittered. "That's kinda scary, ain't it?"

The proprietor came over. Juliana ordered a Salade Dalat and a Tiger beer.

"That still doesn't tell us why you came here, though," Neil insisted.

She gave him a helpless look. "I hate to say this," she said, "but it's really none of your business." She hesitated a moment, then murmured, "I had some things to think through."

"You could have gone where there's no war," he said. "You could have gone to Borneo with the Peace Corps."

She made no reply.

"Come on, man," Shoogie blurted. "You know the look. Shit! She came here because she's hard core."

Neil hadn't been thinking of her that way. But he had been around combat men enough, even as a kid, that he could pick one out in a crowd. He wasn't sure what it was, but he could spot one. Maybe it was the level gaze. Maybe it was the fact that their pores seemed to have sweated harder than other people's. His Uncle Willie, the family disgrace on his father's side before Neil, who had graduated from West Point, been through two wars, and still retired a lieutenant colonel, had told him that in World War I the combat men said they had been to the fair and seen the elephant.

Juliana's pores weren't blown out, but she had the same level gaze. He had never, that he could recall, seen that look on a woman, but somehow this girl had been to the fair and seen the elephant.

She smiled often enough, and when she laughed, she had a low throaty chuckle that stirred him. But in repose her mouth had a cynical cast. She had the look of someone who expected life to rise up and smite her at irregular intervals. She looked as though she had no faith remaining in anything save her own audacity.

She looked at Neil and asked, "Gotta cigarette?"

He tugged a Marlboro from its flip-top box in his shirt pocket.

"Light?"

Shoogie shot her a sidelong glance and slid his lighter across the table to her. It was a Japanese imitation of a Zippo, with an enameled Snoopy on it, snoozing on top of his doghouse, with a thought balloon captioned, "Fuck it!"

She lit her Marlboro, examined the lighter and shot Neil a glance not unlike the one Shoogie had given her. She nodded toward Shoogie. "I can tell about this guy," she said. "He's just a crazy, but why are you here? Aside from the funny suit you seem like a fairly normal person."

Shoogie grinned his cracked and broken grin. "Our boy here is a third-generation West Pointer," he said.

Neil wished Shoogie had just let him give her a flip answer and let it go at that. It was nothing he wanted to talk about.

She glanced at his shirt collar. "I thought West Pointers were all officers."

Neil shrugged sheepishly. "Only if they don't get thrown out. My roommate cheated on a physics exam. I knew it and didn't turn him in."

Her eyes shot up. "They threw you out for that?"

He nodded.

Shoogie just would not leave it alone. "Anyway," he went on, grinning that wolfish grin, grinding it in. "Getting thrown out of West Point helped him escape the family curse."

"I wish you would just this once shut the fuck up," Neil snapped. Shoogie grinned placidly back.

"Which is?" Her eyes glittered sardonically.

He shrugged again. The restaurateur brought their order. Neil was grateful for the break. He dug into his sandwich. He hated to tell this story. People looked at him differently after they'd heard it."

But she wouldn't let it drop either. "What is your family curse?" she insisted.

"My grandfather, the first Lieutenant Thompson was killed at Belleau Wood. My old man was killed in the Normandy Invasion. Both were West Pointers."

Her eyes narrowed. "Oh, wow! You're crazier than he is." This woman had the most direct gaze he had ever encountered.

He shrugged. "I had some things to think about too. Anyway I owed 'em three years."

She hesitated for a second. "My father was a Marine in World War Two."

There was a split-second sober pause. "Marine grunts are first-rate," Neil said.

Shoogie added, "Their fuckin' officers have a maximum I.Q. though, and I think it's about ninety."

The conversation lagged while they ate their lunch. When they were through Neil said, "We're having a Stand Down party at the Project tomorrow. You ought to come. I'll pick you up and see you don't get bit."

She gave him a glance and shrugged her slender shoulders, her breasts riding under her shirt with the motion. "Okay."

"Pick you up at seven-thirty," he said.

She glanced at her watch. "I've really got to get back to school," she said. "I've got a class."

Neither of them ate a bite, or lifted a glass as she walked in a sliding saunter to the bike, swung her leg over and hit the starter button. She expertly gunned down the street.

"Man, whad you ask that dippy bitch to our party for?" Shoogie demanded after she had roared away.

"Well," Neil said, "if the opportunity presents itself, I'm gonna fuck her 'til her nose bleeds."

Shoogie grimaced in distaste. "She's got a face like a cupful of diced assholes."

Neil shook his head. "You were kind of rough on her."

Shoogie snorted. "I'll tell you somethin', Hoss. There ain't but two or three round-eye women in this province, and the word gets around on em pretty fast."

Neil raised an eyebrow. "So?"

"Don't go thinkin' it's love. If that little honey had as many stickin' out of her as she's had stuck in her she'd look like a fuckin' porkypine."

Neil hadn't wanted to hear that. He didn't believe it either. It was just the sort of thing that every dipshit who'd hit on her and not scored would say.

They finished their meal in silence and drove back to the Project.

Stan the Man said he couldn't remember what czaz was either, and to forget it.

Chapter Five

It was five minutes to nine when Colonel McLeod came out of his office, beret jammed into the right cargo pocket of his jungle fatigues.

Neil and Shoogie looked up from folding chairs just outside the railing that separated the office area from the waiting area.

"Let's get some coffee," McLeod said. He nodded toward the door and forged on through the gate in the railing. They walked across the courtyard and into the messhall. McLeod did not head for the officer's table, but sat down near the door, with his back to a wall so he could survey the room. A tiny Vietnamese waitress brought them a pot of coffee and a plate of sweet rolls, fresh and glistening with thick flecks of unrefined sugar. The colonel ignored them, but Neil had slept through breakfast, and he grabbed one. Shoogie ate two.

McLeod lit a Ruby Queen and leaned back in his chair. "We got a rush call for a hot mission; I want you two to volunteer for it."

"Where?" Shoogie asked, his voice muffled by the roll in his mouth.

"No place you very much want to go," McLeod replied. "I'll tell you where if you take it. Your old pal General Frenier wants to see what recon can do."

Shoogie snorted. "Show and Tell."

McLeod let a thin trickle of smoke out of each nostril. "Oh, it's a legitimate mission. He wants confirmation on that NVA division that's after his firebase. He says it will help him utilize our services better if he sees how we operate. So we're sending one team in early."

Neil sipped his coffee and said nothing.

Shoogie looked at McLeod speculatively for a long time. "You never sent a team back in two days after they came out before."

The colonel nodded. "No, and I wouldn't do it now if I had a fresh team. I requested a delay and it was denied. I explained why and it was still denied. He says he's got companies been on operations for up to a month."

"Yeah, but they generally try to outnumber the other guys," Neil put in.

McLeod's eyes blazed for a second. He wasn't used to his orders being questioned. Then he dropped it. "Anyhow," he said, "I'm asking you because you're who pissed him off. You and me and the Project and Vietnam."

"What's he want?" Shoogie demanded. "If he don't like this war, what's he want?"

A thin, ironic smile curled across the colonel's face. "He wants World War Two with helicopters."

Shoogie shrugged. "Okay, we'll take it. Why not?"

"Thompson?"

Neil nodded and shrugged. "Ever'body gotta be someplace."

McLeod smiled. "Okay, go pull your team in. It looks like this op has one more patrol. I'll have the sergeant major postpone the party 'til you get back. I'm not going to run the TOC with a bunch of hungover drunks. You're in at last light tomorrow night."

* * *

Shoogie had the three-quarter ton truck floorboarded, but it would only do forty. They were way out from town, tearing along the highway, and Neil wore his entire patrol harness, complete with grenades, Randall, loaded CAR-15--selector on auto-- propped on his leg, pointing into the jungle as they passed by rubber plantations and open rice paddies, dry and stubby in the sun. This stretch was a lot more dangerous than the road to town.

They roared on and on. Finally, out of boredom, Neil asked, "Whatever made you join the army in the first place?"

Shoogie paused and hitched over the wheel reflectively. "Well," he said, "I usta have this little fifty-two Merc. Had her primer-coated, chopped and channeled. Had a three-quarter-race cam, dual carbs, dual Smitty exhausts, and dual madonnas on the dashboard. It was the fuckin' rod supreme in Dallas." He eased down in his seat and went gimlet-eyed. Neil could see him in a letter jacket and slicked back greaser hair, revving his engine at a stoplight.

"One night this little shit pulls up beside me in a old Ford, and him and me commence to badmouth each other's cars. You know, I'm giving him shit and he's givin' me shit. He had this little honey with him, and she didn't wanta see speed; she wanted to see blood. So pretty quick it got personal. Right away I'm out the car, and got my old trusty tire-chain with me. But I realize, wait a minute, motherfucker; if I hit that little dude with this chain and the cops come, it's all over. So I dropped it."

He paused for dramatic effect and looked to check his audience. "Anyway, this little fucker turns out to be a human buzzsaw. By the time the cops came I was down on the ground and his sweetie was tryin' to bash my head in with a spike-heel shoe.

"We was in the middle of a juvenile delinquency scare in Dallas then. He was twenty-three and I was sixteen, so they let him go and put me in jail.

"We beat it easy enough, y'understand. I never hit him with the chain, and him and me both started the fight about equal. In fact, we didn't neither one of us know who started it.

"But it was already all over the papers and I was, like, the most famous juvenile criminal in Texas.

"Anyhow it got bad after that. One night I'm standin' in the parkin' lot at the North Commerce Drive-Inn, and there's a fight goin' on. You know, it's like one o'clock on Sunday morning, and these assholes are drunk and some of 'em's from Highland Park, and some of 'em's from Richardson, and they're at it. So somebody calls the cops and they come and I'm goin' to Oak Cliff, so I got no stake in the fight, not even standin' close to it. But the cop car pulls up beside me and the cop leans out and says, 'Your name Swift?' I says yeah, and he says, 'Get in.'"

Shoogie's eyes blazed with a strange combination of amusement and indignation. "Man, they didn't even stop the fight. They just took me downtown. Anyway that made for another little round of headlines.

"So Monday, after I got out, I get this phone call. Dude says, 'You must be about the lowest son-of-a-bitch alive, Swift. The only thing lower than you has to be the woman that borned you. So I'm gonna come out there this evening and kill your mother.'"

"No shit?" Neil exclaimed, over the road noise.

"No shit! So I called the cops. She wasn't really my mother. She was a foster parent, but she treated me right, and I sure didn't want no harm to come to her. When I told him who I was the desk sergeant just laughed. So I said, 'Okay, motherfucker, but when somebody's head goes rollin' down Fourteenth Street don't say I didn't call.

"Anyway, nothin' ever come of it, but I figured I better split. So after that I went to Louisiana, lied about my age, and enlisted, went Airborne, and when I was old enough I got in the Forces."

"Where the hell is this place?" Neil asked, taking a long look down the road.

"We're about there," Shoogie replied.

Two miles later he turned off down a gravel road. It was a long straight tunnel between enormous trees; the green, sun-dazzled canopy almost closed over them. It would have been a perfect place for an ambush, but Neil put the safety back on his CAR-15, collapsed the stock and slung it around his neck like a guitar. Montagnards walked along the road; no ambush here.

Little old ladies, their breasts flat and wrinkled as empty tobacco sacks, long shiny black sarongs down to their ankles; young men, some in loincloths, some in shorts, strangely designed handmade axes on their shoulders; young girls with tawny breasts, and children with dusty legs, all walked the road.

Shoogie started loading the three-quarter with everybody who was going their way. They swarmed over the sides, laughing, joking, happy with the novelty of a ride.

At last, two more miles down the road they came to a bend and a large village with a high bamboo fence around it. There was a little bamboo guardhouse by the gate, the guard in old but clean fatigues and cap, with a carbine slung across his back. He swung the gates open. The words BUON T'PEK were scrawled on a one by ten board nailed over the gate.

As they drove through the gate Neil was surprised to see a large green John Deere tractor, with a disc harrow attached. It appeared to be clean and well maintained. The ground in the village was irregular, but covered with a fine, deep, green grass. Besides the wicker and thatch longhouses, mounted six feet from the ground on thick poles, there were several plastered and thatch-roofed structures down on the ground; a school, a chapel, and some storage buildings. All were painted Air Force blue. Neil smiled; the Project's scroungers had been on the case. Healthy-looking chickens and ducks ran squawking and quacking out from under the slow-moving three-quarter. Neil saw several pigs that seemed to be crossbred between the potbellied tribal swine and healthier Western types.

"Man, "Neil said, "this is the richest, cleanest Yard village I ever saw."

Shoogie grinned proudly. "Most of the young guys work for the Project," he said. "They've got a little money and a lot of free advice. They've made the most of it. You oughtta seen this place two years ago. It's come a long way."

Shoogie parked in front of a thatch-roofed longhouse, high up on pilings, with a rattan porch against which a deeply notched log, leaned.

Nay Thai came out on the porch and grinned at them. "Sergeant Swif', Sergeant Tom-son," he said happily. "Welcome my house. Come in."

Neil and Shoogie climbed the log and ducked in the door.

Other longhouses that Neil had been in had one large room, but this one had been partitioned off. There were rugs scattered around on the floor, and from somewhere way inside the longhouse American pop music played on a battery-powered record player, Herb Alpert's Tijuana Taxi. Not exactly Neil's favorite, but he could tolerate it for these people.

Some aluminum tubing lawn furniture was grouped around a small wooden table under an aging photo of an elderly, imposing-looking Montagnard in a suit and tie, circa 1925.

Nay Thai, in flip-flops, slacks, and a sport shirt, indicated the chairs.

Shoogie shook his head. "Let's sit by the light," he said. They sat crosslegged on the floor, next to a big open window, which came to within eight inches of the floor. Nay Thai excused himself. Minutes later he came back and sat next to them. "Wife come quick with numpai," he said. "You want rice wine or beer?"

"Beer, if it's all right," Neil replied. He'd tried the tribal wine and been given his bracelet, but the stuff tasted awful, and his initiation had given him a hangover that lasted three days. Shoogie loved it.

Neil's eyes lit on a fifty-pound bag of cement, leaning by the window for some upcoming project, covered with fine gray cement dust. Its label read PORTLAND XIMANG. He smiled at the Vietnamese spelling of a prosaic word like 'cement.' The whole culture in a word, he thought.

Very soon a pretty young woman with a dark tribal complexion, wearing her hair in a Sassoon cut, came in. She wore a black and white checked minidress and white sandals. They looked like Capezios, but surely weren't. She carried a tray with a bottle of Tiger beer and a used Old Crow bottle, full of a cloudy yellowish-brown liquid, and three semi-clean glasses.

Nay Thai introduced his wife. Neil didn't catch the name; to him it sounded like a cough. She sat the tray down, poured their glasses full, and left.

Shoogie took a long pull on his numpai, as did Nay Thai. Neil sipped his Tiger.

"What up?" Nay Thai asked.

"We're going back in," Shoogie said. "We came out to alert the team. Briefing tomorrow morning at oh-nine-twenty, briefback at thirteen-thirty, insertion at last light."

Nay Thai absorbed this information without visible emotion. He'd been doing this a lot longer than Neil, and he had to know how bad it was. "Team come now," he said. "I ask for numpai."

They sat and drank for awhile, talking idly and watching out the window as children played in the shade under the adjacent longhouse, ducks and chickens paraded across the lawn, and hogs drowsed in mud puddles.

A kittenish little girl, about five, with saucer eyes, came to the edge of the mat they sat on, and stared at them in wonder. She wore a pink western dress, without underpants, a practical omission in a house with a rattan floor.

"My girl," Nay Thai said proudly.

"She sure is pretty." Neil grinned at her and waved his fingers. "Hi, Honey."

Her eyes went wide and she backed away, but did not get up or leave.

"What's her name?" Shoogie asked.

Nay Thai grinned. "H'rin," he said. But we give her nickname, 'Debbie.'"

"Debbie?" Shoogie's eyebrows rose.

"Yes," Nay Thai replied. "I name her for American lady, sing and dance."

Neil got up slowly, smiling shyly at the little girl. She ducked her head again. He touched her nose with his forefinger and she giggled and looked up at him.

He stuck out his tongue, goggled his eyes and wiggled his ears. Her eyes flew wide as she hid her laughing mouth behind her hands. In a few minutes she was riding all over the longhouse on his back, laughing delightedly.

Neil was still throwing the shrieking, giggling little girl around when Ksor Drot, Frenchy, and Y Buhn came. Old Ksor Drot was the only one in tribal dress. Except for his bare feet Frenchy was in uniform, complete with beret and

French para badge. Y Buhn wore jeans, boots, and a sport shirt with the Project crest embroidered over the pocket.

"Numpai!" Ksor Drot grinned, showing the gap where his teeth had been filed down in accord with the old tribal custom. His had been the last generation, which did it. He dragged up an enormous ceramic crock, several hollow reeds, and a pan of water to fill the crock with when they drank the level down. Neil had been told that there was no alcohol in it at all, only dried cakes of some hallucinogenic substance. But to Neil it felt like a weird drunk.

Like it or not he was going to have to drink the stuff. Neil put the little girl down, gave her a resounding buss on the cheek, and came over to the crock. She followed him over, but Nay Thai waved her away with a frown.

As guest of honor Shoogie was first. He sat down on a small log placed in front of the jug. Ksor Drot put a cup in the water and poured it into the jug, filling it to the rim. He then selected a long slender dried reed and jammed it down through the mixture to the bottom. He sucked all the rice husks and crud through the straw and spat them on the floor, then swung the reed to Shoogie.

Shoogie sipped, putting his thumb over the end of the reed when he stopped to say something, so the liquid wouldn't run out. He lit a cigarette, which was supposed to help, and frequently stopped to take a drag. Neil lit one also, so he'd have an excuse to take frequent breaks when his turn came. Shoogie finished one cup in a few minutes. Then it was Neil's turn. One cup wasn't too bad. He got the pukey stuff down fast and sucked smoke into his lungs. They kept passing the straw, next to Nay Thai.

After his third round Neil excused himself to find a friendly bush. He'd almost got there when his stomach rejected its contents and the numpai came pouring up his throat, turning it raw, and stinging his nose. He threw it all up, urinated, and, considerably refreshed, staggered back to the longhouse.

* * *

Neil spent the next evening getting his gear ready, concentrating on the tasks at hand, trying not to think about the mission except in a tactical way, coldly and analytically. The other thoughts kept crowding in; he kept shoving them back. He had a couple of drinks and went to bed early, so he'd be rested in the morning. He read something for awhile--what he couldn't say--then snapped off the light.

He lay naked, tossing in his bed, dimly hearing the familiar slam of firing mortars, watching the sickly light of flares cast weird drifting shadows on his wall, just as passing auto headlights had when he was a child.

He remembered a recurring dream from his childhood. He'd been in the fifth grade and his seventh school, always the new kid, and had dreamed repeatedly that the thirty-four children in his class had run him down like a pack of wild dogs and torn him to pieces.

Maybe that's why he didn't really hate the North Vietnamese. He thought of them as his playmates.

They'd all been new kids when Neil started military school in the sixth grade, but he was the only *experienced* new kid. That first night some of the other boys had been homesick and crying, but it was a breeze for him. He'd felt at home in a uniform ever since.

He wasn't really afraid now, just jazzed. He knew from previous missions that he would have to get on top of a rising panic on the chopper; that's when it came for him. But he was wired tightly now, no doubt about it. Finally he got up, lit a cigarette, and put on a pair of cut-off tiger pants and flip-flops. He wandered outside the teamhouse and leaned, smoking, on the sandbag wall. He watched shadows creep outside the perimeter, moving in the light of drifting flares.

As soon as one set of flares died another set flared, higher and to the right, drifting and smoking under their little parachutes. He had been a month in country before he stopped seeing Cong moving in the shifting shadows under the flares.

Shoogie came out, a towel wrapped around his waist. "Gimme a light," he said.

Neil flipped his zippo under Shoogie's cigarette.

Neil drew sharply on his own cigarette as Shoogie lit his. Tensely, he said, "You can't sleep either?"

Shoogie nodded. "I like the woods, but sometimes, the night before we go in, I get so fuckin' scared I think I'm gonna puke."

Knowing the answer before he asked, Neil asked anyway, "If it's so bad, what do you keep doing it for?"

Shoogie shuddered. "This is my life, man," he said. "I don't want no other life. I had that and felt like I was already dead."

The ghostly light drifted across Shoogie's face and Neil drew on his cigarette. In that light his friend's features took on the appearance of rigor mortis. It occurred to Neil with virtual certainty that Shoogie would die soon. He was pretty sure Shoogie knew it too.

Shoogie flipped his cigarette out into the darkness. "Let's go get some sleep. We gotta early start tomorrow." He walked off into the darkness. Neil followed.

But even back in bed Neil couldn't sleep. He'd seen this phenomenon before, the rigor mortis in a man's face, and then the man had died.

Chapter Six

They clattered over the last checkpoint, a waterfall dimly perceived in the fast failing light. One minute to go. Then the ship flared and drove straight down into the hole. Neil jerked the quick release on the rope ladder and swung over the side. He was three rungs down when every automatic weapon in the NVA inventory opened up.

He kicked loose and dropped through the cool evening air, slamming into the slanted earth on the side of the hill, hard, falling sideways as the rounds snapped over his head. He heard soft plops as the others hit all around him. Then they were up and running crouched over for the shelter of the woods.

Pain ran up Neil's right ankle as they moved. Then he was in the trees. Snapping, scratching branches swept his hat away, and it fell, dangling on his back from the parachute suspension line around his neck. A branch put a deep gouge in his cheek, but he barely noticed it.

Twenty meters into the brush they fell to earth, silently gasping labored breaths. Neil grinned like an idiot. He felt so happy he thought he would die of it. He had forgotten himself again.

Behind them there was a huge WHOOM! and orange light exploded thousands of shadows into the trees. Neil turned to see the chopper flame, falling sideways into the jungle, showering sparks and secondary explosions. Then it settled into a single stationary fire, and Neil lay with his face in the dirt, the damp earth pressing into his nostrils.

Adrenaline had so flared them that it seemed he could smell each individual tree and bush. The firing died and the noise of the rapidly burning chopper died also, except for the occasional pop of the door gunner's machinegun ammo cooking off. By then, in the jungle, it was dark. Then from a half dozen directions at once came the lilting sing-song of Vietnamese conversation. Tiny lights from small perfume bottles stuffed with string and gasoline were lit in the woods around them. Two flashlights fanned the area and then flicked out again. The nearest small light was four yards off to the left. It cast enough of an aura for them to see a three-man machinegun emplacement, dug in. They had been waiting for them.

The guy holding the perfume bottle set it in the dirt. Shoogie's silenced "K" tapped politely, six rounds. One of the NVA coughed twice, but there was no alarm. Neil heard some slight stirring ahead and he reached out and grabbed a patrol harness. He felt someone grab his, and they started their slow painful walk through the gap in the NVA perimeter left by the unmanned machinegun.

The NVA troopers in the hole sat slumped over in their firing positions. The team moved with excruciating slowness. Feet going into the earth toes down, they felt for soft spots, moving branches slowly with their free hands. They moved for perhaps fifty meters. It took an hour and a half. Neil knew when the chopper didn't get back McLeod would be on the radio. He also knew that Shoogie wasn't about to try for radio contact this close to the enemy.

He pictured the anxiety in the headquarters, and the choppers flying over this area tomorrow. He pictured the relief when they made their first scheduled contact in the morning. If they could. Christ, there were NVA all around.

Finally Y Buhn found a thicket and they crept into it to try to sleep. All night Neil lay touching Ksor Drot's leg and Frenchy's arm, his weapon ready to fire. He wore his harness. He shut his eyes and tried to sleep, but it was no use. It was so still. The Viet conversation died down. He had to think about it then. Would they get out? He mentally figured the odds. It was tough to do. He'd been in some baddies, but none as bad as this. Well, fuck it, he thought. Everybody dies. He thought briefly about Juliana's hair and her legs, then shut that out and fell into an uneasy sleep.

He woke long before daylight and watched the first dim outlines of the brush around them emerge out of the black, then turn gray, then green. No sign from Shoogie, so nobody moved. They lay and waited. All around they heard NVA getting up, talking to each other. Jesus, Neil thought, if we're in the middle of a bivouac area there's no telling how long we'll be stuck here.

There was early-morning mist in the trees, and swirling on the ground. The NVA built their small fires and cooked their rice, still talking and walking around. But none came closer than twenty feet to the thicket. As the mists burned off they put their fires out. Somewhere off in the distance an authoritative voice spoke in Vietnamese, and people began moving. It sounded like they were forming up on a trail. They made no attempt at stealth. The death of the machinegun crew didn't appear to have been noticed. This didn't look like any place to hold roll call. The voices started moving past, for what seemed an interminable time. Along toward the last the wind started to play tricks on Neil. He could swear he heard one say, "Say, bruh, you see that mu'fu' burn?"

Then it got very quiet. Neil turned around to see Shoogie shrug out of his pack and pull a plastic bag of freeze dried rice from it, tear off a corner of the bag, and pour in water from his canteen. Then, while the rice swelled, he reached for the radio. Neil rolled over into a firing position. If he hadn't known what was being said he'd have thought it was the wind sighing in the trees. "Ghost Six, Crazy Horse. Orange Juice, over!" Orange juice was a code word that meant the mission had been compromised, request emergency extraction. From there all it took was acknowledgement and the choppers would be on the way. He waited for Shoogie's 'Roger, out.' It didn't come. Instead he said, "Negative, over."

Neil looked at him. Shoogie mouthed the words, "Do we have casualties?"

Jesus Christ, Neil thought. What's the matter with those people? When a man asks for an emergency extraction you don't ask a bunch of stupid-ass questions. You get him out.

Shoogie's eyes went narrow and his mouth bitter under the green crud on his face. Then his mouth twisted into a smile. "What the fuck you expect me to do?" he muttered into the radio. "They know we're in here." There was another pause. He said, "Roger, acknowledge, continue the mission. Out!"

Neil got out his notebook and wrote on a blank page, "FRENIER?"

Shoogie shrugged and took out his pocket knife. He started slicing a small sausage and mixing it with the rice. Neil made a cup of Tang and ate half a bar of chocolate. Then he lit a heat tablet and made instant coffee. The tribesmen mixed their rice as Shoogie had. When they had finished breakfast they carefully scooped out a hole and buried their refuse, then covered the fresh holes over with leaves.

Shoogie took out his map and compass, oriented them, and made an entry in his notebook.

Then they got up to move out. They'd only picked their way about twenty feet forward when they heard voices moving fast down the trail again. They froze. The voices passed by, and just as they started to move out they heard more voices on the right. Jesus, Neil thought. They're all around again.

They didn't seem to be searching, just two or three guys moving down a trail, but Neil heard the slap of weapons two or three times.

The team moved out again, came across a trail. Both Y Buhn and Shoogie got across, then they had to get down while three NVA walked by. They carried water buckets, one on either end of a long pole. They walked by, chattering and laughing. Neil waited until they had passed, then sent Ksor Drot and Nay Thai across, and barreled over after them. Frenchy was right behind. If they could get off this hill and over on the next one they might have room to breathe. They made another fifty meters that day, then crawled into a thicket on the side of the hill and went to sleep, nervous and jittery. Shoogie requested extraction at the morning contact.

He was again told to continue the mission.

Neil was enraged, the more so because he couldn't express it. They'd found out what was in here. They couldn't move. For awhile he wondered if this was part of some plot of the general's to ruin the Project. But he realized that by the general's way of thinking they'd been sent out on a five-day recon, and barring death or act of God they were going to recon for five days.

They made another breakfast and started moving down through the undergrowth on the side of the mountain. Soon the growth got thicker. They heard water bubbling in the river below. Shoogie checked his map and nodded. Neil got his out. There was a spot on the next mountain over that would be good for an extraction, if they could get there, if Frenier would allow them to leave.

The ground sloped rapidly at their feet and they had to swing their way down, grabbing vines and bushes with their hands. They heard the sound of the rushing creek grow louder.

When they reached the bottom they froze and crouched slowly. There was a small trail running down by the water, and a sound of voices came from the brush. They faded into the bushes and froze again. The first one rounded the trail. He wore a khaki highnecked jacket, floppy hat, khaki pants and tire sandals; he had an AK slung over his shoulder. He was over six feet tall, and he was black.

Neil remembered stories of Foreign Legionnaires who had switched sides. Maybe this guy was Senegalese. The second one came around the bend. He was a Caucasian, skinny guy with long hair. He carried himself awkwardly. The black guy was at ease in the woods. The white guy was too young to have fought with the Legion. Four more came down the trail, all Viets. Two of the Viets sat down on the rocks, weapons ready, while the others started to get out of their clothes. They were here to bathe.

Neil never knew who or what made the noise. The black had just thrown down his hat and leaned his AK up against a tree. He froze. The white guy was halfway out of his shirt. The two Viets were in somewhat the same position. They all froze. They looked across the river, carefully scanning the bushes. Neil avoided locking eyes with any of them. He waited for them to forget it and start getting undressed again.

The white guy finally started to get out of his shirt, and the two Viets followed suit. But the black kept looking across the river. Finally he reached over and picked up his AK. He held it at the hip, still scanning. The two guards sitting on the rocks started looking again. One flipped his safety off. The white guy was the only one oblivious to it all. He continued undressing. The Viet on the rock next to him took his safety off. The white stopped and the Viet put his AK to his shoulder. It looked as though he had decided to spray the bank, just to see what might happen.

Neil heard the tap of Shoogie's "K". The Viet grabbed his chest and fell backwards off the rock. One foot hung on the rock while another slid down the side and didn't move anymore. Two purple-black holes appeared on the startled Caucasian's chest. He fell down on the bank. The other four jumped quickly behind cover.

"Oh, God!" the Caucasian screamed. "Help me! Somebody help me!"

Jesus, Neil thought. English! American English!

They didn't move. The black guy and the other three were under cover and waiting for the team to make a move. The team waited, listening. The worst danger was that the Viets would go for help. There was a burst of AK fire and Neil dug his head in the dirt. There was a crashing noise to his left. He looked. Ksor Drot was dead.

Nay Thai's grenade launcher went *poonk* twice before the first grenade of three exploded across the river. White smoke ballooned up from three different places, six feet apart, along where the others were. Neil heard a scream across the river, and the rustle of voices.

Shoogie's voice, low and very calm, said, "Split! Left!"

Frenchy was furthest right. He poured out a magazine, and then crashed through the brush to the rear. Neil emptied his magazine and moved out. The team put out a continuous stream of fire. It sounded like one M-16 with a two-hundred-round magazine. The Viets returned fire, but high, the team's suppressive fire ruining their aim. Neil scooped Ksor Drot's body up and threw it over his shoulder. It didn't weigh much for a dead body, just a tiny little old man with no front teeth and his ear lobes pierced and stretched into loops. Neil had run back into the brush with a lot of trees between him and the bad guys by the time Y Buhn fired the final magazine. Dimly he heard a rich baritone call, "We gone git chew, mothah*fuck*ahs!"

They highballed straight through for half an hour, then stopped. Shoogie called on the radio for a McGuire rig extraction. The team started moving again. There were signal shots from the rear. Then immediately, answering shots from very close ahead. Neil remembered what Shoogie had said about that.

Shoogie altered their course and slowed down, moving more cautiously. Then they heard choppers beating their way through the air.

Shoogie started looking for a break in the trees. He took a while to find one, and it was small. Shoogie got on the radio and Neil popped yellow smoke. Slowly, in a pall, it drifted up through the gap in the trees. Soon gunships whirled around them; streams of machinegun fire and rockets poured into the jungle. The first recovery ship jockeyed in over the gap in the trees high overhead. Neil felt like half of a heavy weight had been lifted from him. He grinned, almost giddy from the thrill of it. They were going to make it. All but Ksor Drot.

Sandbags dragged the three ropes with their heavy nylon loops on the ends, big enough for a man to sit in, down through the trees. Downblast whipped and wound the loops and the long nylon ropes above them. Neil, Frenchy, and Nay Thai dragged them down. They started to take a little fire through the trees. Apparently the other bunch had got one or two men inside the gunship orbit.

Shoogie and Y Buhn fired back. Nay Thai started putting out grenades from his launcher. Neil didn't like having those enemy rounds snapping over his head while he worked. He and Frenchy got Ksor Drot's body hooked into the rig by a couple of snap links. Neil sat down in one of the heavy nylon loops and locked his right wrist in a heavy nylon cuff, near the top of the loop. It would hold him in the rig, even if he got hit, or slipped out of the seat. He might be hanging from a broken wrist, but he wouldn't fall.

Neil sat on the right; Ksor Drot's body was in the middle sling, and Frenchy sat in the left. Neil gave the thumbs up and the chopper started up. When their feet cleared the ground they swung forward a few feet like kids on a playground swing. Then the chopper surged upward and trees and branches whipped Neil as he put his free elbow over his face. Then they were free and in the air.

He looked down as the jungle dropped away underneath and his sling started to wheel around slowly. Three men could link arms and legs and stop the spin, but two and a corpse couldn't.

The three had spread apart, Neil hanging lowest because of his weight, Frenchy next lowest, and Ksor Drot's body above. Neil was blown around to where he could see the other recovery ship surge out of the hole, the solid clump of the other three dangling underneath.

They were high; it was cold. The land and sky whirled around until they found a safe and open place to set down. Then they got in the chopper and collapsed against the ropes by Ksor Drot's body, and went home.

McLeod's C and C ship whirled in ahead of the recovery ships. Then their skids touched down. Neil and Frenchy laid Ksor Drot's body out on the pierced steel planking chopper pad. Then Neil knelt and took out his poncho. He spread it on the ground, picked the body up, and laid it on the poncho. He cut off Ksor Drot's stiff, bloodied web equipment and threw it to the side.

A jeep, with a single white star on its red license plate, was drawn up just far enough back from the helipad to avoid the downdraft. General Frenier stood beside the jeep in his shiny boots, swagger stick tucked under his arm.

An ambulance drew up beside Neil and his men. Two Montagnard medics withdrew a stretcher from the back. Neil looked up, feeling his eyes narrow and his mouth twist. Here, at last, was someone he could be angry with. "Hold it a minute!" he commanded.

An American medic got out of the driver's side door. "We'll do that, Sarge," he said.

Neil flared in a sudden rage. He whirled on the medic and snarled, "I take care of my own man, motherfucker." He knelt again, got some parachute suspension line from his pack and wrapped the corpse in his poncho. It took a few minutes to wrap securely. This was a moment for ritual, and Neil had none. He slapped the body on the shoulder and said, "You were all right."

He picked up the equipment and slung Ksor Drot's AK over his shoulder, standing up. "All yours, Ace," he said to the medic.

The other chopper had whopped in on the other side of the pad. Shoogie and the others walked up and Nay Thai intoned something in the hacking tribal language. When he was through Neil handed him Ksor Drot's gear. .

Neil noticed that Shoogie's leg was bleeding. It didn't appear to be serious, and he walked normally.

General Frenier advanced to meet them. For a moment Neil thought the general was going to speak to him. But he stopped Shoogie. He eyed Shoogie's right hand, but when no salute was forthcoming he demanded, "What happened out there, Sergeant?"

Shoogie slouched and appraised the general from the corner of his eye. "There's a leak somewhere," he said. "They was dug in on the LZ. They was waitin' for us."

The general shook his head. "There was no leak, Sergeant," he said. "Security was perfect on this operation."

Shoogie cocked his head further and put his hands on his hips.

Colonel McLeod strode up, moustache bristling, and saluted quickly. The general returned it without taking his eyes off Shoogie.

"There was Americans out there with 'em," Shoogie said, "a spade and a white guy. They used American slang and talked with American accents. We killed the chuck."

McLeod frowned.

The general's eyes clouded over. He pointed his swagger stick at Shoogie and exploded, "Damn it, Sergeant! I came here for intelligence, not wild tales."

Shoogie hitched the sling on his K. "We went out and got this man killed...and you don't wanta believe it. Fuck you, General. I'm gonna go get my leg bandaged." He started forward toward the dispensary.

He now walked with a noticeable limp, which he had not before. The rest of this team followed. Neil's shoulders were hunched against the blast he knew was coming.

"Hold it right there," the general purred. The note of command stopped them dead. They turned to face him.

"McLeod, I want this man disciplined," the general barked. There was an edge in his voice.

Colonel McLeod met him gaze for gaze. "Sir," he said, "Sergeant Swift has been under continuous strain for a number of days. Further his record is superb. He has never given an erroneous report..."

"McLeod," the general exploded, "I don't wish to discuss it. If you don't punish the man yourself, I'll courtmartial him."

McLeod took out his notebook and scribbled in it. He looked up. "Sergeant Swift, come here!"

Shoogie walked over and saluted. "Yessir," he said.

McLeod tore the sheet out of his notebook and handed it to Shoogie.

Shoogie saluted and walked away.

The colonel turned back to General Frenier and said, "Sir, to courtmartial Sergeant Swift now would constitute double jeopardy under the Uniform Code of Military Justice. I have administered nonjudicial punishment in the form of a written reprimand."

The general whirled to face Shoogie. "I want to see that," he barked.

His aide ran over and snatched the paper from Shoogie's hand. He ran back, smoothing it out, and handed it to the general. Frenier looked at it and his face flared red. "McLeod," he snarled, "I am going to make a very serious effort to have you relieved, and this outfit broken up. This is the sorriest excuse for a military organization I've ever seen." He wadded the note up and threw it in the dirt.

McLeod quivered with barely suppressed rage, but he managed to curl his mouth into an insufferably suave smirk. Neil had never seen a man flush a military career with more style. He was probably flushing any chance Neil had for a commission with it.

"Sir," the colonel said, "sorry or not, this organization furnishes sixty percent of the tactical intelligence in Two Corps. The unit was organized by order of the Commanding General, MacVee, and I was selected to command it by the Commanding General, MacVee. We offer a service. If you don't like it, why … don't … you … not … use … it?"

"Pah!" the general snorted. He whirled and strode toward his jeep, got in it, and rode back to his waiting helicopters.

Neil turned to Shoogie, whose eyes bored holes in the general's back. "Wha'd the old man's note say?" he demanded.

Shoogie grinned and picked up the note, smoothing it out and reading aloud. "Dear Shoogie: Don't do it anymore. --McLeod."

Chapter Seven

The party started at five-thirty. Freshly showered, Neil sat nursing a Tiger beer, scowling, still angry, still scared, one leg thrown over the arm of a wicker armchair, and watched it begin.

The Club was a huge room, paneled in varnished quarter-inch plywood, for which Shoogie had traded two AK-47's to an engineer outfit. The gray rock bar had a black leather-padded top. On the wall behind the bar was a ten-foot-long handpainted copy of the June 1966 Playmate of the Month, a redhead, prone, nude, leaning on her elbows, airbrushed breasts jutting, one leg cocked with the toe pointing gracefully skyward.

The painting seemed flat, her mouth was a little off, and she smiled vacantly into the room. Aside from Neil no one noticed. It was the idea of it they liked.

The walls were decorated with the Theta flag and captured weapons, some chrome-plated, mounted on plaques. There was also a captured NVA flag, a captured VC flag, and an old VC unit flag. And a few good paintings of Vietnamese village and paddy life. The artists had done a much better job with this material than they had with the centerfold. The rear wall was completely covered in red flock, and on it were 62 wooden plaques, each with the Theta bereted death's head and a brass plate giving the name, date, and security considerations permitting, location, of the death of a Theta man. Sixty-two was quite a few, considering that the Project had a maximum of sixty-six Americans assigned at any one time, and had only been in existence for two years.

The party was slow to start. A few men still wore their uniforms, having a drink after work and before showering. Others wore civilian clothes. Occasionally one of their Vietnamese girls wandered through the room, smiling professionally, or maybe not smiling at all. Behind the bar an Akai reel-to-reel tapedeck played top-forty tunes, unspooling a frantic jangle of electric guitars and drums, and whiny unschooled voices.

Most of the men wore slacks, sport shirts, and G.I. haircuts. Half the older NCO's wore airborne tattoos, acquired on the drunken night of a jump school graduation in the fifties. The young guys didn't wear them. A few, like Neil, wore their hair longer. Both groups wore moustaches; the older guys wore handlebars, and the younger ones Zapatas. Most wore party shirts they'd had tailored in town, with the Theta crest and the man's nickname embroidered on the pocket. Neil wore sandals, white levis and a black t-shirt.

He lifted the cover on his watch, glanced at it, then rose, walking through the double doors and down the hall to his room. He flipped his shoulder-holstered Browning 9mm over his head, and grabbed his CAR-15. Out through the back way he grabbed a jeep and headed for town to pick up his date.

* * *

She lived in a large yellow-plastered house down a long hilly, rock-studded street. The house was on the fringes of a big Montagnard village called Buon Allay A.

Neil drove the old black jeep down the rutted mud streets of the village. There was every type of screwball architecture; regular jungle-style Montagnard longhouses, low square shoddily-built plaster Vietnamese houses, more ornately constructed French-style structures. American missionaries and IVS volunteers had rented most of these. Their salaries, though small by American standards, were huge here.

Even so, they lived not so richly as Vietnamese provincial officials, or the lowliest G.I. in this garrison town. Most of the IVS volunteers were Americans, but a Canadian flag hung in front of one of the houses. Perhaps they thought Charlie would care. A young man in a modified blond 'fro, wearing a pair of faded jeans and a Quicksilver Messenger Service t-shirt sat barefoot on the porch, smoking a handrolled cigarette. He gave Neil an abrupt wave and a tight little smile as he drove by.

Neil grinned back and threw him an offhand salute.

Juliana's house wasn't hard to find. There were only three streets in the village. All he had to do was drive until he had a chance to turn left, then stop in front of the first house on the corner. It was a low yellow stucco structure with a porch trimmed in white. The architecture was French art deco, but the building looked as old as Angkor Wat.

He knocked on the door and heard a faint feminine voice call, "Come on in!" Walking in, he felt immediately comfortable. Almost at home he might have said, except he had not been comfortable at home.

Lots of wicker stuff, most of it Montagnard. A rice-carrying basket sat next to the couch, converted into a magazine rack; a flat wicker rice-winnowing basket sat on the coffee table, with a potted plant on it. There were hanging plants around the room, suspended by macrame.

From somewhere in the back came the sound of the Jefferson Airplane. His album. He listened carefully. From here he couldn't make out the words, but synched right in with the music. The new singer, Grace Slick, was great, even better than Signe. Her voice harmonized with Balin's perfectly. He wanted to charge back to the bedroom and put his ears to the speaker.

"I'll be out in a minute," she called, louder now that he was inside. A door slammed and he caught a flash of long tanned, wet thigh under a towel as she slipped down the hall. He caught his breath.

He continued his inspection of the living room. An intricately patterned red and yellow sarong woven by the Cham people, a rectangle of cloth about three by five feet, hung on one wall. The missionaries sold them to raise money for the Cham and Montagnard peoples. Neil had sent one home himself, but his mother had washed it, and all the homemade dyes had run. Pinned to this one was a barechested poster of Jim Morrison of the Doors, striking an attitude in shiny leather pants and a wide belt decorated with silver conchos.

"There's tea in the pot," she called. He glanced at a tray on a table beside the couch, which held a Japanese teapot and tiny porcelain cups. He poured himself a cup, wondering if the hand-carved Moroccan box next to the sewing basket under the coffee table was a stash box, and if so would it be a good idea to get high? About half the guys in the Project were lifer NCO's, and one thing they wouldn't understand or tolerate was a potsmoking sergeant. He let it ride.

He took a sip and cringed as his tastebuds were hit by a totally unfamiliar flavor, dry leaves and rocket fuel. "Jesus!" he cried, "What the fuck is this?"

"Ginseng," she called from the bedroom. "I get it from the Chaos" Her voice dropped a register. "It's very invigorating. It's a famous aphrodisiac."

He shook his head and puckered his lips as though to whistle.

She came out in a green-silk brocade dress, her long red hair parted in the middle and plaited into one long braid, straight down her back. She wore scuffed black flats, and was without makeup. The slit in the cheongsam ran two-thirds up her thigh. He noticed her shins were barked and bruised under her tan, and he liked that. She had given the Montagnards more than English lessons. She had worked in this village.

On Taiwan the dress she wore could have been worn by anyone, from a teenager to a great-grandmother. But in Vietnam only prostitutes wore them. Her reputation might not have been earned, but it had certainly been cultivated.

"Hello," she said.

He smiled. "*Hiam droi jian muon*," he said, taking her arm, turning toward the door. "I think we better get moving before dark."

She looked surprised. "You speak Rhade?"

"Jarai. I picked up a few phrases from Nay Thai."

They walked to the jeep, and he handed her into the right-hand seat. He walked around and climbed in on the driver's side. Extracting a pack of cigarettes he offered her one. "*Ih djup hot moh*?" he asked, then grinned. "That's the first two sentences in the phrase book."

She smiled back and took one of the bent filtertips, cocking her head toward him. "Thanks," she said, then, looking at the Colt and the Browning," I see you brought your guns."

He nodded, starting the jeep. "It doesn't happen often, but you can get shot at on this trip." He put the jeep in gear and drove off.

Her eyes narrowed. She drew on her cigarette and threw her head back to catch the breeze. Since the vehicle was combat-rigged, with the windshield lashed down to the hood, there was quite a bit of it. She cupped the cigarette with her hand, then gave up and threw it away. "I can't fit you into the hired killer role," she said.

"Well," Neil replied, "killing people isn't my primary mission, really. But I'll tell you this, there's a lot of people in this country that <u>need</u> killing. What I can't figure is why you're here."

She had been thinking while he talked. She shook her head, then looked at him suddenly, and the hungry look in her eyes startled him. "Have you ever?"

"Ever what?"

"Killed a man?"

He looked at her, surprised that she could ask a recon man such a question. "Not so far today."

"Don't be smart."

"Yes," he said. He saw no point in telling her that the last one had been yesterday.

She made a face. "Did you like it?" Her eyes were shining. He didn't know what to make of that. He didn't want her to be a death groupie.

He shook his head. "No, I didn't like it. I thought I might, but I didn't. The exhilaration is all in the risk."

"Ever think about doing something else?"

He nodded. "I enrolled in a summer art course at San Francisco State after I left West Point. But I quit."

"Why?"

"My instructor said I didn't have the discipline."

She laughed.

He laughed too. "Self-discipline. I didn't have any of that after the Academy. I just stayed stoned for two months."

It got dark as they rode in silence the rest of the way. The jeep lights caught the gate guard as they drove in. Neil cut the lights and the guard waved them through. The jeep crunched on gravel as they drove to the club. Light poured through the windows, and the noise level had risen greatly. The same top forty tape was playing, but twice as loud. A burst of dirty laughter came through the windows.

He got out and walked around the jeep to help her out. She haughtily ignored his arm and dismounted from the jeep. She swept toward the door.

"Halt! Who is there?" The voice came from above them. Neil looked up to see Rick Simmons, a new guy in the Mike Force, standing on the roof above the door, obviously very drunk.

"A friend with a friend," Neil said.

"Advance friend and be recognized," said Simmons.

Neil took one step forward.

"Halt! Who is there?"

Neil saw that this could go on for some time. "Simmons, tinch-hut," he commanded. Simmons promptly came to an exaggerated position of attention.

"One step forward HARCH!"

Simmons took the step and promptly plunged off the roof to land flat on his face at Neil and Juliana's feet. He appeared unconscious. Neil stepped over him, guiding Juliana toward the door.

"Shouldn't we help him," she asked.

"He'll be all right,"

These parties were fierce. A fantastic amount of tension built up on an operation, and McLeod gave them two or three days to blow it all out before they got serious again. Recon men, between patrols, were like Rock musicians in a Holiday Inn in Cleveland on the forty-sixth day of a sixty-day tour.

He doubted she had ever seen a party quite like this one.

He opened the door and she walked inside, into a burst of light and noise. She stopped. Along the left hand wall a group of men were taking turns ramming their heads through the wall. It was a plaster wall, and Neil could see the setup coming. Most of them were from the Project, but some of them were helicopter crews, guests at the party. In a very few moments one of the pilots would be steered to a portion of the wall with a support beam behind it, and probably knock himself out, to the sustained laughter of the Special Forces guys.

Tim Geer waved at Neil. “Hey, Thompson,” he called. “Wanta run your head through the wall?”

Neil waved back. “Another time, perhaps,” he said. He steered Juliana in a wide arc around the pool table and toward the bar. She gave him a glance, but this time she did not resist his arm. He steered her with ease across the dance floor. They passed a few couples gyrating badly to the music, and others on rattan couches against the walls, shrouded in darkness, in various stages of what is often described--erroneously in this case--as the act of love.

"Who are all these girls?" she asked.

Neil stopped and looked around. "Well, let's see," he replied, fingering his chin. "There's Sergeant Becker's shoeshine girl." He indicated a young woman with large hemispherical buttocks, wearing translucent white silk jeans with nothing underneath. She was doing the frug or some other rock'n'roll dance--Neil didn't know their names--with a man who resembled a tattooed cinnamon bear.

"Becker's a kind of interesting specimen," Neil told her. "He carries a Walther PPK all the time, and when I first met him that bearlike creature told me he had seven notches on it."

Trying to appear blasé'," she said, "That doesn't seem so many in this crowd."

"Yeah," Neil agreed. "That's what I told Bear. But he said, 'Becker don't count gooks.'"

Her face was a disapproving blank.

There were not as many women as men and there were two couples of men doing the jerk, or what Neil supposed was the jerk, by the bar. One of the couples was Shoogie and Colonel McLeod. The colonel thrashed sedately, grinning under his moustache. He wore black pajama bottoms, VC tire sandals, and a hideous yellow and purple floral pattern Hawaiian shirt. Shoogie's hair was wet from the shower, and he wore only an olive drab towel. He held a toilet kit in the hand that kept the towel together.

Neil forged a path to the bar. Cigar and cigarette smoke filled the room. There were several men at the bar. They stared into, or over, their drinks with paralyzed intensity. Juliana wanted Tiger beer also, so Neil ordered two.

The song ended. McLeod and Shoogie came to the bar. Shoogie, half-gassed, planted a wet kiss square on Neil's left ear, while the colonel ordered himself a martini.

"Don't ever die, you sweet motherfucker," Shoogie said expansively. "Don't you even catch cold."

Neil kissed Shoogie's ear and muttered, "Careful darling. Our secret..."

Shoogie snorted, reached over the bar to snag a beer, and disappeared, presumably to dress.

As they sat at the bar Juliana reached up and started to undo her braid. As she did so her hair fell in long Botticelli-like waves, and Neil felt longing. Juliana sighed. "What was that all about?"

Neil smiled. "Just something we do in bars to bug people. We're supposed to be so fucking macho…"

He thought about kissing Colonel McLeod on the ear, but decided against it. The colonel didn't think all their little games were necessarily that cute. He would probably prefer, for example, that his helicopter crews not require hospitalization. Still it was his rule never to interfere with their parties unless someone's survival became an issue.

The colonel caught his eye. "Ah, Thompson," he slurred. "Do you think it wise to bring a normal person to one of these vile exhibitions?" He turned to Juliana. "How do you do, my dear? My name's McLeod, and I'm afraid I'm in charge of these hoodlums."

She smiled genuinely and took his hand. "Juliana Kos," she said. "Are these degenerates the famous Green Berets?"

"I'm afraid so," McLeod replied. "You must understand they live under great stress." His return smile was sardonic.

She fumbled for a cigarette. "What are they all so afraid of? You're the first one who's met my eye since we arrived."

"There is actually only one thing most of these men are afraid of," said the colonel, "and that is the American female." McLeod's butane lighter materialized under her cigarette.

She gave it an irritated glance, then accepted the light.

Neil interjected, "The Colonel has a theory that wars arise when sufficient numbers of men will do anything to get out of the house."

"What? Oh, bullshit!" Juliana exclaimed. She seemed both outraged and amused at the notion.

"It's true," said McLeod. "Duty calls. That's the only ploy that never fails. Women don't like their men to leave for football or fishing expeditions. The only excuses that really work are to go to work or to war."

He sloshed his martini, holding forth. "The trouble with going to work is that you actually have to work. The trouble with going to war is you can get killed. But, there are lots of men who would rather die than work, or stay home either, for that matter."

"Shoogie says," Neil put in, "that there's only two reasons to go indoors, to get laid or make money. And there's only one reason to make money."

McLeod eyed Neil's carbine and coughed. "A-hem!"

Under his predecessor, a young major of the come-on-guys-let's-go-get-'em school of leadership, men from the Project had gotten drunk in the club and shot rats out of the eaves with submachineguns. McLeod had banned weapons in the bar.

"Oh, yeah," Neil said, flushed, and nodded to Juliana. "I'm tired of carrying this thing anyway," he said, shrugging the shoulder from which hung his CAR-15. "You wanta come back and see how the hired killer lives?"

She nodded and followed him through a curtain of multi-colored plastic strips and down the narrow hall to his room. "That's quite a man there," she said.

Neil nodded. "I remember the first time I ever met him. I was a yearling at West Point. He was on duty one night when I was reading *Street Without Joy*, Bernard Fall's book about the French in Indochina. I'd kind of spaced out. There was a snowplow out on the South Area and I was watching gray snow whirl around in the yellow revolving light on top of the it.

"That was right after the Marines landed at Da Nang, and we were all wondering if the army would go. 'What's the difference?' my roommate wanted to know. 'It'll all be over before we graduate anyway.'

"The major--he was a major then--was just coasting around the barracks. You know, he's not a big man, and he's very quiet. He's been passed over for promotion, but he acts like the one-eyed man in the kingdom of the blind; and he gets all these plum assignments.

"He came in, picked up the book and sat down on the corner of my desk. 'We're making the same mistake these people did,' he said. 'If I had my way, nobody would go to Vietnam but volunteers. They'd have to spend their first six months in a village, just living and working with the people. I mean pulling rice and shoveling shit. After that the villagers would vote on whether each man got to stay or not. Then they'd have to stay until the end of the war, which I figure would be maybe twenty-thirty years.'

"I asked him if he thought he'd get many volunteers for a deal like that, and he said that with men of that caliber you wouldn't need many.

"He said we always got in trouble in these ceiling-fan countries because the State Department didn't trust anybody who couldn't be bought.

"After I joined the Project I heard a rumor that he'd left a Vietnamese girl pregnant when the O.S.S. pulled his team out in '45. That's supposed to be when he started on the sauce."

He led her down the hall, past Shoogie's room, to his. He flipped the curtain of multi-colored plastic strips aside and led her into the room.

"I thought you soldiers had to keep the barracks clean," she said. She walked over and cocked her head sideways to see what he read. Aside from the stuff on revolutionary warfare and the Tao Te Ching the only hardback was Korzybsky on semantics. She picked it up and asked, "Yours?"

He went to the record player, shuffling through the stack for something to play. "That's Shoogie's," he said. "I haven't read it yet."

"Shoogie's?"

"Yeah," Neil said. "He surprises you. I've played him about a hundred games of chess and only tied him once."

He put on the danceable side of an Ellington album. He took her closely in his arms and started to slowdance. He put his cheek to hers.

"MmmmmmmmmmmHmmmmmm."

He held her close, barely swaying to the music. She looked up and he kissed her. Her mouth opened and his tongue found hers. He hadn't expected that. He held her again and they danced some more. She danced close, and he was filled with urgent longing. Before the first syllable was out of his mouth he knew it was a mistake. But unbidden, from somewhere deep, came the words, "I love you."

From her reaction you'd have thought that he had slapped her.

"Not me," she said defensively. "Not again." She stepped back and stood with her hands on her hips. Desirable, oh God, she was desirable. He realized that if he'd kept his mouth shut he could have had her. But there was no way to get back there now. His suggestion of intimacy had scared her off.

His face twisted in disappointment and embarrassment. Her's blazed. Whatever it was, she was blaming him for all of it. The moment had passed. Even if he tried to undo it, change what he'd said, it wouldn't work. Damn!

"You're a pretty good dancer," she said softly. They swayed to the music until the end of the number.

When they got back to the party he coldly inquired, "Drink?"

"Yeah!"

He went to get a couple more beers.

When he returned, he handed her one and sank deep in his seat, staring fixedly ahead. Dimly through the noise he heard her say, "Neil!" but he didn't respond. He sat in an agony of frustrated longing. "I just wanted a nice time," she said.

After that she sat, sipping her beer, looking around at what was happening.

The party had settled into a lot of hard drinking and very little dancing. All the clowning of the early evening had died. Everyone appeared to be trying to get as drunk as possible as fast as possible.

Neil noticed a lieutenant staring at Juliana and gave some thought to breaking his left leg just above the knee.

There was only one couple dancing now. Bear was dancing with a tiny short-haired Vietnamese girl. Her dress was an almost exact replica of Juliana's. Whore, he thought. He watched them.

Shoogie came through the double doors leading to the barracks wing with his arm around a tall, willowy girl. Her features were European. Neil's guess was that she was half-French and half-Chinese. She had none of the breakable delicacy of the Vietnamese about her.

The girl wore her hair to her waist. She wore a pink blouse and white raw silk slacks, tailored to fit well, rather than be whorishly tight. She had style.

Shoogie steered her to their table. He had a half-angry strung-out grin on his face. The girl adopted a fashion-model stance. There was something feverish in her glance, and she gave Shoogie a look which was an almost unimaginable mixture of hatred and adoration. He grinned back, like a man with the upper hand.

"This here's Xuan," Shoogie said to Juliana.

Neil stood up with a wry smile and offered the girl his seat, then snagged two for him and Shoogie from an adjacent table. Juliana surveyed Xuan with abashed curiosity. Xuan lowered her eyes.

"You are very beautiful," Juliana said, speaking slowly to be understood. "Why are you with these barbarians?"

Xuan shrugged. "Mama-Papa dead. Husband dead, baby dead. I no dead." She spoke in a dead monotone.

"Haven't I met this young lady before," Neil asked Shoogie.

Shoogie nodded. "She used to be with Al Wier," he replied. He turned to Juliana and continued as though he were discussing the absence of someone who had gone to the seashore for a couple of weeks. "Al got hit a month ago. His arm was blowed off, and he bled to death running." He pointed to the red flock wall with the plaques. "That bottom right-hand plaque is Al's.

"Anyhow I picked up Xuan's contract, you might say."

Juliana looked sick. "When I met you guys I thought you were acting crazy, but you aren't acting."

Shoogie turned to Neil and grinned. "Say, old buddy, you don't seem like you're doin' too hot. You mind if I take a crack at it?"

Shoogie was drunk and it was dark. He did not respond to the sound of Neil's voice when he grated out, "Mind? Why should I mind?"

And indeed, why should he? Neil had no claim on Juliana. She did not want him on any basis that made sense to him. She and Shoogie were both free agents.

Neil sat glumly, staring ahead. He was so horny. He always got horny in the woods. He was getting very drunk. "Y'wanta dance?" he demanded suddenly.

She jumped as if electrified. "No!"

"Okay, fuck it," Neil muttered, getting up. "I'll dance with this other bitch." He got up and walked over to the cinnamon bear and the skinny little whore. "Dance?" he asked.

The Bear rose. "I'd love to," he said.

"Not you, Shitbird. Your date."

"Oh, whyncha say so?" said the Bear, sitting down. "Sure, go ahead."

Neil slid into the rhythm of the Mamas and the Papas 'Somebody Groovy", doing the Dirty Bop, the only rock'n'roll dance he knew. She giggled and hunched back.

He reached out and snagged the zipper on her dress, unzipping it all the way down. She laughed and spun back around, a broad phony smile on her face. She shrugged out of the dress and kicked it to the side. Still moving to the rhythm, she pointed to Neil and motioned for him to take off his shirt. All eyes were on them now. Men beat their beer bottles on the bar and tabletops, shouting, "Go! Go! Go! Go! Go!"

Neil slipped out of his t-shirt and threw it in the corner. The little whore was skinny and slightly bowlegged, but she moved well. She reached up and unsnapped the black bra she wore. The bra fell to the floor. She was practically breastless, but she shook what she had. A roar of approval went up from the crowd.

Neil spun and looked at Juliana. She watched with numb detachment. He spun back around, kicking off his sandals. He undid the top two buttons of the fly, but there was no way to get his jeans off and keep dancing.

"Hey, Bear!" Shoogie called across the noisy room. 'Did you know Thompson's a well-known diver?"

"Yeah!" the Bear called back. "I heard that."

"He's a champion skydiver."

"Yeah, I heard that!" screamed the Bear.

They kept on dancing.

"He's a world-famous scuba diver."

"So they tell me!" Bear bellowed.

"I don't believe he's did no muff diving though."

"That right?"

Ordinarily Neil would have just shot them the finger and got another beer. But this time he was in such a rage that he was willing to humiliate himself on the off chance he might humiliate Juliana.

Shoogie got up and advanced slowly toward the dancing couple. So did the Bear, from the other side. "We gotta make sure Neil is fully qualified," Shoogie bellowed to the room at large.

"Yeah!" echoed the Bear.

Shoogie grabbed the girl's right arm and leg; Bear grabbed her left. Her eyes were wide, but she was laughing. They hoisted her high and rushed her to the pool table. Brushing a junior officer aside, they pinned her to the table and stripped away her white lace bikini panties. She was naked except for one high-heeled satin pump. Her legs were spread wide. A shout went up from the crowd, like that of a desperate submarine watch officer, "Dive! Dive! Dive! Dive! Dive!"

Neil went in, tasting the oily tang. A pubic hair went up his nose, causing his eyes to water.

He looked up just in time to see Juliana going through the curtains with Shoogie.

Chapter Eight

Neil didn't exactly turn the wheel toward Juliana's. He more or less slumped against the side of it and the machine slewed into the rutted mud road. It was raining, not hard, but the jeep had no top and no windshield. Water hit his glasses, and the windstream blew drops across his vision like tiny comets, as they caught whatever light there was.

It was night, he was angry, and he was very, very drunk.

He had been about to jump Shoogie out at the Imperial, but he wasn't really angry with Shoogie. Just as well be angry at a cat. Finally, drawing doodles with the ring of evaporation on the bottom of his beer bottle, he said, "Man, I shouldn'a told you I didn't mind you hittin' on her. It really pissed me off. I wanted to start something with her."

Shoogie gave him a wry look over his beer. "I told you about that cunt," he said.

Neil smiled tightly. "Are you going to see her again?"

Shoogie shook his head, no. "I don’t like them fuckin' hippies," he said. "I wouldna' nailed her, but I wanted to take her down a peg." He snorted in derision, and looked at Neil closely, as if debating whether to continue or not.

"Absolutely the most hostile fuck I ever had."

Shoogie looked at him and grinned sheepishly, as though he had been the victim of a huge practical joke. "Just when I was about the get my gun she twisted and squeezed me out. "'Show's over,' she said. I grabbed her by the fuckin' arm and climbed back on.

"'Look, Cowboy,' she says. 'I got mine, so fuck you!'"

Shoogie shrugged. Neil had to smile. He had never before known a man so sure of himself that he could tell such a story without shame.

Neil laughed, a short barking laugh, not so much in amusement as in relief from tension. Somehow this made it... He didn't know what this made it. But it was not the betrayal he had thought, just interesting weird behavior.

"I said, 'Bullll---shit!' Shoogie went on. I grabbed her and started fuckin' her again. She didn't fuckin' move. She just laid there. Then she reached out and lit a cigarette. God damn!" He paused a moment, and his eyes narrowed down very tightly. "I'd already fucked Xuan twice that night and m'ole peter just gave out. Then after awhile I got so pissed I went and got Xuan and fucked her again. That was the second most hostile fuck I ever had." He shrugged his shoulders and examined the rim of his glass. "Cary fuckin' Grant," he said regretfully.

Neil took a long relaxed swallow of beer and leaned back in his chair, laughing silently. It was the sort of laugh that comes after surviving a car wreck. He realized that what he'd just heard was as close to an apology as anyone was ever going to get from Shoogie Swift.

He sat there and got a good deal drunker. Shoogie went off with one of the whores who populated the Imperial bar. For awhile Neil thought he would never want to see Juliana again. He felt she could be, and should be, better than that.

He decided the only thing to do was to go out there and talk to her about it. So he lurched off into the night, taking their jeep. Shoogie would figure out what happened to it, and if he didn't, fuck 'im.

But on the way he got to thinking about the patrol again, wondering about the Americans with the Cong. Were they G.I.s who had deserted? He hated to think that.

Were they some kind of Berkeley Red Guards who had put their money where their mouth was?

Then his thoughts drifted to Ksor Drot. He had been fighting for over twenty years, first for the French, then the Americans, when he got killed. Neil had known him to be a kind man; he had met his grandchildren. Neil wondered if Drot's grandchildren would have to fight for twenty years too.

Thus preoccupied he arrived at Juliana's. He got out of the jeep and lurched toward her door, water cascading over the poncho and soaking him from the knees down. Once he stopped the jeep his glasses immediately fogged. He took them off and wiped his eyes.

He stumbled on her steps, and, feeling both angry and clumsy kicked her door. There was no answer, no answer at all. He knocked on the door and called, "Juliana?"

There was a rustling noise inside and the door opened a crack. It was dark inside, but he could make out her baleful glare. "Oh, it's you," she muttered.

He was still angry and drunk, but after three months in recon he calmed down and sobered up fast when things didn't look right. "Where's the lights?" he demanded. "Why are you hiding?"

She sighed and backed up a half step. "Some Viet Cong came into the village. They said that if the Americans didn't get out of here they were going to burn the whole village down."

"Let me in!" Without pausing for a reply he entered the house. "They won't bother you tonight," he said. "Turn on the lights."

"How do you know?" She made no move to comply.

"It's my business to know. Turn on the goddam lights."

She went to the table and lit a kerosene lamp, filling the room with orange light and long shadows. He swished the poncho over his head and threw it in the corner, then sailed his wet wool-smelling beret on top of the pile. The legs of his jungle fatigues were cold and clammy, but the thin poplin would dry in a few minutes. He reached in his shirt pocket and got a cigarette, tapped the filtertip twice on the crystal of his watch, and lit it. "How many were there?" he demanded. "What exactly did they say? Who did they talk to?"

She sat on the couch. "Why are you asking all these questions?"

"Because, goddammit, everything they do is significant. Why the hell are you here all alone anyway?"

"What do you want me to do," she snapped. "Go to the missionaries' house and huddle for warmth? We don't have any guns. At least here with the lights out I can hide."

Neil smiled, pleased to find a civilian who hadn't panicked or fallen prey to the herd instinct. He sat on the couch opposite her and she told him everything that had happened. She shot him resentful glances, but she had been badly frightened, and any help was welcome.

They had come into the village, assembled a group of Montagnards and harangued them for hours for associating with the imperialists. They had threatened to destroy the village if it didn't get rid of the Americans.

There had been three of them, with one carbine, one pistol, and one bullhorn among them.

Neil chuckled when he heard that. He could fill in the rest of the description from the way they were armed. "Black pajamas and needed haircuts," he said. "They're locals, which doesn't mean they're not dangerous. It will probably take them three or four weeks to make their move. But you'll have to move out."

She gave him a stubborn glance. "I've worked too hard for these people to be frightened off"

"Yeah?" he said. "What's going to happen to your people if they kill you and burn the village out? You'll be safe enough in town, and you can still teach."

He intended to check his conclusions with Colonel McLeod, who knew more about the V.C. than anybody. But he was sure she'd be safe for awhile. The V.C. never ran any kind of operation, no matter how simple, without weeks of planning and rehearsal. And they never did exactly what they said they were going to do. They'd do something similar, usually in a different place, at a different time. But they didn't blab their real plans.

"I'm almost one hundred percent certain they won't be back for at least three weeks. After that I'm pretty sure they *will* be back. But just in case, there's a couple of grenades in the jeep. I'll get those."

She looked up, startled. "I'm not going to kill anybody."

Disgusted, he replied, "Okay, okay, one of 'em's tear gas. Maybe that'll stall 'em long enough for you to get away."

He shivered from the damp, even though it was oppressively hot and humid. "Could I have some tea?"

She smiled at that. "Okay!" She rose and went into the kitchen. "It'll take a few minutes to boil. Why did you come here in the first place?"

All the pent-up anger he had felt at the Imperial had faded. There was something so touching and vulnerable behind her defiance that he wanted to shield her from anything that might do her harm.

But in her there was also a hard little knot of rage that he could not penetrate. Even now she seemed to fear warmth toward him more than she feared the Viet Cong. "I was going to give you a hard time about going off with Shoogie. But, what's the point? I guess I'm just disappointed…I wanted something real."

She came back into the room. He looked at her and saw no sympathy, and all the sad story he had dammed up inside blocked again. "What's your beef against men, anyway?"

"You're all assholes."

"Probably true," he replied. "But being nice gets you nothing with women. I was nice to you and got fucked over. Shoogie treats women like shit, and he has to beat them off with a stick. I oughtta shove a grapefruit in your face. Then maybe you'd take me seriously." He raised his hand as if to strike, with no intention of following through.

She grabbed a pair of scissors out of the sewing basket at her feet, and announced, "Just you try it, Buster."

He decided it would be a good lesson for her if he took the scissors away, and possibly paddled her sweet fanny into the bargain. Only he was kidding and she wasn't. He swept his hand toward her wrist, fairly swiftly, but slow enough not to bruise her arm.

She struck with lightning speed, a glancing blow which plowed a three-inch furrow across the bone on the bottom of his right forearm. Blood cascaded down the arm and into his lap.

He laughed. "Seven missions without a scratch, and look at this!"

"Serves you right," she muttered doubtfully, putting the scissors down.

"Get a towel, will you?" he requested.

She glared at him again. He held his arm out to keep from getting any more blood on his uniform, and splattered the couch. She went and got the towel quickly.

He clamped it tight to the cut. "This sucker's gonna need some stitches," he said. "I can't get back to the Project tonight. It's after curfew and too insecure. If I don't get shot by the bad guys, I'll just get shot by the good guys." He paused to think what he'd need to sew the cut himself. "Get me a heavy needle and some coarse thread, a pair of pliers, and a pie-pan full of alcohol. I guess I can do it with that."

She winced. "You're going to sew up your own arm?"

His eyes narrowed. "You want to do it? I could bleed to death by morning. Just get the stuff, will you?"

She rose to go to the kitchen. "I don't have any medicinal alcohol. Is vodka all right?"

He smiled. "Sure, I'll take it internally too. You might roll up a couple of joints. This is gonna hurt. And there's only two things I can't stand, pain and discomfort." He smiled wanly at the old joke.

She came back into the room with a pan and a bottle of vodka. Then she threaded a needle with coarse green thread from her sewing basket.

He took a long swallow of the vodka, then poured roughly three-eighths of an inch into the bottom of the pie-pan with his right hand, while pressing his left forearm into the towel in his lap.

"You really want a joint?" she asked.

"Yeah," he muttered. "If I get real drunk I won't be able to do this, but if I get stoned enough it'll still hurt, but I won't care, and I won't lose motor control."

He pulled his arm away from the towel, and seepage immediately started again. She was fumbling in her stash box and didn't notice. Her hand shook so badly she couldn't roll a joint.

"Damn," she said. “We'll have to use the pipe."

"Whatever," he muttered.

She packed her little hash pipe with finely sifted buddha weed and they each took three hits.

"Okay," he said, as soon as his ride on the up elevator started, "you're gonna have to…hold this cut," he groped for the word, "…closed, while I do the stitches. Let's try to clean it up a little. Here!" He lifted his arm for her to hold the towel.

"Yicch!" she muttered.

"C'mon, man, show some guts."

She held the towel. He put his fingers in the alcohol, then picked up the needle and started the first stitch. He wished now he'd never started this business. He could probably have made it to the medic at the MACV Compound; he'd just wanted to show off. He'd also figured if he broke her down a little he might get some straight answers. He was so drunk and stoned he felt like he was looking at the needle a long way off, down the barrel of a shotgun. The first time he attempted to insert the needle he tried to put it in an inch over the arm. Finally he got it in. It hurt with a dull, searing, one-pointed agony.

"Motherfucker!" he muttered. His fingers slipped, but the needle held. He grabbed the pliers, swished them around in the pan, gripped the needle near the eye and pushed it through. "Oh, shit, that hurt!" he said.

She shook even harder. "Can you tie it off," he asked. "I can't do that with one hand."

"I guess I'll have to," she replied.

She tied the first stitch off. "How many of these are you going to do?"

"Three ought to do it."

Her fingers, bloody as his arm now, were shaking. Her lower lip trembled. Then her eye caught his. "Okay," she said.

He grinned. For her courage, for her style, inside of him some last defense tumbled. For whatever that was worth.

He attempted to set the needle for the second stitch. Thinking took his mind off pain more than booze or weed did. "What the hell are you doing?" he demanded, as much for conversation, for distraction, as anything else. "There can't hardly be a man in the world with more characteristics you despise than Shoogie Swift. If you just wanted to get laid you could have done that at Harvard or Berkeley or wherever the fuck you came from. What are you trying to prove?"

She tied off the last stitch and clipped it.

"Let's clean this mess up," he said.

"That looks easier said than done."

He was feeling a little shaky, and he wasn't sure that maybe they'd messed up, and that he had lost too much blood. But it seemed important to him to be cool enough to clean up. He threw all the tools in the pan. The pain in his arm was searing, and he wished for a local anesthetic. He splashed vodka all over the cut and stitches, took two swallows and choked. "Jesus!"

She looked at him with concern, but made no move to offer assistance. "Bad, huh?"

"Yeah," he replied. He paused. She had been about to tell him something. "Who was he?"

"Who was who?"

"The guy that was gonna be your perfect daddy?"

She slapped him square across the face.

"Jackpot!" he grinned.

The hardness came into her eyes again. She looked at him for a long time, deciding whether to speak. Then she did.

* * *

Her class was out at 11:20 and she didn't have another until 1:30. She left Hamilton Hall, thinking only to find a shady spot to read until lunch.

This simple plan was destroyed by a large and noisy crowd surging past, carrying placards decorated with the peace sign and slogans like "U.S. OUT OF VIETNAM", and, U.S. ATROCITIES IN VIETNAM." There was idealism and marijuana smoke in the air. Being recently arrived from Carthage, Missouri, she had never seen one of these demonstrations before. She caught the excitement immediately.

Leading the crowd was a young man, tall, blond, longish hair, but not rock'n'roll long. Electric blue eyes shot sparks as he carried a flag that Juliana had never seen before, blue on top, red on the bottom, with a yellow star in the center. A low rumbling chant began from the group. "HEY! HEY! LBJ! HOW MANY KIDS DID YOU KILL TODAY?"

She too had seen burned out villages, dead babies, and crying mothers on TV. She had seen U.S. Marines torch a village. She jammed her books in her backpack and joined the throng marching amid the stately buildings. She felt the warmth of comradeship, excitement, and the thrill of power. Then a girl striding beside her, with long chestnut hair and an India print dress, a very tan girl with no shoes, handed her a joint and she hit it, sucking smoke to her toenails. *Whoïinnnggg!!!*

Her feelings intensified by a factor of six and her brain slipped into rock'n'roll time.

She passed the joint on and a guy who looked like he'd spent the last six years in a closet handed her an opened square of aluminum foil with little crumbly chunks of what looked like orange Kool-Aid on it. She looked at it stupidly.

"Lick it up!" he said. "It'll do your head nice." She bent over and licked the foil clean.

"What is it?" she asked, raising her head. It had an odd taste, or possibly absence of taste; it gave her an empty feeling in the pit of her stomach.

"Berkeley Sunshine," he replied with a wink, "The best."

"Best what?" she asked, but her benefactor was whirled away in the crowd. *Best what? Best what? Best what?* But she knew.

She dodged and squeezed through the press of bodies toward the front of the shouting, chanting throng. Three times people handed her joints as she moved forward. She was high and everything in her vision was starting to wriggle and slide. The colors leapt at her. Then someone started to sing, and it was something she could grab onto and remember, so she started singing too. "We shall not, we shall not be moved," over and over. It seemed simple and beautiful, she thought, so simple and beautiful.

She felt a metallic tingle in her gut, her nostrils dilated, and all the detail in the surrounding buildings jumped out at her.

The metallic taste passed and the queasiness faded. All was beautiful. These people were young and right and good; archetypal, noble. Colors were brilliant and clear and the world twisted in weird ways, gnarled, wriggling, and bizarre.

The buildings were ancient, abandoned, buried in ivy, the crowd a new form of barbarian horde, and the sky Van Gogh swirls.

She looked down at the sidewalk and Turkish rug patterns appeared in the brick. She surged forward, carefully slipping between people in the chanting throng, feeding off their energy.

The throng jammed in front of Lowe Library and the guy with the laser eyes carried the flag up the steps. He and another student mounted the steps and the other guy handed him a bullhorn. Laser-eyes handed the other boy the flag. He was gorgeous, in khaki pants and a Penny's work shirt, red bandanna at his throat. A slight breeze lifted the hair over his neck. He was tall and thin, maybe six feet, with slim hips and broad, bony shoulders. His face showed intellect and imagination, strength and courage, ambition and energy. He was the most perfect human male she had ever seen.

She turned to the guy beside her and said, "Who's that?"

"Todd Carpenter," he said. "From Virginia. He founded the SDS Chapter." Her mind recorded every word, even though it was hard to follow the echo in his voice, his face slipping around. His hand moved before her, leaving strobelike tracers. Her attention went back to the steps and the guy with the blue eyes. He was speaking, and phrases stuck with her…"immoral war…innocent victims…duty to resist." He spoke well, but she knew she could help him with content. Gotta do something about those clichés.

"BLAW WAW SQUAW MAW!" More powerful speakers drowned his voice. She looked to see a line of New York policemen on the flank of the crowd. Slightly in front and to the side of this formation an older man in a gold-braided uniform spoke into a bigger bullhorn than Todd's. "RAW GRAW MAW BLAW!" he said. The crowd looked at him stupidly for a moment. He began too bellow into his loudspeaker again, this time in an agitated and belligerent manner. Juliana could see his face, could tell he was nobody to mess with; but to this crowd of spoiled upper and middle-class kids he sounded just like their mothers when they said, "I mean it now," and really didn't. This guy's voice went low at the end. Juliana thought, he's fixing to break balls and heads. She laughed. "Damn, this is exciting."

More from Todd's little bullhorn. "Sit down and link arms," he said. "They can't break us if we stick together." Other students, longhaired and bellbottomed, but obviously not stoned, moved briskly through the crowd, instructing everyone they passed to sit down and link arms. She sat with the others, and hooked arms with a couple of other kids.

Then the junior leaders sat down and linked arms too.

On the other side of the crowd, away from the cops, a TV panel truck drove up, then another. Crews boiled out of the back. Cameramen adjusted their braces and strapped in. Soundmen fiddled with knobs, and walked crablike behind the cameramen, anchored to them by black cable. The correspondents stood off to the side during shooting, taking notes and protecting their coiffures.

Everything stopped while the TV people set up. Cops and demonstrators alike waited stupidly as the engines of their fame were put in place. Then they started again. Todd picked up his bullhorn and put a ring in his voice as he instructed the people who were already seated with linked arms to hold fast.

The cops reached into the crowd and attempted to drag students out of the pile, but the linked arms maneuver held them fairly well. A few were dragged loose and packed off to paddy wagons, but most held.

The older cop with the bullhorn pointed to Todd and ordered. "Get that yimp!"

Two burly cops forged none too gently through the crowd, to mount the steps. Todd sat down and huddled in a ball, the "non-violent crouch" of the civil rights march days, but the cops grabbed him under the arms and bumped him down the stairs, then dragged him toward a paddy wagon.

Instinctively and unquestioningly Juliana dropped the arms she was linked to and started stepping over people to get to that paddy wagon.

Surging through and over the crowd, she was lost in awe and majesty, lost in the veins in the leaves of trees and in the texture of their bark, in the patterns of flakes and rust on the body of the paddy wagon that made this paddy wagon different from all others.

Strong arms hooked under her armpits. Another cop grabbed her feet. He was a young guy, and he looked uncomfortable. His brass buttons were funhouse mirrors for her face. "Golly, officer," she exclaimed, "the buttons on your pig coat are beautiful in the sunlight."

He looked at her and cracked a grin. "Sistah," he said, "whatever you're on, we're takin' you where you can sleep it off."

He jerked his thumb toward the open door of the paddy wagon, and he and the other cop hoisted her in.

She was immediately plunged into a box of gloom and darkness. Her heart fell, and she started to feel her sense of wonder slip away into the murk. Then she spied Todd sitting at the front of the box. There were six or eight other students already there, but her attention focused on just him. He sat alone and dejected. The others were laughing. It was a big joke to them. They'd be booked and released, one night in jail at the most.

She worked up next to him. "Hello!" she said.

He looked up and grinned. She melted.

He beckoned her over. Out in the sunshine, looking at him on the stairs she'd been a wild creature. But here now, in the dark cubicle, swaying as the engine thrummed and they were led off to jail, she felt very small and afraid. As she recognized her fear it started to escalate into panic.

He looked at her, eyes brimming with compassion "You're tripping," he said.

"I know it," she whispered, and held her fingers to her lips.

She snuggled into him and put her head against his shoulder. She felt warm and protected. She closed her eyes and a row of cartoon duckies in ever-changing colors tracked across her eyes, then changed into bearlike creatures and then a kaleidoscope of stars and comets.

She opened her eyes to see she was shut into a dim container with people sitting in rows, and the shock caused her to burrow further into his shoulder. He smiled at her and held her tight and she closed her eyes, looking for her cartoons.

He stayed with her all through the booking process. "Are you gonna be all right?" he asked.

She grinned and shrugged. The police station was almost as depressing as the paddy wagon had been. For awhile she amused herself by looking at wanted posters, just as design patterns. She looked into the face of a mass murderer, and his soul was mesmerizing, evil beyond anything.

Todd grabbed her elbow. She looked away, into his face.

"Don't look at that," he said. She saw the concern in his eyes and started to move into his arms.

"Not here," he said, "not now." He grinned. "Look into your hand."

"Why?" she asked.

"Look at the lines. What do you see?"

The lines in her hand were jumping and wriggling in the most astonishing way. She watched them until an officer came with a clipboard and asked her the usual questions. Fortunately he started with "Name?" If he'd begun anywhere else she'd never have been able to get into the rhythm of it. She answered by rote, past peaking, past all her rushes, churning along on a stream of colors and weirdness, able to pull it together and maintain if she had to, losing it immediately the minute she let go.

An hour later, on the street, he asked, "You okay?"

She started thinking about going back to the roach-infested closet she shared with two other girls and tears formed in her eyes.

"C'mon!"

She didn't even ask where they were going. She just hooked an arm over his and went with him.

* * *

His apartment was also small and roach-infested, but it was a garden level, with a small outdoor space and some greenery. The old brick wall had ivy clinging to it, forming a cool green pit. Sitting on his aluminum garden furniture they smoked a joint and drank a glass of white wine. She saw that he was checking her over, saw that he didn't want to hurt her or freak her out, knew he was going to make his move, and waited and smiled. She was calm and felt the beginning of the old smoky "I want it!" feeling.

His stereo was an eight-track he had bought in high school because he had one in his car. It had a prolonged skip when it changed tracks in the middle of a song, but it would play the same album unattended forever if that was wanted, and sometimes it was. He put on the Moody Blues *Days of Future Past*, which clicked right into *Nights in White Satin* and she merged with the music. They finished their joint in the garden. He rose from his chair, took her in his arms and led her inside.

The walls of the living room were covered with SDS charts and graphs, page proofs of the last issue of the *Barricade*. But she ignored those.

No charts in the bedroom, but there were two good speakers. The sound seemed to vibrate through her and she was lost in it.

An old handmade quilt covered the bed, and the room was a bit dank and musty smelling, but he lit some incense and the mustiness was subsumed in sweet funk.

She had no memory of taking her clothes off. One moment she was standing there in jeans and a T-shirt and the next she lay on the bed looking at the soft flesh of her lover's belly, framed in the V of an open zipper. He kicked off his sneakers, pulled his shirt over his head without unbuttoning it and shucked out of his khakis as he fell on the bed, smiling. No shorts, no undershirt, no socks. One minute clothed and beautiful, the next naked and beautiful.

She'd had two lovers before, one timid and hesitant, the other clumsy and hurtful. But Todd was her first gentle, accomplished lover. He moved slowly with the rhythm of the Moody Blues and she was lost in it, all her senses still expanded by the drug, so that wherever he touched her she ached with pleasure and longing. Wherever she touched him her hands found a quiet strength. It was as though her body had been transformed into an instrument of the music, now *Nights in White Satin*, now *Tuesday Afternoon*.

* * *

Even later, when it went bad, then worse, she remembered that first year of gentle nights. Todd was genuine. He really cared. He cared about her; he cared about civil rights, and now he cared about the Vietnamese. The only one he didn't properly care for was himself. He drove himself. He kept up with his classes, ran the paper, organized, worked on committees for national demonstrations.

Many nights she excused herself and flopped on the bed as he and some committee poured over rosters, typed letters, and schemed. He started speeding about a year after she moved in. At first it was just whites, 25 milligram dextroamphetamine tablets. He would usually come off them about four in the morning and grab a couple or three hours of sleep before he went at it again.

Then the press started and he was dropping black mollies to get up for interviews with *Time* Magazine. He grinned at her, and it was like his same old grin except this time there was something guarded, something calculated about it, and she knew he was conning her, playing for effect. She put it out of her mind though, because she loved him, and it *was* charming.

But she could see Todd changing as fame arrived and he took more speed to keep up with it.

Todd was gone a lot, to meetings, to demonstrations. She couldn't go to all of them and keep up her studies. She took speed once with him, but she hated it, just hated it. She felt strong, jammed with energy, as though energy were gushing through her body like water through a huge fire hose, but it made her nervous and ill-tempered. She became so crabby that she told him everything she didn't like about him in about three minutes.

"You're self-centered," she said. "You pretend to be this caring concerned person, but underneath it all you're just as selfish as the rest of us. You want what you want when you want it, and you don't care about my needs, or want to hear about them." She stayed right down on his case until he finally left the apartment, and after that she didn't do any more speed.

But he did; he made the Law Review and played Led Zeppelin loudly at 3:00 a.m. while babbling political pronouncements with no basis in fact, philosophical maunderings with no basis in logic, reminiscences of boring and pointless times. He developed a whole new set of friends for these activities, long-haired, pale, greasy guys in black leather, all of them rapping a mile a minute in the middle of the night, heavy metal rock'n'roll thudding in the background. This always seemed to happen when she had a test the next morning.

She became distracted and worried. She worried about the future, about her grades, but mostly she worried about Todd. She loved him, and she knew he loved her. He had proved it so many times, with his tenderness and caring, with little thoughtful surprises. But the speed was building a wall between him and his own emotions.

She remembered the time she had taken the black mollie and the ugly feelings that had been released. She remembered thinking at the time that if she ever really wanted to kill somebody all she'd have to do was shoot speed, and that's what Todd was doing now, crystal meth, into the vein. It terrified her to think of it. She was so distracted that she started to forget things, her pill for instance.

Then she forgot to have her period and she forgot the first three doctors appointments.

* * *

"So you're three months along," said Dr. Esther Weintraub," and you look like shit. You've got dark circles under your eyes; you're still smoking pot. You've got to clean up your act, my dear, or you're going to hurt the baby." Dr. Weintraub, a thin, fervent woman in her early thirties, stubbed out her own cigarette and smiled. "Really."

Juliana nodded. "I've been so… I don't know."

"Now you know."

Juliana nodded.

"Eight hours every night, no dope, no booze, no cigarettes. Eat right and don't worry."

Juliana nodded again. She hadn't intended to get pregnant, but she was. And inside her there was a quiet joy. She could feel the life growing in her, and she knew that when she told him Todd would share her joy. This could be the change that fixed everything.

* * *

He looked up from his books, eyes blazing, mad from speed. "You bitch," he said. "You couldn't wait to ruin my career, ruin my life." He was out of his chair and he hit her in the face. Another blow to the head knocked her down. Then he kicked her in the belly and walked out of the apartment.

So sudden she hadn't got her hands up to defend herself. She lay, almost unconscious, aware of a sharp pain in her stomach, as though she had been stabbed with a spear.

She lay for a long time, waiting to feel better, waiting for him to come back. Only he didn't come back, and she felt worse. She felt something warm and wet spreading over her crotch. She touched it with her hand. It was her blood, also her future and the life she had planned. It occurred to her that it might be her life altogether. She lunged to get up and fell back again. Then she scooted on her back across the floor until she could knock the phone off an end table. She picked up the handset, righted the phone and dialed "O".

"Operator."

"Operator, this is an emergency. I'm miscarrying and losing blood…about to pass out…tell'm break down the door…I'm gonna pass out.

"Operator…" and the phone dropped from her fingers. She awoke in the hospital with a tube in her arm.

When he came in, straight, and apologetic, with flowers and his patented winsome smile, she turned away and pulled the covers over her head. She didn't listen to, "I'm sorry," or, "It'll never happen again," or "I love you. I want to marry you," or "We'll have lots of kids…later."

She almost came out from under the covers on, "It'll never happen again," to tell him why it would never happen again, but no, she would deny him even her anger.

She felt empty; not just depressed or angry, but hollowed out, used up, burnt.

Then she saw a picture in the *Times*, with a Vietnam story about the American missionary doctor, Pat Smith, holding a baby suffering from extreme malnutrition. In anguish and longing her heart reached for the child.

Maybe she was supposed to do something more than march and hold a sign. She wondered if the Peace Corps was in Vietnam.

She called the New York Peace Corps office and was told that they were not. But the lady said there was another organization that did much the same work in Vietnam, the International Volunteer Service, and gave her the number.

* * *

Neil slid over on the couch and put his throbbing arm around her shoulder, very carefully.

"Goddammit!" she snarled, leaning forward, putting her head in her hands. "I never cry. I never cry."

He didn’t' know if the gesture meant she was avoiding his arm, or not. He took the arm down and leaned forward to look at her face behind her hands.

She cried in great racking sobs. She bent further and rested her head on her arms and her arms on her knees. When she looked up she threw her head back and sniffled. Her eyes were red, and tears ran down her cheeks, slow rivulets that clung to her chin and dropped onto her knees, making tiny dark wet spots that quickly soaked into fuzzy circles on her jeans.

She got up. "I've got to bandage that cut," she said coldly. She gathered up the pan with the vodka and the pliers. She threw the sewing stuff back in the basket. "One pot of coffee coming up," she sniffled.

When she came back he sat forward and drank his coffee. He looked to see if it would be okay to put his arm around her again. But he couldn't read her expression. He decided not to try it. She might construe it as a pass, and the last thing he felt like right then was making a pass. He wouldn't want one either accepted or rejected.

"You can spend the night," she said.

He looked up, startled.

"I need a friend to hold me," she said.

* * *

The Vietnamese bed was big, wide, flat, hard, and lumpy, with a musty faded floral pattern bedspread, and an enormous white gauze mosquito net suspended over it.

Neil spent the night naked, curled around the object of his desire, she in a pair of peach-colored bikini panties and a t-shirt. He held her long, luscious body, with his right arm under her neck, and the throbbing left one twisted in an incredibly awkward way, to keep the pressure of the bed off the pain.

"You really like me, don't you?" she asked in the dark.

Startled, he replied, "You think I'd take this shit off somebody I didn't like?"

He waited for her reply, but she was asleep.

Chapter Nine

"Jesus, look at these poor motherfuckers," Shoogie said with an expansive wave of his hand. They walked away from their Huey toward a three-quarter-ton truck the brigade had sent to pick them up. Their camouflage uniforms were clean. They were shaved, their weapons oiled and spotless. Their gait was relaxed and casual.

But the soldiers around them looked harassed and miserable. They all wore helmets and jackets, even those working with picks and shovels to repair rocket holes in the runway. The camp was neat enough, big squad tents laid out evenly, the proper sandbag walls around them. But the hilltop had been scraped clean by bulldozers, and the winds had scattered a fine red dust over everything, including the people. It was laid over the tents, into hair, into the gritty oil of faces, into knuckles.

Their truck was covered with it. The recon team itself was starting to pick up the dust. Nowhere on the hill was there grass or a tree to relieve the manmade desolation. Even the once lush hills in the distance were pockmarked and burned by bombs and artillery. There was a burned out Montagnard village visible on a hillside half a mile away.

Neil and Shoogie squeezed in beside the driver. The rest of the team climbed in back. The young soldier started the truck and drove away.

Neil looked over into the back at their stoic Yards. Ksor Drot's son, Nay Go, had asked to be transferred over from the Mike Force Battalion, and Shoogie had accepted him. He sat quietly in the back, a little bigger and heavier than Ksor Drot had been, with unfiled teeth and unlooped ears, but very much like him, quiet and solid.

Shoogie pointed off in the distance. "Who burned that village over there?"

The driver glanced in that direction "We did," he said. "The people was supposed to be Cong sympathizers."

Shoogie drawled, "If they weren't before they sure as shit are now."

The driver frowned.

They drove to a tent a few hundred yards back from the runway.

"You know what this is all about?" Neil asked.

"Nope!" Shoogie replied.

They all dismounted from the truck. The general's aide came out of the tent and Shoogie threw him a lazy salute.

The lieutenant grinned and returned the salute. He was much more relaxed, almost a different man. "Sergeant Swift, Sergeant Thompson, come in."

Shoogie excused himself to Nay Thai and the four tribesmen went into a flatfooted full squat outside the tent, firing up their crooked pipes and banana leaf cigars.

"You with the general?" Neil asked the lieutenant as they filed in.

The lieutenant laughed. "I'm not his aide anymore," he said. "I'm the new assistant brigade intelligence officer. And I want you guys to meet my boss."

Sitting behind a battered field desk was a skinny, slope-shouldered little guy in an olive drab T-shirt with MAJ SWANK stenciled on it in black. A field cap with a brown cloth major's oak leaf and black parachute wings sewn on it sat back on his salt and pepper crewcut. His features were sharp and his face badly pockmarked. He stood up and extended his hand. "So you guys are McLeod's best," he said, shaking Shoogie's hand.

Shoogie grinned. “You’ll have to ask him about that, sir.”

“I have and you are. Now lookahere!” He picked up a pointer and tapped a map. “This here’s Hill 987. They’s Gooks on it. I need to know how many and what for. Accordin’ to that prisoner you guys brought in they wanta knock out this base. If so, I wanta know when and how. This here smartass lieutenant says you guys can find out part or all of that for me. If you work for McLeod you probably can. How about it?"

Neil scratched the back of his head. “What’s the general think of all this?”

The major cocked an eyebrow and deadpanned, “He wants intel. How I get it, that’s my business.”

Shoogie went over and looked at the map closely. “Looks like about a two-day job,” he said. He took out his notebook and copied down the mapsheet number. “We gonna work it through the Project or direct through you? You guys set up for this type operation?”

The major shook his head. “Not yet, but we need to be. I been thinkin’ of havin’ a long-range recon platoon formed to work direct for me.”

“Okay,” Shoogie nodded. “This’ll give you a head start. We need a twenty-four hour radio monitor, and a full-time on-call extraction chopper. You oughta have one for every three teams. Just workin’ one team like this is sort of inefficient as far as your support base goes.”

Shoogie and Neil talked to the major and the lieutenant until two that morning, outlining the details of a recon operation, and getting their signal instructions worked out for this patrol. The major filled two steno pads and started another. The lieutenant sat wide-eyed through the entire conversation.

There was a long period during which the major stood with his back to them, making squiggles on an overlay with three different colors of grease pencil. Neil's eyes were drawn to the lieutenant. He looked at Shoogie as though he were having a mystical experience.

Shoogie caught the look. He exchanged a glance with Neil, and then edged over to the lieutenant. The lieutenant's eyes widened as Shoogie wrapped an arm around his waist, kissed him lightly on his left ear, and muttered, "You know, motherfucker, I *like* you."

The next time Neil glanced in the lieutenant's direction he was gone.

Finally the major crashed on a folding cot, and the team rolled up in poncho liners on the floor of the tent.

Next day they started getting ready. The lieutenant had returned with the daylight, and was fascinated by every detail of their preparation. Shoogie took an entire stick of camouflage greasepaint and mashed it into a crumbly ball, smearing it over every inch of his exposed skin, on his neck, behind the ears, down in his nostrils, and in his hair. "That stick would last most guys a year," said the lieutenant.

"The texture's better if you cake it on," Shoogie replied. He surveyed himself in the mirror. He put his hat down over his eyes and, just standing in the tent, looked like something growing out of the ground. If there was a switch in his head marked 'recon' and another marked 'garrison' he'd already switched to recon. He turned like a bush blowing in the breeze and lifted the cover on his watch.

They went in at last light. It was kind of a sloppy insertion, because the brigade's chopper crews weren't used to that type of operation. They went halfway up the reverse slope of the hill and crashed into a thicket for the night.

It was a rough climb the next day, all up. And the terrain was much more open, much of the undergrowth burned off. They were constantly on edge, for there was very little cover. He could see for maybe fifty feet through the trees.

They passed through one section where napalm had started a brushfire that left a light gray ash on the ground, which puffed under their boots as they walked. But the ash was too fine and light to leave recognizable footprints. Out on the edge of the burned-over area, low flames licked at the brush, dancing around rocks. Fine smoke drifted through the jungle. But they ran into no Charlies. Lots of tracks, but no Charlies.

Early that afternoon they found the top of the hill. Drifting up from below they heard the lilting tones of Vietnamese conversation and the clink of shovels.

Shoogie got out his binoculars and looked down the face of the hill. Wordlessly he handed the glasses to Neil. It was all under the trees, and none of it would be seen from the air, but everywhere Neil looked he caught partial glimpses of the arc of swinging shovels, patches of Viets moving with water buckets, and cooking around small fires. They were spread thick all over the forward slope of the hill. Neil couldn't tell for sure how many, but it had to be at least a regiment, maybe a thousand guys.

Shoogie took his binoculars back and led them five hundred meters back down the hill. Then they moved laterally until they found a trail. They set up beside it. They had to move back further than usual because of the openness of the terrain. They were way too far back to even consider a prisoner snatch. Too open and too many Gooks around for that anyway.

It wasn't quick this time. They sat there for three hours. Once during that period a platoon went by, struggling with long wooden boxes of rockets, four men to a box. Neil counted six boxes.

After the platoon they waited again. Three men came up the hill walking with a quick jerky gait. The one in the middle wore the red collar tabs of an officer, and carried a Tokarev pistol in a leather holster. The two others had AKs. Shoogie cut all three down quietly with his “K”. Then he moved onto the trail. Two of them were still moving, so he put a round in each of their heads. He motioned for Y Buhn, Frenchy, and Nay Go to drag them back off the trail while he, Neil and Nay Thai covered their tracks. The officer carried a message pouch. Shoogie cut that off him. With usual Vietnamese thoroughness they all carried letters and the little diaries they kept so compulsively. And wallets. The tribesmen grabbed all the rings, watches, and ballpoints. Then Shoogie jerked his head down the mountain. Time to go.

* * *

When they re-entered Major Swank’s tent Shoogie went over to the corner to shrug out of his gear. Neil took their little collection of wallets and notebooks to the major’s field desk; the weapons he left outside with the Montagnards, who squatted over them in a semi-circle, smoking. The Yards would split a 5,000 piaster reward for each weapon, about fifty bucks apiece total, roughly a month’s salary. They talked about it in low tones in a language filled with chokes and hacks and glottal stops.

Neil dumped the notebooks and wallets out on the major’s desk. "Some of this might be pretty useful. The officer was a meticulous notekeeper.”

“Okay, good.” The major leaned forward and pulled the family pictures from the NVA officer’s wallet. He looked them over carefully; one older man, older woman, wife, and little girl. And a picture of a civilian man in an open-throat white shirt and flip-flops, in front of the cathedral in downtown Ban Don. “Hey, Sternberg,” he called to the lieutenant, who was earnestly pecking on a portable typewriter at the next rickety field desk. The lieutenant stopped and looked up.

"Go run this stuff through the Two Corps agent suspect file, will you?"

Neil's eyes snapped back to the major. That was not the sort of file a brigade intelligence section would normally have. "Where'd you get that, sir?"

The major leaned his chair back on its rear legs, put his hands behind his head and grinned. "J-2, MacVee. You know how it is; all intel flows uphill and never gets back to the people who can use it. So when I came down to the brigade I brought my own."

Neil took the picture from the major's hand. He was fascinated by intelligence work. "Let me do it," he said. "Who knows, I might find a familiar face."

The lieutenant got the file out for him, and he sat down on an olive drab folding chair. The file was a collection of odd-size photographs, some wallet size, some streaky black and white polaroids, some that appeared to be shot from a roof across the street with a telephoto lens. Neil went through, looking for a thin man, about forty-five, wearing glasses and swept-back hair.

What he found was Xuan.

She was a little younger and a little heavier. Her hair was up, and she wore a high-necked khaki Mao jacket, but it was her.

Neil felt cold. Of all the whores at the Project she was the only one he actually liked. "Hey, Shoog," he called. "C'mere."

Neil handed him the 5X7 card with the photo stapled to it. He took it and his eyes narrowed. He handed it back.

"This is real good stuff," the little major said, looking up from his writing. He was copying the North Vietnamese assault plan they had taken from the message pouch into another spiral notebook.

"Accordin' to this jazzer here they gonna run a full division in here to take this camp. That's their lead element up on that hill, the 305 Regiment. That's a pretty good outfit."

The lieutenant sorted through the other stuff at his table, the letters, diaries, and wallets, none of which had any money in them when they got them back from the Yards.

Neil slouched in a green metal folding chair, smoking a cigarette. Shoogie had his "K" broken down, and was wiping carbon off its bolt. "You could heliborne assault into the back side of that hill real easy, and take it," he said tonelessly to the major.

"That's a rodge," the major said. "That's going to be my recommendation

* * *

The lieutenant colonel, Frenier's operations officer, was perfect, like the general, except that whereas the general was sexless perfect the colonel was voluptuous perfect. Somehow he had got starched fatigues out here, and he stood ramrod straight, with just the hint of a pout on his lips, as Shoogie, leaning back on the rear two legs of a folding chair, jabbed a green-coated finger at him and said, "Sir, they're dug in solid on the forward slope of that hill, but they ain't expecting nothing on the back side. You go up the front you gonna get a shitload of people killed. Go up the back and you got it dicked."

The Ops Officer gave him a look of mixed puzzlement and exasperation, wondering why he had to explain himself to somebody who looked like a bush. "That's true, sergeant. "But it's too late to change the plan and get the change approved now. The time loss would obviate the principle of surprise. They don't know we are coming now. If we change the plan we may find them dug in both ways. Besides, to go up the reverse slope would be a violation of international law, since the reverse slope is across the Cambodian border." He concluded with finality, as though the matter were settled, and moved his pointer.

"Hmmmmmmph!" Major Swank cleared his throat and stood up. "That's only on the Army's maps, sir. The Air Force maps have both sides of the hill on our side of the border. My recommendation is the reverse slope."

From where he had been sitting quietly on the front row of folding chairs, the general purred, "We're in the army, Major. We operate from army maps."

Shoogie leaned forward. "The fact is they don't nobody know where that border is. It ain't never been surveyed. It could be anywhere within five klicks east or west of that hill."

Still shrouded in shadow, without turning his head so much as a millimeter, the general said, "Gentlemen, we are wasting time. My decision has been made. We take the forward slope."

Chapter Ten

Xuan giggled, sitting on a barstool.

"Go on, have one," Shoogie said, handing her a drink from behind the bar. He had showered and put on clean fatigues when they got back from brigade. She took a sip of the seven-seven he had made for her.

She made a face. "I never drink before," she said.

Shoogie nodded. "Drink it, Baby. It'll help."

She looked at him quizzically, then gulped the drink.

Neil, in a clean uniform, walked in the door and put three six-foot lengths of manila hemp on the bar. "Hi, Xuan," he said.

She nodded hello.

"This be enough, won't it?" he asked Shoogie.

"Yeah."

Neil went back out. A few minutes later he came back in with a field telephone with two six-foot wires running from the posts. He sat that on the bar too.

"Finish your drink, Baby," Shoogie said gently.

She eyed the equipment, her eyes shifting from puzzlement to apprehension, and took another gulp of the drink.

Neil brought a straight-backed wooden chair over and put it next to her.

"Sit on the chair, darlin'," said Shoogie.

"Her eyes went wide. "For why?"

Shoogie nodded and sipped his drink. "Because I tell you to," he said, with a very low edge in his voice.

She sat in the chair.

"Now sit still," Shoogie said. "Neil is going to tie you up."

Neil took the first piece of rope and started to secure her hands behind her.

She giggled, frightened, and a little excited.

"Why you do this?"

"Well," Shoogie said, voice steady, eyes half lidded, "We found out you're a spy. Now we're going to find out what you know."

She sat rigid in fright for a moment, then sagged in the chair. When she sagged the ropes loosened.

"Well, shit," Neil said. He retied them.

She looked at Shoogie again. She was obviously frightened, but on some level she still trusted him. "I love you," she said.

Shoogie picked up the field phone and moved it near her chair. "I know that, Baby," he said. "I love you too. This ain't got nothin' to do with that."

Christ, Neil thought. Listen to this!

Shoogie dragged the chair over by the field phone and took the earrings out of her ears. She jerked her head to one side, but he grabbed her hair and held her. He picked up a piece of double-E-eight wire and threaded it through her pierced earlobes. Then he looked at Neil and said instructively, "This here's a variation of the Western Union pigtail splice." He very carefully wound the bright copper and steel wires around each other. When he was threading the wire a stray steel filament stuck the lobe of her ear. "Oops, sorry," he said, and wound the offending stray back to the main wire. Then he finished the connection.

She did not cry, but she looked as though she might. "Shoogie," she asked again, "why you do this?"

Shoogie scowled. "I ain't gonna let somebody do it that likes it," he said. He picked up a yellow legal pad and a government issue ballpoint. He went around and sat in one of the wicker basket chairs in front of Xuan and lit a cigarette. He waved a hand at Neil to sit by the phone behind her.

Nervously Neil sat down by the phone. He put his left hand on top of the phone and took the crank in his right.

"Name?" Shoogie inquired. She told him. They went smoothly through address, date of birth, place of birth and so on. She readily admitted being an intelligence agent, and that she was a dedicated Viet Cong.

They hit a snag when Shoogie asked who her contacts were. She squinted her eyes and held her mouth in a thin line. Shoogie nodded. Neil whirled the telephone crank and Xuan lept in her bonds. She did not cry, nor did she cry out, but she slumped in the ropes, almost unconscious from pain.

Shoogie winced. He composed his face and said, "Easy, Ace, just enough to get the information."

Xuan was almost out in the chair. Shoogie got her drink and propped her up again. When she recovered he asked the question again. She shook her head again. Shoogie nodded and Neil gently turned the crank. She arched in her chair again, and again it was Shoogie who flinched.

For the first time in his life Neil knew what it was to despise himself, because somewhere in the depths of his consciousness he was enjoying this. He could not allow himself to be involved in any more of these "interrogations" or they would become a need. Now he knew why well-trained professional interrogators preferred to use any method other than torture, quick and easy though it was.

Her contacts were the Chao brothers. The attack on Hill 987 was expected. The little old white-haired lady who did Frenier's laundry and starched his fatigues also saved scraps of paper, and listened carefully.

Shoogie cut Xuan loose. "Okay, Baby," he said. "You got half an hour to pack up and go."

Her face was bathed in sweat, hair down in her eyes. "Go?" she said.

"Hey, Shoog," Neil exclaimed, "we're supposed to turn all prisoners over to the Viets"

Shoogie took her arm. He turned to Neil. "We got what we need. We turn her over to the Slopes, they'll just rape her thirty-two times and beat her to death with bamboo rods. Fuck that!"

Neil shook his head. "She'll just spy somewhere else."

"I don't think so," Shoogie said. "When the word gets out she talked she'll have to hide from her own people."

She was so dazed she could hardly move. "I'll help her get her stuff and go," Shoogie said.

"I'm not believin' this," Neil said. "She's a fuckin' spy."

Shoogie gave him his narrow squinty-eyed look. "Go get yourself a pistol with a silencer and meet me at the TOC. We got work to do."

* * *

They found Colonel McLeod in the TOC, watching the Ops Sergeant plot positions of deployed teams.

"Are you sure?" he demanded when they told him what they had found out.

"Yessir," Shoogie replied. "They know the attack is coming. The information came right out of Frenier's headquarters, from the housemaid."

"Where's the girl now?" McLeod asked. "I'd like to talk to her myself."

Shoogie shrugged. "She escaped, sir."

McLeod arched an eyebrow. "Escaped?"

"Yes sir. We just turned our backs for a second, and by golly, she was gone."

McLeod smiled wryly. "That right?" he asked Neil.

"Yessir," Neil said, and then added, "by golly."

The colonel chewed the ends of his moustache and paced the map-festooned concrete bunker. The young captain and his sergeant had become aware that something was up. They watched him anxiously. "All right," he muttered, almost to himself. "Frenier never admitted to being wrong about anything in his life. He won't stop the attack, or go up the reverse slope. He'd throw away his whole brigade first."

He turned to his Operations Officer. "I want the entire Mike Force, minus one company, on the pad ready to go in one hour. We're gonna deploy as a battalion." He grinned. "Get the sergeant major. I'm gonna lead the assault force and he's coming with me."

He turned to Neil, who understood the Old Army and its politics. "We're not going to get any thanks for saving Frenier's hide. If anything he'll ruin me all the quicker…"

He smirked. "Well, fuck 'im! We're going up the reverse slope of that hill and clean house. We'll save that brigade as many casualties as we can."

Neil saw any chance he might have for a commission going down the tubes, but for McLeod it seemed worth it.

McLeod sat down at his desk, scribbled a message, and handed it to the Ops Officer. "Have this sent to Frenier a half hour after we're gone." Then he turned to Neil and Shoogie. "You two want to go? It ought to be a nice party, and we'll all be lookin' for work after it's over anyway."

"Wouldn't miss it for the world, sir," Shoogie said. "We need to run an errand in town first, though."

The colonel looked at his watch. "Make it quick!" he said.

* * *

Twenty minutes later they blew by the Rotary Club sign on the edge of town. "Our airlift will be here in two hours. McLeod wants you and me to go in with the lead company."

Shoogie passed everything on the road. Little kids saw the look in his eyes and dropped their thumbs. "Who's got the lead company?" he shot at Neil without turning his head.

"Bear."

Shoogie slowed down as they entered the traffic circle. He gunned around the corner by the cathedral. He and Neil got out a block from the Chao's. The two of them padded silently, stoop-shouldered, down the street. Shoogie's "K" was draped over his shoulder, and Neil wore his pistol in a shoulder holster. They wore serious expressions, and people made way for them.

They turned in at the Chao's and stepped into the showroom. The old gentleman in the homburg and the undershirt sat behind the counter, manipulating an abacus, and marking the figures down in a notebook.

"Boys upstairs?" Shoogie asked.

The old man nodded.

Halfway up the stairs they stopped and screwed the silencers onto the barrels of their weapons.

They pushed through the screen door as they entered through the kitchen, rattling six-packs of empty coke and orangeade cartons stacked behind the door.

"Hey, George! Bernard!" Neil called.

Bernard's high, slightly lisping voice answered from inside. "We here."

They walked through the dining room and around a Chinese screen. George and Bernard sat on the couch, George leaning forward with his elbows on his knees, a cup of green tea warming his hands. Bernard sat, petting a Siamese kitten, one leg tucked under his body. His tea sat on the table. They both looked up and smiled. "Did you ever find out what czaz meant?" George asked. They were both sweaty. A basketball and wet towel lay beside the couch.

Neil opened his mouth to tell Bernard to put the kitten down, but Shoogie cut in, "Yeah, we brought you some," and fired.

George's body jerked four times as Shoogie walked a burst up from his belly to his head. His body was almost ripped apart.

The kitten jumped as Neil drew the .22 and fired twice into Bernard's amazed face. One round went in his mouth and the other into his left eye, both of which were wide open.

Shoogie looked at his watch. "We better hurry. I wanta talk to Bear before we take off."

Chapter Eleven

Spread out like the right half of a V of geese the nineteen helicopters in their formation looked like successively smaller toys, until one of the toy soldiers sitting crosslegged in the door reached down and scratched the leg under his fluttering camouflage trousers.

Neil wished the Montagnard behind him would quit shifting around. His feet hung over the door and every time the guy moved Neil got shoved a fraction of an inch closer to the edge. It made him queasy.

The hill loomed in front of them. As they approached from the south air strike after air strike went in on the east side of the hill, big jet fighters circling high above the action, peeling off and screaming in, one at a time, to loose their bombs and then bank shrieking over the jungle. Huge orange and black blossoms of napalm bloomed and died in series across the face of the mountain, and high explosives left ragged holes in the matted earth below.

Neil had seen their fortifications. They weren't being hurt that badly.

Their choppers dropped lower. A flight of gunships barreled in ahead and went into orbit around their small landing zone. Rockets and machineguns cracked and hammered, and their own ship's two machineguns opened up as they flared.

A barren scar of earth rose beneath them; Neil pushed out six feet up, dropped to the dirt, then ran with the others for the shelter of the woods. He went to earth behind a tree on the edge of the LZ as his ship and the other that had come in with them lifted off. The cloud raised by the helicopters swirled over him and left a gritty film of dust on his glasses and down his neck. He untied the triangular bandage from his CAR-15 and wiped his glasses off, then retied the bandage cowboy fashion, around his neck. He finished just in time to get another dose of dust as the next two choppers came in.

"Hey, Shoog!" he called.

Shoogie looked up irritably, then grinned as he realized there was no reason not to talk when they were out with this mob. "Yeh!" he muttered.

"You look funny," Neil said. They wore no camouflage stick on their faces. There had seemed no point in it since the reaction force didn't wear it. They had drawn the line at wearing helmets though.

It took ten minutes for all the troops to get on the ground. After that Bear formed his company, which led the column, and moved out through the woods. The jungle was comparatively open, for Vietnam, and they moved in three files of one platoon each. Bear kept his company headquarters behind the first squad of the first platoon. They marched Bear first, his radio operator, Shoogie, a grenadier, Neil, their Montagnards, and behind them the second squad's point man.

From the moment the choppers lifted off they heard the shattering, earth-shuddering blasts of air strikes and artillery, plus the occasional *popopopopop* of AK fire, and the chatter of M-16's coming from the other side of the hill. That was good. Most of the NVA wouldn't have seen or heard them come in, and while they had undoubtedly been spotted, the NVA were too busy to pass the word.

They moved easily on the trails for half an hour, moving always upward, keeping the left and right files barely visible through the trees. The Mike Force company moved well, Neil noted, and while they made a lot more noise than a recon team, they weren't likely to draw more attention than they could handle. There was no talking, and they managed to keep their feet off the big sticks and out of the leaves.

Looking around the grenadier, Neil watched Shoogie humping along. It seemed strange to see him walk without putting his toes down first. His walk was dreamily detached. When they took their first break Neil sat down and lit a cigarette. He felt guilty, smoking in the woods. Taking off his hat to mop his brow, he looked over at Shoogie.

Their team leader sat with his elbows draped over his knees, hands dangling like dead birds. For a moment the same pain played over his face that had when they shot the juice to Xuan. That was replaced by a soft expression Neil had never seen before. Whatever Shoogie was thinking about, it wasn't the business at hand.

Bear's PRC-25 radio crackled.

Bear took the handset from his Montagnard radioman and muttered, "Uh-rodge Ghost, this Gunsel. Go!

After a pause he said, "Acknowledge, send Crazy Horse your location. Wilco. Gunsel out."

"Got it," Shoogie muttered stiffly, still uncomfortable with talk in the woods.

He clicked his tongue once, to get the attention of the team, which had automatically taken up firing positions off the trail when they stopped. Then he jerked his head back down the trail. Soundlessly they rose. Frenchy took the point and Shoogie fell in line behind him. The others took their usual positions and the team moved out. On the trail Frenchy set the short, choppy, bobbing pace of the V.C. It took them only a few minutes to walk back through Bear's company to where McLeod had set up his headquarters.

Normally the Mike Force was employed in company strength, so there was no battalion headquarters as such, just McLeod, his ops officer, the sergeant major, a radioman, and a security squad.

McLeod squatted, Montagnard fashion, flatfooted, over a plastic-covered map, grease pencil in hand. It was the first time Neil had ever seen him in a patrol hat, and the first time he had ever seen him look relaxed and happy. He nodded to Shoogie. "This look like what you saw up there the other day?"

Shoogie looked at the map closely. "Yessir," he muttered. "But that was then; this is now. They had plenty of time to put some security out to the rear. They know we waxed those clowns, so they must know we know how they're deployed.

"McLeod nodded. "That's what I'm thinking too. I need to know what's up there now. You feel up to a daylight infiltration?"

Shoogie didn't answer immediately. He squatted over the map for several minutes, examining it carefully. "Okay," he said. He rose and reached into an ammo pouch for his camo stick.

* * *

The team dropped out the doors and scrambled for the woods when the chopper was six feet off the deck.

They moved fast until they approached the top of the hill mass. Then they got cautious. Hard as it was to believe, it had been less than forty-eight hours since they were here. It would have taken awhile for the NVA they had ambushed to be missed and found. Even if the bad guys had drawn the correct conclusion from that, the most they could have done was to put out a few observation and listening posts. The team's mission was to find these, and the holes between them, before the Mike Force got this far up the hill.

The brush was so thick they punched through it on a compass azimuth. Shoogie set the course, but Neil checked his compass too. They had moved about two-thirds of the way up the hill and altered their course to move generally south.

Twice Shoogie stopped. He and Nay Thai went forward, noted the positions of an LP and came back. Neil watched him in awe; the son of a bitch was the best. He had picked out the most likely positions for listening posts from the map, and moved right to them. If he had guessed right there would be a gap where a draw ran between two fingers of the hill. The Mike Force could use that for cover when they moved up. If the NVA were smart there would be an LP there, and the team would have to take it out without being discovered, quickly and quietly.

They moved about halfway down the slope of that draw, not really expecting to make any kind of contact yet. The silence was shattered by the sound of an RPD, a Soviet-made automatic rifle. Neil hit the ground as he heard the snap of rounds overhead. Somebody really smart had put that weapon and crew there.

There was no noise; the RPD didn't fire again. Neil's nostrils opened up clear and he gulped air in frantic swallows. The chill hit his stomach, and time stopped. He waited for a signal from Shoogie, but it didn't come. He lay waiting, but heard no sound. He wondered if Shoog had been hit. But if that were the case Frenchy or Nay Thai would have come back down the line and told him. If Nay Thai had been hit Nay Go would have seen it. The only explanation was that Shoogie, and probably Frenchy and Nay Go, were trying to circle right and come in on the LP's blind side to take it out.

Normally Shoogie would have taken the whole team. Maybe he wanted to try to take them out before they could make their report. But they were bound to have heard the firing up on the hill. If the NVA headquarters tried to contact its LP and got no response they'd know what had happened. It was time to waste these clowns and get out, and the team wasn't moving. What the fuck was going on?

Neil had his CAR-15 ready. He was poised, ready to spring, and nothing was happening. His heart had almost stopped. He wanted action; he wanted to move. He wanted anything, anything at all, to break this tension. His breathing was too loud. He tried to tone it down. Then he heard the chatter of an M-16, then the *popopopopop* of an AK. His whole body was shaking.

Then things started happening. Nay Go came back toward Neil, carrying Nay Thai's body. There was blood all over him; he was obviously dead. No way was Shoog going to like that. He and Nay Thai had been on the same team since Day One. Then Shoogie burst through the woods. His eyes had gone to ice. He got on the radio and called for an extraction, then he jerked his eyes back up the hill.

Neil nodded. Nay Thai had been number one with him too. From this close in they had maybe twenty minutes before the chopper showed up.

They left Nay Go there with Nay Thai's body and the radio. Frenchy took the point, Shoogie right behind him, Neil next, and Y Buhn in the rear. They moved very quietly around to the left. As usual they moved soundlessly, slowly. Neil's guts tightened; they were using a lot of time creeping around in the woods. Shoogie would push it to the limit, every time.

Neil had the feeling things were coming unraveled. He had been scared before, but this was the first time he had been so scared he could barely keep on top of it.

Two sharp thuds slammed into his chest, and almost simultaneously he heard the burst of an AK firing. With no transition at all he found himself flat on his back in the jungle, his head resting against the root of a mahogany tree.

Goddam, he thought. While we were looking for them they were out looking for us.

He heard the tap of Shoogie's K and the pop of Frenchy's AK, and looked at the ragged holes in his shirt, raw black tears in the camouflage, rimmed with fresh blood. He heard that gurgling sound when he breathed. Oh fuck! Sucking chest wound. He quickly tore open his shirt. One sucking chest, and one in-and-out pec; lucky they missed his heart. He grabbed for the pressure bandage on his belt and tore it open.

By that time Shoogie knelt by his side. He nodded toward the hill and gestured two X's for kills, then mimed that the RPD was still there. He grabbed the bandage from Neil's hands and slapped the bright aluminum side of its wrapper over the wound. The foil would be airtight when wrapped solidly. Then he stripped off Neil's shirt. The straps on the bandage fluttered down like tentacles on a limp pink octopus. Carefully Shoogie tied the bandage around Neil's chest. It was starting to hurt, a horrible deep dull ache.

Shoogie held out a morphine syrette.

Neil thought about trying to move through the jungle, maybe having to fight on morphine. He'd rather not do that if he could help it, and he could bear the pain as long as he had something to do. He shook Shoogie off.

Neil gingerly shrugged back into his shirt. Y Buhn picked up Neil's gear, and Shoogie jerked his head toward the LZ.

They went back to Nay Go and Nay Thai's body. Things were starting to get a little vague to Neil. He wasn't exactly on top of it.

Shoogie took his map from his pants cargo pocket and picked out what he hoped would be a place where the chopper could get a McGuire rig through the trees. Then they heard a signal shot coming from back up the hill, where they had first heard the RPD.

Shoogie pulled Neil to his feet and raised his eyebrow in a question. Neil felt really rocky, but he could walk faster than these guys could carry him. He nodded.

Shoogie jerked his head in the direction of march.

They started back through the woods. Then they heard another signal shot. This one came from in front of them. Neil smiled sardonically through the pain. Shoogie had always said that the time to worry was when the signal shots had you bracketed. Shoog checked his map again and spoke quietly into his radio, then changed directions, off to the left this time. Neil stumbled along in a vague haze of pain, dizzy from loss of blood.

A long time passed slogging through the jungle. It could have been five seconds or five years. It was all the same to Neil. Suddenly they were in a clearing. Well, not exactly a clearing, but there was a break in the trees, and the light streamed in through only one canopy of jungle, like a stained glass window with all green panes, and right at the top there was a tiny patch of blue sky. Not big enough for a chopper to get in, but enough to drop a McGuire rig through.

The first chopper appeared and Shoogie got out his signal mirror. He talked on the radio until the chopper passed directly overhead and the crew could pick up the flash of his mirror. It made another quick orbit and the McGuire rig crashed down through the trees.

Then the RPD opened up. Nay Go and Y Buhn both went down, dead. That woke Neil up in a hurry. He grabbed his CAR off Nay Go's body and opened up in the direction the shots had come from. They stopped, at least for a second.

Silence would be wasted now. Shoogie dropped his K and picked up Nay Go's M-79. "You motherfucker!" he screamed. Then, to Neil, "Get in the rig!" Neil dropped the weapon and worked his ass into the sling, cinching his right arm into the cuff, in spite of the pain. Frenchy got into the next canvas loop, his eyes as big as tennis balls. Shoogie fired another round from the M-79 in the direction of the RPD.

"Get in the fucking rig!" Neil screamed. He felt rotten about leaving the Yard's bodies behind. That was not their custom, but there was no time, and McLeod would send a patrol back for them tomorrow.

Shoogie grabbed a bandoleer of M-79 grenades from Nay Go's body and got in the sling. He put his arms around the outside of the sling and *ponked* out another round from the M-79, toward the RPD.

"The cuff!" Neil screamed.

"Fuck the cuff! I'm busy." Shoogie screamed back. He jerked his thumb up. Neil and Frenchy each grabbed Shoogie's sling to keep them from spinning individually. They rose through the trees as Shoogie broke the M-79 open and put in another round. Neil started to scream at him to use the cuff again, but even if he could have heard he wouldn't have listened.

The treetops whipped past, and soon they were one hundred, two hundred, three hundred feet below. A slow burst of what was probably the RPD came arcing out of their hole. Neil could hardly hear because of the noise of the chopper. There were two rounds of green tracer in the six-round burst, and one of them arced up and into Shoogie's leg, right below the groin. A look of pained surprise crossed Shoogie's face, and Neil heard, or maybe only saw him mutter, "Shit!" as blood from a severed femoral artery spurted once and he tumbled backward out of the sling.

Dropping away below, Shoogie arched into a skydiver's delta, face to earth, head slightly down. He had four seconds, and as his body became smaller, falling away, he brought the M-79 to his shoulder and squeezed off a round, which, to Neil, looked like it exploded right in the space where the tracer had come from. Shoogie disappeared into the treetops.

Neil lost consciousness.

Chapter Twelve

He woke up in the back of an ambulance. The siren was screaming and there was an IV in his arm.

The deputy commander of the 5th Special Forces Group, a dour, awkwardly spoken lieutenant colonel, was in the receiving section when they brought him in. "You did an outstanding job out there, Thompson," he said. He put his hand on Neil's shoulder, while two medics in whites cut his tiger suit off with surgical scissors. Neil got an inward flash of amusement at the thought of how he must look, lying naked on a gurney with a flesh-colored bandage on his chest, his face, ears, and the backs of his hands covered with camouflage greasepaint.

"What's happening on Hill 987, sir?" he asked the colonel.

"Christ, kid, I was hoping you could tell me. McLeod commits three companies without notifying this headquarters until they're already on the ground. He's gonna get his ass burned for that. Frenier's on the horn and he's hoppin' mad. He called Special Forces a bunch of goddam glory-hunters. Nobody knows what the hell is coming off."

If Neil hadn't been so badly shot up the DCO would probably be giving him a hard time. One of the medics stuck a needle in his arm.

"The brigade's assault was compromised, sir," Neil said. "The 305 Regiment was dug in on the forward slope of that hill, waiting. We had confirmed intel on that, and very little time to act. Colonel McLeod is going up the reverse slope. If that brigade survives it will be because of our diversion. It's all documented. If anybody's the glory-hunter it's him, not us."

The DCO seemed extremely relieved when Neil muttered the magical word "documented". Then things became pleasant and very vague. Neil slipped into unconsciousness.

When he woke he was in a hospital bed, between crisp, clean sheets, with an IV in his arm and an itchy drain in his chest. He asked the first medic who passed his bed what had happened to his outfit. The medic said he didn't know, and sent a nurse who didn't know either, and who knocked him out with a shot.

The next day they took out the IV and brought a burlesque of American food on a tray. He asked what had happened to his outfit. The medic didn't know, and after breakfast they gave him another shot and a six month old *Reader's Digest* to amuse himself with until he nodded out.

The next morning a doctor came to check his drain. Neil asked him what had happened to the Project, but he had never heard of the Project, and the nurse gave Neil another shot. When he awoke General Frenier stood beside the bed with two colonels and an aide.

"Oh, fuck!" Neil muttered.

"Read the award," Frenier snapped.

The new aide lieutenant read General Order number such-and-such, from a clipboard, in the barking tone affected on such occasions. Frenier pinned a Purple Heart and a Silver Star on the sheet over his chest, and one of the colonels took a picture with a Polaroid camera, immediately tearing the paper-covered film out and staring at it stupidly while it developed.

"I don't get it?" Neil muttered, nodding toward the Silver Star.

The general cleared his throat. “Would you gentlemen please excuse us for a moment. I’d like to speak with Sergeant Thompson alone.”

The three officers immediately disappeared down the passageway between the four bunk cubicles, the colonel still trailing his fluttering Polaroid strip.

Neil didn’t know what to say; he was too well-trained to start screaming at a general. Frenier didn’t seem to know what to say either. He swallowed a couple of times and cleared his throat. “I guess I owe you an apology, son,” he said at last.

Son? Neil thought. Jesus!

“Those bastards were really dug in up there. It would have taken a division with artillery and air support to get them out. But we caught them in the open with our artillery prep when they tried to shift their defenses to repel McLeod’s feint. As it was my brigade took thirty percent casualties.”

“How is Colonel McLeod, sir?” The words escaped Neil before his anger could censor him.

“He may lose a leg. The sergeant major bought it. They went up for an aerial recon in his C and C ship. Both pilots were hit by machinegun fire, and the ship went in. McLeod’s the only one who made it.”

“Goddammit!” Neil muttered.

“Naturally after all this I’m not going to raise the question of his acting without authority. I’m putting him and Sergeant Swift both in for DSC’s. And on my own authority I’m awarding you and the sergeant major Silver Stars.”

Neil was flabbergasted. Now that everybody’s dead we’re all pals, he thought. What the fuck is this?

At that point one of the nurses busted in again and gave Neil another shot of Demerol. The general gave her an annoyed look, but Neil admired her cleavage and a tiny portion of her brassiere before she turned him over to stick a needle in his butt.

By the time she had gone he had it figured out. "You're getting another star out of it, aren't you?"

"Probably," the general admitted after a brief embarrassed silence. "Almost certainly."

Sure. If McLeod weren't accused of acting without orders, then he had to have been acting with orders, and who's orders could they have been but that great military genius, Brigadier General Marcus A. Frenier?

Neil sighed. "What happened to the Mike Force?"

"Heavy casualties."

"Did Bear make it?"

"I don't know who Bear is."

Neil was starting to feel sluggish.

The general gave an embarrassed little chuckle that Neil found totally out of place in this conversation. "One thing I have learned out of all this is that Swank is correct. I need an organic reconnaissance capability."

That's no shit, Neil thought. You won't get any help from Special Forces after this.

"I want to organize a Long-Range Reconnaissance Platoon, and I want you to command it."

Neil was dumbstruck: his commission.

"I've got I don't know how many worthless officers running round my headquarters. I need every man I've got with enough sense to dress himself, just to keep the paperwork flowing. I do not have a man available who could do the job. Not only that, but you gave one of the best briefings I've ever seen."

It all seemed to be coming from a long way off, and to not mean much. He managed to get out the words, "Honor offense?"

The general cleared his throat and shrugged. "I think you've redeemed yourself for that. Besides, the requirements for a reserve commission are far different than those for graduation from West Point. At Annapolis what you did isn't even against the rules."

Neil smiled. There it was, a second-class commission, for his slightly smudged "honor".

He wanted a commission, but he didn't want Frenier's commission as the price of keeping his mouth shut. His mind formed the words, "Go shit in your hat!" But before they escaped his lips he was asleep.

* * *

Neil drifted back in through several layers of consciousness. The first realization that hit him, again, was that Shoogie was dead. He felt grief, then anger. If the rabid little motherfucker hadn't been so hell-bent on revenge he'd probably be alive today. Then he remembered telling Frenier to take his job and pack it up his ass. Had he said that or only thought it? Frenier was right though; Neil would be the best man for the job. If somebody who didn't know the business set it up, or somebody who didn't have the balls to stand up to Frenier, that whole platoon would go home in bags.

Ah, well, fuck 'em if they can't take a joke.

Neil opened his eyes to find a nurse and doctor standing at the foot of the bed. The nurse was a hard-bitten old major and the doctor was a Sigma Chi golden boy. Neil figured him for five years out of someplace like U.S.C.

"Take him off demerol and start fifty milligrams darvon," the doctor said. Then when he noticed Neil was awake he smiled. "Good news, sarge," he said. "I'm putting you on the next evac flight home; you leave Wednesday."

Neil was shocked into tight focus. "No!" he snapped.

The doctor and nurse both looked surprised.

"Look, I'll be back for duty in a month. I don't want to pick up pine cones at Ft. Bragg."

The doctor shook his head. He was obviously a draftee with no understanding of the professional viewpoint.

"Our policy is to get all seriously wounded home as soon as possible."

Neil frowned. "I got stuff to do here."

The doctor and nurse exchanged glances, then the doctor shrugged. "I don't make policy"

"I'm not kidding about this," Neil insisted.

The doctor shrugged again. "Catch-22 in reverse," he said. "Anybody who wants to be here is too nuts for combat. I'm not only going to send you home; I'm going to set you up for a nice long talk with the shrink."

Oh, great! Neil thought. With a history of psychiatric evaluation I won't even be able to get into OCS. The only thing that made the army bearable was that none of his classmates had graduated yet. After June they'd be everywhere. Life would be unlivable for him as a sergeant. As for civilian life, well, he had never thought much about it, except that it had always seemed a dull routine with no higher goal than a quick buck. He was rapidly running out of options.

* * *

That afternoon General Frenier showed up again, with an aide carrying an attaché' case full of papers; his discharge as a sergeant, reserve commission as a second lieutenant, orders recalling him to active duty on the same date, and a transfer to the brigade, effective in three weeks.

"Sir," said Neil, "if I'm going to do this job I'll need a serious commitment from you on a couple of points."

The general's eyes narrowed slightly. "What are they?" he demanded.

"First, the LRRP Platoon is all-volunteer, and no man's assigned unless I accept him."

The general nodded, then said, “In view of the mission that seems reasonable. What’s the second?”

“If I say a team comes out, they come out right then; no ifs, no ands, no buts.”

He general gave him a long hard look, then shrugged. “All right, I’ll buy that.”

Neil still had his reservations, plenty of them, but he held out his hand. “I guess you got yourself a boy,” he said.

They shook on it.

He was surprised that his first thought was to call his mom and give her the good news.

Chapter Thirteen

Neil eased the old black jeep over the ruts to Juliana's house.

He was healed enough for limited duty, but not so healed that he should go slamming his jeep around on this hideously rutted road.

He was pale from loss of blood and weak from lying in bed. He would have to work out for at least a month to be ready for the field. The main difference, from a military point of view, was that he now wore the gold bar of a second lieutenant. He expected his transfer to the brigade any day now.

Arriving at Juliana's house he eased out of the jeep and walked, a bit hunched, to her front door. He bopped it a couple of times with his fist.

Moments later the door opened and she looked at him, startled. She leaned against the door. "You look like death warmed over," she said.

He wondered if this gave her pleasure. Why did he feel it necessary to explain himself to this person, justify himself to this person?

"Come on in," she said. "I'll get you some tea."

He sat on her couch and examined a new Braque print on her wall.

"It'll have to steep for a minute," she said. She sat down beside him on the couch and, without thinking, reached down and got her Moroccan stash box. "Would you…?" she asked.

He nodded.

She opened the box and took out a pack of Zig Zag rolling papers and a baggie of Buddha weed. "I didn't expect to see you again," she said. "I heard you'd been evacuated."

"General Frenier fixed it for me to stay," he replied crisply, defensive and trying to conceal it.

"Oh, wow!" she said, and dreamily continued rolling the joint. Then she looked at him sharply.

"Did you do it to become an officer? If you did that's the sickest thing I ever heard. God, it's like you're trying to get killed to fulfill the family tradition."

Neil smiled wryly and shook his head. "No, Frenier offered me the chance to build his recon platoon myself, from the ground up."

She lit the joint, inhaled deep in her lungs and passed it to him. Growling low in her throat, so as not to lose smoke, she said, "That's worse. You sold out."

It saddened him that she would believe that, but he knew it wasn't true. "No!" He shook his head. "It's not as easy as that. Look, he's not a stupid man, or a particularly bad one. He's just set in his ways and this is a different kind of war. He's at least starting to listen.

"When my Uncle Willie was in World War Two there wasn't a man in his company killed or seriously wounded until he got evacuated with malaria. After he left, within a month forty percent of his company was killed or wounded. And his replacement wasn't a dud. He was about average.

"Uncle Willie didn't go by the book; he went by his gut. He never got past lieutenant colonel, but from what I hear he was a hell of a field commander."

Juliana sneered. "Frenier's not like that."

She was still angry with him, but he was sure this would pass. He felt right about his decision, but he wanted her to understand.

"No, he's not," Neil said, "but I am." He shrugged a little sheepishly. "I trained my whole life for this, and I'm good at it. If I take that platoon most of them will go home on their feet. If I don't half of 'em will go home in bags. That's a fact."

Her mouth was tight, and she looked past him into space. She examined him closely. He saw that he had not convinced her. To her the G.I.s in that recon platoon were an abstraction. To him they were a bunch of guys who could go home if he was willing to put his own life on the line for them.

"Will you just stay here until you're wounded again, or killed?" she demanded.

He shrugged. "I don't know."

She gave him an odd fixed look, and he felt a sudden flush. His mind shifted quickly. He noticed she was surrounded by half-packed boxes.

"You leavin'?" he asked.

"Those V.C. came again last week, the ones who threatened to kill me."

"You use the grenades?"

She shook her head. "Some Montagnard friends in the village hid all the American civilians. But now they want us to leave. We're too dangerous to them."

"Moving to town?"

She nodded yes. "My year with IVS is over in a month. I'd planned to stay for another year, but I'm going home. I don't belong here. I needed to see this, but I'm going to finish grad school."

He nodded. He had something he wanted to say. "McLeod once said that when a young man faces death in combat, and lives through it, he thinks he's proved himself because he's faced the worst. But it's not the worst. He said it was third worst. He said losing a woman you really loved was worse than that, and losing a child was worse than losing a woman. In a way both of those have happened to you." He smiled sadly.

"It's my last night here," she said quietly. "Would you like to stay?"

He nodded.

After awhile she made some sandwiches. They talked about movies and books, art and music, drank some red wine and smoked another joint. "I don't know about you," he said, "but this meets all my requirements." He took her in his arms.

She laughed, then pressed against him and kissed him softly. He put his hands behind her neck. Her whole body melted into his and she held him tight. Something in her had surrendered. Then she leaned back and said, "C'mon."

He reached up and undid her braids, so that her long red hair swirled over her shoulders. Then he reached out and undid the top button on her shirt, and then the others. He looked into her heart-shaped, freckled face, her level eyes now melted and liquid, and threw the shirt to the floor.

She undid his shirt. He took her hand and they went into the bedroom.

The room had dank, lime-green concrete walls, but it was filled with wicker tables and chairs, and a couple of wooden chests. She lit candles, a lot of them. Their light flickered in the room. The bed was a big handmade wooden affair, with a rough frame for mosquito netting that gave it a kind of canopied effect.

She started her record player. The first album in the stack was Surrealistic Pillow. She lifted the tone arm to the third track, a romantic ballad called "My Best Friend," and let it play.

Neil sat down and untied his boots. He kicked them off and pulled his jungle fatigue blouse over his head, then shucked out of the trousers.

She lay down on the far side of the bed, staring up into the mosquito net.

He rolled onto the bed, flipping the white gauze around them. He reached for the top button on her jeans.

The night was slow lovemaking. Their bodies grew sweaty so that they slid against each other, slipping outside and inside. Sweat ran down his face and dripped onto hers, and on her breasts. In the candlelight her sweat and his mingled and rolled down his belly to hers. His eyes poured over her face. It was a different one than she'd worn when they first met. There was some trust in it.

She lay smiling, rolling slowly with him, and he could not have told who initiated the rhythm, but she took it and built it as her head thrashed from side to side and her red hair lashed her face and her freckles and the tears in her eyes. She took his hips in her hands and climbed him as he drove into her. She gasped. Her eyes rolled back and she gasped again and moaned. He thought she would never stop, didn't want her to ever stop.

His emotions were touched in places that had never been touched before, that made him wish for things he had never wished for before. He felt that all of him was going into her, that each would have the other's strengths from now on.

He lay in her for a long time afterward, just holding her, her hands fanned over his back. He kissed her eyelids.

Then he rolled off and held her. After a long while she leaned up and he watched her in the dim and flickering light, her hair wild around her face, over her breasts. He watched the concave arch of the shadow of her back, the soft roundness of her shoulders, and the shadow of her breasts on the inside of the gauze netting. She took him in her mouth and within seconds he was hard again. She mounted him and rode him to another crashing orgasm. And that was how the night went.

Chapter Fourteen

Neil ran, wheezing, alongside a ragged and sloppy formation of fifty-five LRRP candidates just as the sun peeked over the rim of the Chu Dle Ya Mountains. In his semi-conscious state he could hold the step and keep up with his troops, but he was not fit to lead them at this hour.

Pappy Flagg had done that for him, and thank God. Pappy was one of those great NCOs who could function optimally from the moment his eyes opened until they closed again.

The first morning, this Monday, Neil had tried to lead the run. He'd run one squad over a tent rope and dumped five of them before he stopped the formation and reorganized.

He wasn't completely recovered from his wound. His chest hurt, and his lungs hurt. There was a hot iron stitch in his side. He turned and ran backwards, ostensibly to check the back of the formation, but really so he could work different muscles, and to let a bit of the formation surge past him.

They ran on the dirt maintenance road just inside the perimeter that circumnavigated Firebase Debbie Sue. The rising sun blazed the dust cloud rolling behind them into a ghostly reddish-gold. A few GIs who had fallen out of the formation stumbled dejectedly in the cloud.

This was Friday of selection week. Those who were still falling out by now would be going back to their units.

When this crowd fell in Monday morning there would be only thirty-five of them, and that would be the platoon; seven teams of five men each. With anticipated casualties, illnesses, and R&Rs, he hoped to get four men per team into the field.

They'd been running for about half an hour, just a couple of minutes left. His wound was burning. But that was what this run was for, to see who would keep going when he thought he was going to die. He was glad to be semi-conscious. It would hurt a lot worse if he were awake.

With the sun other GIs came out of their tents. They stood in fatigue pants and flip-flops, barechested, with GI towels around their necks, hooting and catcalling at the LRRP candidates. "Yoo-hoo, ya run like a buncha girls."

"Hey, slow down, yer kickin' up dust!"

One called cadence way off the count. "*Hawn-tup.........thripfawp!*" trying to break their stride The LRRPs loped on, ignoring it.

Pappy called quick time as they entered the LRRP encampment. They marched into their formation area looking pretty good, shoulders back and down, head and eyes to the front. These were proud troopers, too young for Special Forces, but the same type of guys.

Neil hadn't even been conscious of Pappy's cadence. He'd just run in step, grateful to be at the side of the formation, rather than in the middle, dodging the feet of the guy ahead.

The breeze hit him the second they slowed to march cadence. His sweat was sickly slick; he shouldn't be doing this yet. But so what? He had to set the example, period.

Flagg halted the formation, gave them left face, saluted Neil, and dismissed the troops to get ready for chow.

As the men walked away to clean up Neil approached Flagg. "Sarnt Flagg," he said, "I'll be in the office. I want to go over the Form 20's again before class. Reckon you could bring me a fried egg and bacon sandwich after you eat?"

Flagg gave him a look of fatherly tolerance and amused exasperation. It was a look senior NCOs reserved for second lieutenants of whom they were fond. "Yessir, you want mustard on it?"

"Absolutely."

"You want me to start the coffee before I go to chow?"

Neil grinned. "I'll manage," he said. Flagg was such a good NCO that Neil felt grateful every time he looked at him. A little rawboned guy from some Cajun place in Louisiana, Flagg knew his job cold. And he was a man of great rectitude.

Neil tended to grade everybody he met in the brigade on how he thought they would have done in Special Forces. Flagg would have made it, but in fact Flagg's special talent, his love for GIs, would have been wasted in Special Forces.

He had no family, no wife, no kids, and hard as he could be when the occasion called for it, he clucked and worried over his "kids". He scrounged them extra chow and ammo, and nursed them through bad patches of fear, and Dear John letters.

He hadn't had a chance to do much of that yet for the LRRPs, but Major Swank had recommended him, and filled Neil in on the kind of man he was.

Then Flagg had clucked and worried over Neil and his wound. Neil had won Flagg's loyalty by driving on when he hurt.

Thus far Flagg had anticipated all Neil's orders. Everything Neil told him to do, he had either already done, or done something else that was better.

Flagg set the moral tone for the platoon, because Neil hadn't worked with regular GIs since basic training. Neil was picking up Flagg's attitude toward these kids. He thought they were funny, and he thought they were great.

The first day in the compound when he'd drawn his rifle from the brigade armorer he'd immediately stripped the sling off, and was walking back to the tent that served as his and Flagg's office, carrying the M-16 by the ring just aft of the handguard.

The first GI he passed said, "Don't point it down, sir. The b-bs will fall out."

Neil had walked into the tent and told Flagg about it. Flagg had laughed and topped that with another GI story. He had a million of 'em.

Neil entered the same tent, poured some water in their battered old percolator, filled the top with grounds—-he and Flagg liked it strong—-set it on top of a ring of flat stones and lighted a slightly more than marble-sized wad of C-4 plastic explosive under it. The stuff burned with a hot blue flame. Then he sat down behind his field desk and started going over the Form 20's one more time.

He should have completed this part by now, and in fact largely had. He looked for five things on the Form 20. He wanted high school grads, not GEDs, because a high school grad might or might not know anything, but he'd at least had the discipline to show up and plant his ass in the seat for twelve years. Then he looked for a triple-digit GT, which was what the army called its IQ tests. He looked for high physical fitness scores, and no major disciplinary problems.

And he wanted airborne qualified people. Parachute training was a three-week course in performing simple mechanical tasks while scared shitless, which, in Neil's view, was the essence of combat performance.

But he'd make exceptions to all of that if a case warranted it, and it was the exceptions he was concerned about.

He was trying to find thirty-five guys and he'd started with a hundred volunteers Monday. He had fifty-five out there now, and forty of them met his objective criteria. The others were guys he thought he ought to take a closer look at.

He took the names of the four who had fallen out on this morning run. Three of them had already fallen out on one run. He put them in the discard pile. They'd be back in their home unit by noon. But the other one, Abbot, had gutted lots rougher runs than this one, and he'd started out limping this morning. Neil picked up his Form 20. Good scores, GT 115, PT 350. He'd fired expert with the rifle, and he had a semester of college.

And he could type. He'd volunteered for the LRRPs from a company clerk's job, and pissed off his CO in the process. Neil put his Form 20 in the "Talk to Pappy about it" pile.

All the while the C-4 had been fizzing and popping, coffee gurgling, the smell of hot coffee filling the tent. When it got quiet he filled his mug, liberally lacing it with sugar and powdered milk, in hopes that his stomach lining might survive the experience.

He took the cup back to his desk and picked up the stack of files on kids who looked good, but didn't meet his objective criteria. Some of them were Puerto Ricans who had low GT scores because they hadn't learned English yet when they took the test.

At that point Pappy showed up with Neil's sandwich. "They didn't have no mustard out, sir," he said. "I put mayo on it."

Neil took it and said, "I'll eat it fast." He ripped off a big bite, remembered heartburn and slowed down. "What are we gonna do about these PRs? I know they're smarter than their test scores show."

Pappy poured himself a cup of coffee and choked down a gulp, black and scalding. "Yessir, but I say send 'em all back but Santiago. Them kids didn't speak English a year ago. If they get rattled I don't wanta hafta translate their coordinates from a foreign language over the radio. That Santiago's a horse, and he don't rattle for nothing."

Neil transferred six more files to the discard. Ten down, ten to go.

"What about Abbot? He fell out this morning."

"He pulled a muscle yesterday. I told him to fall out if it got to hurting."

Neil checked his watch. Sergeant Sims had them for two hours of radio procedure before Neil's map reading class. Then it was out for an afternoon of snooping and pooping in the woods. He wanted to monitor some of Sims' class, but he and Pappy could go over these things for at least an hour.

* * *

Neil went to inspect Sims' class just before his own. He was immediately displeased with the class site. It had seemed fine yesterday, but today the motor pool had established a wash point nearby.

Some lunatic staff officer had decided the jeeps and three-quarter ton trucks of his battalion had to have the red laterite dust that was ground into everything on this godforsaken hill washed off. It was completely lost on this fool, whoever he was, that all this water had to be trucked up the hill in tank trucks by kids who sometimes took sniper fire to get it.

It also hadn't occurred to him that every one of these vehicles would be indistinguishable from those that hadn't been washed in about an hour. Pointless activity, signifying nothing.

Worse, the motor pool had set up its wash point slightly uphill from the class, so that rivulets slowly trickled towards it. Perhaps the prudent thing would be to move about fifty meters south, but that would put him closer than he wanted to be to a tent area.

Sims wound up his class with a stirring review of the phonetic alphabet and a final admonition about profanity over the airwaves. Then he gave them a ten-minute break. By that time the rivulets had reached the edge of his formation and Neil decided he'd better move them now.

Too late. One of his candidates idly reached out, picked up a gob of mud and wiped it down a nearby trooper's shirt. "Why you son of a bitch!" his buddy exclaimed, and threw a bigger gob in the perpetrator's face. Somebody else flung mud at random and the group dynamic shifted from lethargy to agitation.

I better move quickly, Neil thought. "All right, men…" he began, feeling a little like Maxwell Smart, and was rewarded by a mudball that slammed into his gut.

Boy, I hope this class doesn't get inspected, was his thought.

There was a momentary shocked silence. Almost nobody thought throwing a mudball at an officer was a very good idea. Well, one person had, but Neil hadn't seen who it was. He considered his options, which were narrow indeed. He could sputter and fume like a fool. Or he could try to ignore it, and look like a weenie.

He chose another option, stopped, packed a dense mudball and threw it full force in the direction the one that hit him had come from.

The moment of shocked silence that had extended until Neil threw the mudball ended when someone yelled, "Yeehaw!" and the entire formation dissolved into a slippery sliding mudcaked fiasco. Neil got hit five more times, but he gave better than he got.

It was at this point that Pappy Flagg materialized to announce, "Sir, the general is on his way to inspect."

Neil immediately grabbed his platoon sergeant and threw him into the mud with a right side judo hip throw. If he lived to be a hundred he'd never forget the look on Flagg's face when he landed in the mud.

Then he turned and bellowed, "Awright, ADDEZE!"

There was no eluding the command in his voice. The noise stopped immediately. "All right, gents, pair off immediately. Raise your hands when you got a partner."

Two things happened. The word that the general was coming had been heard by a couple of the candidates, and that word spread throughout the group at almost the speed of light. Fear spread with it. The general was respected, but not loved, in his brigade. They all knew the ancient maxim that shit rolls downhill.

As is the way of these things all hands but three went up almost immediately. From three separate corners of the group. "Okay," Neil said, "you three team up. Move!"

They moved quickly.

"Sergeant Flagg will now demonstrate the right side hip throw, by the numbers."

Neil and Flagg squared off. "Now, Sergeant Flagg will grab my shirt with his left hand." Flagg grabbed his shirt. "Now, here's the tricky part. He plants his left foot next to my right foot, and steps through with the right foot to the left." Flagg did that, which threw his hip under Neil's belly and lifted him a couple of inches off the ground.

"Okay, take notice," Neil gasped. "He's crouched so that his center of gravity is under mine. If he hadn't done that, I could dump him easily. As it is, he's solid as a rock." Neil jerked and struggled but Flagg didn't move. "Also, this way it requires very little effort to throw your opponent. If you don't get positioned right, you have to drag him over your hip, and even if he doesn't resist, it's hard to do. Ready, MOVE!"

Flagg dropped him neatly in the mud.

An immaculate jeep thrummed to a stop about twenty meters away.

The general got out carefully, his aide leaping out of the back seat behind him. His driver stood stiffly beside the vehicle.

Neil picked himself up and said, "Once more at full speed."

Flagg dropped him so fast he wondered why he'd bothered to get up. All the wind went out of him. Old Flagg had got just a *little* payback there.

Neil picked himself up again. "Sergeant Flagg will now take you through it by the numbers."

"Face your partners, gentlemen," Flagg commanded.

Neil walked toward the general and the aide, very conscious of the mud that covered sixty percent of his body. He saluted and said, "Sir, Lieutenant Thompson reports."

The general returned the salute. "What's this?" he demanded. "You're scheduled for map reading."

"Yessir," Neil replied. "My training area was turned into a quagmire by that car wash over there. I decided to use it to make a teaching point. We're still in selection. We can weed out the finicky ones who won't mix it up in the mud."

The general gave him a long thoughtful look. "Commendable initiative, young man. But the next time you take it upon yourself to change the training schedule, you run it through my Training Shop."

"Yessir," Neil replied.

"Carry on!"

Neil saluted and went back to his formation. Flagg was taking great delight in dumping his trainees repeatedly in the mud.

Neil and Flagg ran them through three more throws, even after the General was gone. At the end of two hours every man there was exhausted, bruised and muddy from head to toe. And they had fifteen minutes to get ready for lunch.

"Get 'em in formation, Sergeant Flagg. I've got something to say."

"Aw right, Fall In, Goddammit!" Flagg commanded.

The candidates moved quickly. They knew they had screwed up. The lieutenant had covered for them—and himself—but the thing was he'd been cool about it. This incident would pass into legend in the Brigade LRRPs.

He contemplated them with his feet spread wide, hands on hips. "We've had our fun, gents, and as far as I'm concerned the incident is closed. But we can't be doin' this kind of shit any more. The way the army works is that I have to pretend to be Mr. Big and Important and you have to pretend to believe it. We all know we're just a bunch of clowns, but if we follow the structure we'll come out heroes. Okay?"

"YES SIR!" they bellowed in unison.

He had them. They were his.

Chapter Fifteen

Neil had conceived his reconnaissance platoon as a smaller version of the Project Theta Recon Company; seven teams instead of twelve, five man teams instead of six—usually four when they were deployed. But, as it developed, dynamics were quite different from the Project.

Just for openers he wasn't working for McLeod. McLeod was only a lieutenant colonel, but he was also one of General Westmoreland's fair-haired boys. The Project was funded by the CIA, which meant, in effect, that it had virtually unlimited, all but unaccountable, funds. When they wanted something they bought it or stole it, and nobody bothered them about it.

Neil's Tactical Operations Center was not a miniature version of the Project's lavish bunker. It was a squad tent, surrounded by sandbag walls, furnished with several folding chairs, a couple of folding field desks, a radio, some filing cabinets, and a map.

Actually he thought the Brigade Supply Officer took fiendish delight in giving him short shrift. The way Special Forces units were supplied was envied throughout the army.

Neil quickly set out to remedy this situation, and every other. He awoke in the morning with a head swarming with ideas. First he would have to seduce and corrupt his helicopter support. Not easy, because he didn't have an entire helicopter company in direct support, as the Project did. His platoon drew support willy-nilly from aviation units all over the Central Highlands.

So he set out to make his platoon a good bunch to fly for. With their briefing, a chopper crew got a sandwich and an iced coke. With the debrief you got a beer if you wanted one. Out of cigarettes? Have one of mine.

Except for the Supply Officer he had a certain amount of honeymoon with the Brigade Staff. They were tired of having their companies blunder into ambushes, and wanted the recon platoon to succeed, or at least to trigger the ambushes with four guys rather than a hundred. Neil used that honeymoon to get his men authorized black berets and tiger suit fatigues. Bingo! An instant elite.

He checked with finance to make sure his airborne qualified men got jump pay. And he pushed Personnel to get the rest into jump school.

Another thing he made clear to his men from the start was that a share of captured weapons and NVA gear went back to the platoon for trading material. He didn't have his own mess. His men ate with Headquarters Company. He was going to have guys coming in at all hours, beat up and shot up, having eaten nothing but LRRP rations for days. He wanted them fed right away. And fed well.

Neil had come to the brigade with an extra duffel bag full of NVA weapons. The headquarters company mess sergeant soon found himself in possession of a Tokarev pistol, an AK-47, and a complete inventory of somebody else's war stories.

Neil ran his ideas by Flagg, who quickly sorted through them with a more practical eye. Some things were beyond them, at least for now. They were, after all, thirty-eight guys at the bottom of a long chain of command.

Flagg was not wild about the idea of their building a new TOC before the platoon was even trained, particularly not an underground bunker that would have to be dug by members of the platoon.

Neil let him win that one, for now.

When his thirty-five men were selected, added to himself and Flagg, and E-6 Sims, the Operations Sergeant/Radioman, he had five weeks to get them ready for the three-week MACV Recondo course. Neil's idea was that they should all graduate, with honors. He formulated a training schedule, which he hoped would achieve that end.

Neil signed himself on to go through the course with his men, even though as a former assistant patrol leader in the Project, he was qualified to be an instructor. The benefits of going through as a student; forming a bond with his platoon, observing their performance more closely, demonstrating a willingness to share hardship. All these things made it worthwhile.

The month prior was a constant round of classes, most of which, at first, he had to teach. The last two weeks his patrol leaders were teaching most of the classes.

The training patrols grew longer and more dangerous. First, daylight local security patrols around the firebase. Then daylight insertions in areas believed to be safe. Then overnight patrols a little further out, all within the Brigade's artillery range fan. Then into hotter areas. They made rope ladders out of cable and pipe, scrounged McGuire Rigs from the Project, and used them in training, breaking in aircrews as they went. By the last week before going off to Nha Trang for the school they were running real operations, dropping into areas where the enemy was believed to be, to assess their strength and location.

Neil didn't really like to have more than two teams out at a time this early in the game. His helicopter support wasn't that smooth yet. The kids were still nervous, and if he got two teams in trouble at once he couldn't fly out and extract both. If both he and Flagg were out at once, that left Sims alone in the TOC. And Sims wasn't experienced enough to make life and death decisions.

But that had to be balanced out with training requirements and increasing pressure from Brigade Headquarters for real operational missions. Once the company commanders found they could go in with some idea of what they faced, they didn't want to do it any other way. So Neil put teams out three at a time. He tried to send one on a milk run, and he cut a deal with Major Swank for either Swank or his assistant to watch the store if both he and Flagg had to be in the air for an extraction.

* * *

The sun was just shading into twilight, gearing up for another glorious sunset as Neil left the mess tent. He paused for a second to lean on a sandbag wall, pick his teeth, admire the magnificence around, and reflect on the coming evening. If all went well he would sit on a folding chair, read a magazine, and listen to the radio sputter all night.

He flipped the toothpick into a butt can and continued his stroll back to his TOC. He found Flagg crouched over the radio when he entered the tent.

"What's happening, Sarnt Flagg?"

"Red One broke squelch," Flagg said. "Choppers have been advised, but they aren't spooling up yet."

"Fuck me!" Neil exclaimed. Keying the mike on a radio, "breaking squelch", a coded number of times was a way of notifying the TOC that the enemy was too close for voice transmission. It created a very audible break in the electronic sputter that constantly came from the big radio, and no noise whatever in the field.

Neil went to the pile of field gear by his desk. He took the magazine out of his M-16 and checked the spring for tension. Then he went through his gear for eight magazines with eighteen rounds each, strobe, panels, frag grenades, smoke grenades, two canteens, first aid kid, survival kit, and a couple of LRRP rations. He had his harness rigged with an infantryman's little butt pack to hold all that. It was survival gear in case his airplane went down.

Gear ready, he threw the harness over his shoulders and checked the map for the last location of Red One. They couldn't have moved more than a klick since their last sitrep. The nearest LZ was about 800 meters from their last known location, and in the direction they were supposed to be moving.

He took his own patrol map out of its plastic bag and refolded it so that Red One's AO was centered. He was as ready as he could get before he received a call for help. Then he sat down and lit a cigarette and listened to the radio sputter.

He didn't have to listen long. "Jazzbo, Jazzbo, Red One Alpha. We are Hotel Alpha. Out." Hotel Alpha—hauling ass.

Neil picked up a field phone and called the chopper pad. The crew chief of the on-call Huey answered his ring.

"We got a team in trouble. Crank 'er up!" he barked into the phone.

"Good luck, sir," Flagg shouted as Neil left the tent and vaulted into his jeep.

It took him only a minute to drive to the chopper pad. The rotor was already whirling, engine whining higher into a horrible clatter when he arrived.

Neil parked about fifteen meters back from the Huey. He caught grit in the face as he ran up to the pilot. "Where to?" the pilot yelled, over the rotors.

Neil whipped out his own map and located where the team was supposed to be, then found it on the pilots aviation map, which had no grids or contour lines.

"Got it!" said the pilot. "Let's go. I wanna have these guys in the air before it's too dark to see."

Neil jumped into the passenger compartment and strapped in. He had an aircrew helmet in the back with the headphones rigged so he could talk to both the crew and the team on the ground. The pad and the huge scar of the firebase, cut by roads and rows of regularly spaced tents, a couple of tanks and a few 105mm artillery pieces, dropped away and jungled mountains rose and dived beneath them.

Neil got on the horn as soon as they had altitude. "Red One, Red One, this is Phoenix Six Actual. How copy, over?"

No answer.

They were where the team was supposed to be, but there was no response. Neil was suddenly gripped by fear for these men. In all his angling and agitating for a commission it had never crossed his mind that men would inevitably die from his mistakes, and how would he feel about that?

The pilot's voice crackled in his ears. "I don't see a goddammed thing."

"Me neither," Neil responded. He switched to the ground channel. "Red One, Red One!"

"Phoenix Six, we have you visual. You're about a klick south of us on an azimuth of zero-one-three degrees, over."

Neil looked south, but saw nothing. "Pop smoke, over," he said.

"Roger that," came the response.

Immediately Neil saw two smokes, a yellow and a violet. Charles was up to his old tricks again.

"What's your color, Red One, over?" he asked.

He was calm now. He knew what to do. Moreover, if the least touch of panic crept into his voice the guys on the ground could catch it.

"Yellow, over." The kid sounded rock solid in the headset. Neil noted that his map reading wasn't too cool, but his nerves were. He had chosen this guy well.

"Are you in contact, over?"

"Negative, Phoenix Six, but they're nearby, over."

"Roger that," said Neil. "Call for some arty about fifty meters west of you, over."

"Roger. Break, Break--Red One to Royal Standard. We have a fire mission. One zero zero left from concentration........."

Neil checked the reference. It was close enough to adjust from. They were almost over the patrol now. Neil was frantically looking for a break in the trees large enough for the Huey to drop a rope ladder.

"I see a break approx one-two-zero from their smoke at nine o'clock. Whattaya think?" he said to the pilot over the intercom.

"Roger, that'll work," the pilot replied.

By that time the patrol had directed its first artillery marking round, and was adjusting fire on the pursuing enemy. Neil could see the rounds impacting below. They were surely tearing up the treetops, but he doubted that the Cong were having to do much but keep their heads down. "Red One, this is Phoenix Six," Neil said into the mike. "Move one-zero-zero meters on an azimuth of zero five degrees for pick-up. We got maybe ten minutes of daylight left. Over."

"Roger. Wilco. Out," came the reply.

Wishing that he had the comforting ring of three gunships he'd had on the Project, Neil said to the pilot, "Let's throw a little machinegun fire behind the patrol. We got nothing to do 'til they get there anyway."

"Okay," the pilot replied. He banked and dived. The Huey slick came up behind the patrol's last known position and the door gunners started raking the jungle with thirty cal. Neil pumped two magazines into the jungle out the left door. All of this ammo was probably wasted, but maybe the noise wasn't. Even a momentary distraction might make the difference in the team's escape.

Down on the ground the team would have abandoned all attempts at stealth and would be crashing hell for leather through the brush. Trying to maintain direction in that bush while moving fast was virtually impossible. But if they buzzed the pick-up point the team would have something to home in on.

The lengthening shadows below were making the little clearing hard to see, even from the air.

"Give us another smoke, over," Neil said.

"Roger," came the response. Yellow smoke drifted up through the trees. This time there was only one.

"Move two-zero meters on nine-zero degrees," Neil said.

"Roger, movin' out."

A minute later the team entered the break in the trees, a strobe blazing-blazing-blazing in the patrol leader's hand.

"Let's go get 'em!" Neil screamed. The pilot was already diving toward the clearing.

Neil fumbled with the ties on the rope ladder. The crew chief untied the other side. The ladder dropped just as the ship flared.

The door gunners fanned the edges of the clearing as the team clambered up the steel rungs of the ladder.

So far the ship didn't seem to have taken any fire. Then the crew chief yelled, "Oh shit! Oh, fuck!" as his arm shattered and blood flew. Neil looked over. Everybody was on the ladder.

"Get the fuck out of here!" he screamed, firing his M-16 at the treeline.

With the team still clinging to the ladder, hopefully hooked on by a snap link as they'd been taught, the chopper surged out of the hole. It was only ten minutes back to the firebase, but that's a long time to cling by your fingers.

He quickly grabbed the crew chief's jacket and ripped the sleeve away from the wound. No arterial bleeding.

"Let's get to the nearest LZ and let these guys on the chopper before they fall off," he bellowed at the pilot.

"May be ambushed," the pilot replied.

"Yeah," Neil said laconically, "but I can't let my patrol fall into the jungle."

The LZ was less than a minute away. It was probably under observation, but no one fired on them when they set down. The patrol hopped off when the ladder was three feet off the deck. As soon as the skids touched down the four of them barreled onto the helicopter, which immediately lifted off, the ladder flopping below.

"Damn, sir, that was some scary shit," said the patrol leader.

Neil started putting a pressure bandage on the crew chief's arm. "You did good," he said to the patrol leader.

The other three sat quietly. Their first close call with the LRRPs had sobered them considerably. Neil knew their faces would not be the same tomorrow as they had been yesterday. They would never be the same again.

* * *

Neil and Flagg had prepared their men well for Recondo School. They all graduated, which was rare, and they returned to the Brigade with their morale high. Neil used that leverage to get CAR-15s for his patrol leaders, and a guarantee of couple of days off for a returned patrol before they were eligible for any shit details around the firebase.

Then he started to build his TOC.

This was not a popular move, especially among the troops who had to dig the hole.

* * *

Neil exited the tent that served as the old TOC and walked past the hole on his way to Major Swank's tent.

Passing the hole he heard the sound of digging, spade jammed into the earth followed by a grunt. The digging stopped for a second, and he heard the voice of Sp4 Gilbert, a black kid from St. Louis, say, "This is some ass-dragging shit the El Tee laid on us. Big motherfuckin' hole for him to hide in while we getting' our ass shot off in the bush."

Neil walked to the edge of the hole, hands on cocked hips, looking down on Sp4 Gilbert and his colleague, Pfc Marvin Delroy, a towhead from Kentucky. "You're gonna have to think a whole lot better than that to make it in this outfit, Gilbert. Some day the Gooks are gonna rocket this place. When they do this TOC's gonna be a prime target. If we lose our base station radio the patrols we have out will be fucked. This hole here is to make sure we can receive *your* distress calls, my man. And when that happens I will not be in the hole. I'll be in the chopper, taking hits to haul your funky ass out of the shit."

Gilbert gave him a long look. "Okay, El Tee. Maybe you're right. But diggin' this motherfucker's still a bitch."

Neil shrugged. "That's all of life. Trust me on this. A perpetual R & R would bore you to tears."

"Like to test that theory, sir," said Delroy.

"Finish the hole and I'll get you three days in Vung Tau," said Neil. "Best I can do."

"All right!" they said in unison, and sunk their shovels into the dirt.

Chapter Sixteen

The little O-1E wound down over the jungle, well into small arms range. A lucky burst from an AK could take this flimsy craft out of the sky, and the odds that they would see anything in this dense green jungle were small. The patches where Neil could see more than treetops were few. But this was all he could do now, look and see if he could find anything… and hope. The team had been in a firefight when they called in, and they'd missed two scheduled transmissions since, but maybe the radio had been hit. It was at least possible that they'd be okay. Or that some of them would be.

He was hoping for a flash from a signal mirror, or some smoke, or a flare, anything.

The O-1E leveled out over the treetops and flew a zigzag pattern over the valley. Nothing.

"That's it, Lieutenant," said the pilot over the intercom. He was a twenty-year-old warrant officer, but seemed far older and far younger at the same time. "We're not seeing anything and we're low on fuel."

"All right," Neil replied. "One more pass down the river bed and we'll go home."

"Down the river? How many you wanta lose in one day?"

"Just do it," Neil said irritably. He knew how dangerous it was to fly a fixed course down the river. There were plenty of NVA down there, and they had to be near water.

He hated to subject the pilot to the danger. But these were his men.

Give the guy his due. He made no further protest, but flew around to one end of the valley, put her about fifty feet over the meandering stream and banked and dipped his way down it. Jungle-covered hillsides towered close in on either side, the stream crashing over rocks just under them. Neil could see into the trees, but this was the last place he would expect to find his patrol, and the first he would expect to find the enemy. He craned his neck, looking as deeply into the trees on either side as he could. This would only work if they were alive and trying to signal him. Not very likely he'd spot dead guys in camouflage in the jungle.

He heard the snap of a single-shot rifle and the *popopopop* of an AK over the crackle of his radio. *Snap!* A round tore through the thin skin of the aircraft, pinged off the armored back of the pilot's chair and out through the Plexiglas window. The pilot started evasive maneuvers, but he didn't pull out. He rocked the little plane from side to side, and rose and fell from an altitude of fifty to a hundred feet, but he held his course to the end of the valley, the volume of fire rising all the while. No more rounds entered the cabin, but Neil heard several thump into the fuselage.

He felt a wind on his cheek from the hole in the Plexiglas.

At the end of the valley the pilot said, "I vote we go home."

Dully, Neil muttered the cliché, "Might as well. Can't dance and it's too wet to plow."

On the way back he got Major Swank on the radio, reported negative results and requested permission to take the three teams he had in camp, twelve men, into the area of their last transmission to search for the missing men. The major was a good dude. He said he'd have the patrol, two choppers, a gunship escort, and Neil's patrol gear waiting on the pad when he got there. Neil thanked him.

The odds against finding the men were long, but the thought of waiting by the radio while the General sent in a larger force was terrifying to him. He dare not admit the anguish hovering on the edge of his awareness. Anguish, recrimination, and grief would eat at his soul if he stopped now. His salvation lay in action. And if he found Gooks instead of his guys, satisfaction lay in revenge.

His pilot's voice broke into the intercom. "I'll gas up and fly FAC for your patrol, sir. With only twelve guys you're gonna need some air support."

"Yeah, thanks," Neil said, already planning his route.

"Don't think nothing of it," the pilot said.

He flew a straight in approach to the runway on the flat scar of earth that was their firebase. Three choppers sat on the pad, two slicks and a gunship, and a jeep with two men in it, and one long rank of troopers, twelve men and twelve piles of gear.

Neil's pilot flared a tad high and they dropped two feet onto the runway. Not smooth, but thoroughly reflective of their mood. They taxied past some sandbagged 105s and a crew of barechested kids with dust in their hair, unloading coils of concertina wire and anonymous boxes off a C-123. The pilot opened the flimsy door and Neil climbed out stiffly. It had been a long flight.

"Be glad to have you up there, man," Neil said, standing by the aircraft. "That was some ballsy flying down the river."

"It was fuckin' nuts," said the pilot in an agreeable tone. "I'm nuts, you're nuts. This whole deal is fuckin' nuts. I'm gonna go gas up and tape these holes. See ya when ya get there."

Propwash hit Neil as he taxied away, throwing red dirt in his face. As he turned and walked toward the major's jeep the baking heat settled back in. He ran his hand across his shaggy brush cut and it came out greasy and gritty. He wiped his hands on his pants.

Approaching the jeep Neil flipped the major a salute and without preamble pulled his map from the cargo pocket of his fatigue pants. "I figure the NVA will have the primary LZ under observation. I'm gonna go in here." He pointed out a small clearing that hadn't been used before. "It's maybe half a klick further away from their last transmission than the primary."

From behind the steering wheel the major squinted down over the map. "You sure you don't want just one team and a platoon? You ain't got very many guys here if the shit hits the fan."

Neil shook his head. "Nossir. Our deal. You might have some people on alert, but I wanta keep this within recon if I can. All for one and all that good shit."

The major rolled a Camel into the corner of his mouth. "The Old Man's got Bravo on alert. I had a job talking him out of sending the whole company."

"Thanks," Neil said. He swung his gear out of the passenger seat, put it on and jumped a couple of times to see if it rattled. He wore green fatigues and a black beret. His bush hat lay in the seat. He handed the major his beret and adjusted the cut-down tiger striped patrol hat low on his nose. "Let's get this show on the road," he said.

Another jeep rolled to a stop beside the major's. Neil's platoon sergeant got out wearing tigers, all tricked out. Beside him was a young man similarly equipped. As they dismounted the kid swung a PRC-25 radio onto his back. A slow, wry grin cracked Neil's face. "Ev'body wants ta get inta da act," he said.

Pappy threw him a lazy salute. "Didn't think you were going without me?"

Neil returned it. "Somebody's got to watch the store," he said.

Pappy nodded. "Henderson and DuPont are in the TOC. We'll be all right."

Neil said, "Okay, here's the deal." He handed Flagg his map.

* * *

"Jesus!" Neil said. They'd found them all right, on the ground where they lay after the last transmission. The bodies had been stripped of radios, weapons and ammo, and their packs. They hadn't been mutilated, not this time. Four young men, only one of whom had lived to be twenty. A flood of memories of these kids, finding and training them, moments shared with each one as he'd mastered something he was having trouble with, or been amazed at some technique. Apted, a big dumb ballsy kid, but the most experienced, and the most jungle wise. Berringer, the little guy who had to be counseled to write his folks; Wise, just back from a special R&R Neil had gotten for him because his buddy from Basic had been killed in the 173d; Leeds, the biker.

Neil pushed the memories down, to be dealt with later. He had a job to do here. And the stench was overpowering. He soaked his cravat from a canteen and tied it over his nose. The others did likewise.

Pappy directed one team to zip their teen-age chums into body bags. The other teams were on the ground, fanned out in a circle around them, facing out into the trees, weapons ready. The mood was heavy. Someplace above them droned the O-1E. Charles obviously knew they were in, and they might be fairly easy pickings, but so far they had been left alone. Could it be that the enemy commander had the soul of a gentleman? Not bloody likely.

As Red Two struggled to get the bodies into the bags their faces changed from those of tired, tough boys to those of old men in grief. Neil felt it too, in the pit of his stomach, and in a sour taste in his throat. Somehow this was much more terrible than the fear of his own death. It made his willingness to gamble his life for a commission seem trivial. Was there anything he had done or not done that could have saved these boys' lives?

Funny, he had, for years, hated the term "our boys". His troops had by God earned the right to call themselves men. But in death they were boys again. As their mothers would quickly tell you. Oh, Jesus! He was going to have to write four of those letters.

"We need four one-pole litters," he told Pappy, who put one of the other teams to chopping and stripping the poles. That left one team, plus Neil, Pappy, and the RTO for security. All of Neil's consciousness poured into his ears and eyes. He knew shock, and possibly guilt, would pour over him later. On the Project grief had become a permanent part of his emotional landscape, but responsibility gave it a new twist. Every officer in the army dreamed of becoming a general, but Neil was thinking maybe he didn't have the stuff for it. If you commanded thousands, even the most lopsided victory would leave dozens dead. If losing four guys could do this to you, he didn't see how he could cope with losing dozens and go home to celebrate his "victory".

Neil felt that maybe he'd traded these four for his lousy second lieutenant bars, and he was finding it a very bad trade.

When the poles were cut and stripped, the bodies loaded on ponchos, and the ponchos tied off to the poles, it took two complete teams to carry the bodies. In all likelihood Charles had both his primary and alternate LZs staked out by now. But he had another small clearing that hadn't been used for awhile picked for his extraction LZ. In this terrain, starting at this time of day, they wouldn't get out tonight. Not a good situation. Not a popular decision either, but there it was. No way was he going to risk his people by walking into a likely ambush area just to get out today. He put himself just behind the point, and Pappy just in front of the tailgunner, and they set off in the wrong direction for the new LZ.

Just because they hadn't been hit didn't mean they weren't being watched. He wanted to lose any tail they might have picked up before this route of march pointed toward their destination. This made their route longer. Another unpopular decision.

Made even more unpopular by the fact that this was some of the thickest shit he'd ever walked in. Neil was dragging himself up the hill, taking every step slowly, picking branches out of his face. He couldn't imagine what it would be like if you were schlepping one end of a litter.

So after the first break he took a turn. As an officer he wasn't supposed to do manual labor, and, in fact, drew a disapproving scowl from Pappy Flagg. The kid he relieved said, "Sir, you don't have to do that."

Neil nodded toward the corpse in the body bag. “I'm not supposed to burn shit," he said. "but I can be a pallbearer for my own man."

It was a bitch to travel like this. They couldn't run the ridges. That's where the trails were, and that's where Charles would be traveling. They couldn't run the creek bottoms. That's where Charles had his camps. They had to hug the hillsides and try to maintain a compass azimuth through this horrible thick stuff. Neil only carried the pole from one break to the next. He really needed to be on the compass, on the map, on the radio, watching, listening, thinking.

Maybe he'd made a point carrying the litter, and maybe he'd just been an asshole, currying favor with his troops.

Crossing trails with the litters, which they had to do four times, was a special hassle. Normally you would twinkle-toe across one at a time. With the litters he put gunners on either side of the trail and whisked them across. Then Pappy swept the trail with a palm frond while Neil worked his way back to the front of the patrol. At 1700 it started to get dark and they stopped.

Nobody ate much and most of what they ate they forced down because they knew they'd need the energy the next day. Body bags masked most of the smell, and they'd ceased to be very conscious of it on their hellish journey. But Neil was conscious of it now. The smell of death filled his nostrils and his mind until it seemed to be all there was. He wondered what the others thought. He wondered if they held him responsible for the deaths of these men.

When Apted had picked his LZ, Neil should have caught the fact that it had already been used twice and made him go to the one they were using for extraction now. But he'd been briefing and inserting three teams that day, and briefing Major Swank and the general. Things were hot. He and the major had been up until three the previous morning, planning the best way to get full coverage of the operational area with limited resources, and he'd simply let Apted pick his LZ and accepted it. Normally he thought it best to interfere as little as possible with his team leaders' plans, but this had been Apted's first time out as patrol leader. Neil should have been watching him more closely.

He felt a sudden burst of resentment. Pappy had been there. He was the old head; why hadn't he caught it?

No good, Neil thought. It's your responsibility and you can't pass it on to Pappy.

Thoughts like that chased themselves feverishly through his mind, through the evening, through the night, until the light started to gray into dawn.

When there was enough light they cleared camp and headed out again. The day was another nightmare of wait-a-minute vines and vile sweat. But their route was generally downhill. They were coming into the home stretch, and it didn't seem so bad. The temptation was to abandon caution and burn it in to the LZ. When the point started picking up the pace he held them back. When they neared the LZ he took one man forward for a personal reconnaissance. They crept carefully to the area and watched the little clearing for half an hour. Nothing. It would have taken them an hour and a half to work their way entirely around it, and Neil didn't want to do that. He figured he would be more likely to reveal his own position than to find the enemy's. Odds were they had a couple of people watching the little clearing with the sunlight pouring into it, but if they moved fast they could be out before Charles had time to react with a larger unit. He crept back to his patrol, called the FAC and told him they were inbound, thirty minutes out. The choppers were on alert and the patrol was starting to loosen up. This was the most dangerous time, but the teams were already starting to relax because they could smell safety. Neil was so tense the cords in his neck felt like they were about to pop.

The FAC called that their choppers were coming. Neil halted the patrol on the edge of the clearing and waited until he heard rotors, then popped yellow smoke and threw it into the clearing. He confirmed the colors on the radio and Pappy gave them a mirror flash as they entered the clearing.

As the first chopper settled in they loaded the four bodies and one team, plus Pappy. The first Huey lifted out and sped away over the jungle as number two flared over the clearing. Neil waved his men aboard, still scanning the trees as he barreled on after them. As they lifted out of the hole a solitary shot rang out from the edge of the clearing. Both doorgunners loosed long bursts at the edges of the trees, but he doubted if they hit anything.

* * *

The last of the bodies was being loaded onto the back of a three-quarter-ton truck as his Huey whirled in. He would never see or smell those men again except in his dreams. He would write four letters. He would attend a memorial service in a tent with folding pews, and a folding altar. The chaplain would wear vestments over fatigues and jungle boots. Before the altar would be four pairs of jump boots, and behind each an M-16 stuck into the ground by its bayonet, each with a black beret draped over the buttplate. The chaplain would say soothing words. Everybody in the platoon who wasn't out on patrol or on R&R would be there. The memory of these men would fade in the minds of most of their comrades, who had to forget to believe in their own survival.

But forgetting was a luxury Neil could not afford. He got off the chopper, gave the pilot a little half salute, and the Huey lifted off. Pappy was waiting by the major's jeep. Neil slung his pack over one shoulder and walked across the red dirt to them.

"Good job avoiding contact, Thompson," The major said. "They was Gooks sighted all around you there."

"Yessir," said Neil. "Now I'd like to go back in and bring nape on 'em."

The major cracked a weary lopsided grin. "You'll get your chance, Recon," he said.

They drove to the Intelligence Section's tent, where Neil quickly debriefed the major and typed out a short after-action report. There wasn't much to say. They came, they saw, they picked up their stiffs and left.

He handed the major the report. "I feel like shit about those guys," he said.

The major threw the report in his top in-basket and reached into the footlocker behind him for a half-empty fifth of Chivas. He handed the bottle to Neil, who took a pull and passed it to Pappy. "Don't go blamin' yourself, sir," said Pappy. "You're doin' a good job."

"You can't let it eat at you," said the major, accepting the bottle back for a pull himself. "Only four KIAs in four months is good leadership. It's damn near a fuckin' miracle."

"Yessir," Neil said dully. He knew the major was right. He wasn't going to let himself be racked with guilt over this. This wasn't guilt; it was grief. If he was going to do his job he was going to have to put it aside. "Don't worry," he added. "I'll be good for duty in the morning."

The major smiled. "See you at the club later?"

Neil shook his head. "I've got some letters to write."

"They can wait."

"I want them out of the way.

He and Pappy shouldered their packs and headed back to the platoon area. At the entrance to Neil's tent Pappy said, "Sir, as your platoon sergeant I advise you to get blind drunk tonight and come in to work tomorrow so hung over you can barely move, let alone think."

Neil gave him a shallow grin. "I'll probably follow that advice," he said.

He entered his tent, which was Spartan enough, but roomy and private. Even Pappy Flagg had to share a tent with Sims, and there were eight bunks in those for the lower-ranking enlisted men, although it was rare for more than four to be in at any one time. He dropped his pack on the plank floor and pulled up a folding chair at the GI field desk.

He didn't want to write the parents first. He needed to sort out his feelings in words. He thought about writing his mother, but if he wrote her honestly about this she would probably go into hysterics.

He opened a box of cheap stationery with the brigade crest on it. He wrote in the date and started, "Dear Juliana…"

Neil wrote a calm and dispassionate letter. He wrote not at all of emotional matters, nor did he describe in any detail the sights, sounds, and smells of the patrol. He wrote in a combination of jargon and slang that would be almost incomprehensible to most people. The only clue it contained to his emotional state was that it was seventeen pages long.

He felt a little better when the letter was done, but not much. He was not purged of his emotions, for he had not explored them. Indeed, the purpose of the language he had used was to hold back despair long enough to take care of business.

He turned his attention to the other four letters, concentrating on striking exactly the right note of sympathy, without becoming maudlin. He included one or two vignettes of the kid's life in the brigade, slightly exaggerating the regard in which he was held by his buddies. He would have liked to close on a positive note to the effect that their sacrifice had not been in vain. But he didn't want to lie, so his closing was a bit lame. All in all though, they weren't bad letters.

When he finished writing them he felt empty, drained. He was somewhat purged of the coruscating grief and guilt, but the hollow hurt that replaced it was not much better. He did not know what to do. He really did not want to go to the club and get drunk. But the last thing he wanted was to be alone with his thoughts.

Without preamble or greeting, the screen door to his tent screeched open and General Frenier entered. Neil did not just come to attention, he slammed his body into it. He stood, eyes to the front, thumbs along the seams of his trousers, heels together, feet at a forty-five degree angle. He seized this bit of ritual as a dying Catholic sinner seizes the rite of confession.

"At ease, Lieutenant," said the General. "May I come in?"

Neil relaxed and said, "Yes, sir. Have a seat."

General Frenier stood, clenching and unclenching his fists. He wore his pistol, so he kept his baseball cap on, as prescribed by the regulation for wear of the uniform while under arms. Nonetheless his eyes burned through the shadow under the bill of his cap. He looked crazed. He could have been John Brown on his way to execution.

"Thanks," the General whispered. He undid his slick little black general's belt and holster, and put them on Neil's desk. Then he took off his cap and sat down.

"Would you care for a drink, sir?" Neil asked. He didn't know what else to say.

The question he was burning to ask, though, was what was the general doing here? He wasn't the sort to call on every second lieutenant in his brigade who had a morale problem.

"Thank you, yes," the general said.

Neil got two glasses and a bottle of Jack Daniels from his footlocker. The glasses and bottle were both dusty. He rinsed the glasses with water from his canteen and threw the water through the screened side of his tent. Then he poured a couple of shots worth into each glass and gave one to the general.

"Absent friends," said the general, raising his glass.

"Neil raised his own glass. "Absent friends," he repeated.

"I looked for you in the club," said the general, "but Swank said you were in your quarters."

"Yes sir," Neil replied. "I wanted the letters out of the way, and I needed to think some."

The general gave him a sharp look.

"I wanted to think through if there was something I could have done differently that would maybe have saved those guys."

Critically, the general said, "No doubt you found something."

Neil nodded. "I shouldn't have sent Apted as patrol leader," he replied. "I didn't really have any choice there. But I should have used another LZ."

The general looked stern. "This is not good thinking, Lieutenant," he said. "You will inevitably lose men in the conduct of war, and you will always be able to second guess yourself later. You simply have to do your best and forget about it."

He took a sip of whiskey, paused and took another. "You've done a conscientious job with your platoon. Very few young officers could have done better. I think generally in the army we do a good job, taking care of our men."

His eyes blazed. He leaned forward in his chair. "Not like the God damned Marine Corps, where they never dig in, and all they know is the frontal assault. We don't throw our men away like used Kleenex."

Unless it benefits our careers, Neil thought bitterly. Personally he'd always thought the Marines were pretty cool.

The general drained his glass and stood.

Neil sprang to his feet.

The general buckled on his pistol and adjusted his cap. He placed a most uncharacteristic fatherly hand on Neil's shoulder. "Don't worry about the last operation, Thompson. Worry about the next one. Just don't risk your men needlessly like the God damned Marines." He turned and stumbled through the door into the night.

Where did that come from? Through the screen Neil watched the general lurch away.

Chapter Seventeen

Scanning the reception area Neil felt he was looking at some other army. Until this flight he had not seen soldiers in khaki in a year. Around him the G.I.s with whom he'd flown to the States stood weary and rumpled, barracks bags crumpled at their feet.

The REMFs, the rear echelon clerks, seemed excited and happy to be home, eager to put in the rest of their time in the army, then become hippies. The combat guys wore expressions ranging from wary through angry to bemused. They not only didn't look happy to be home, they didn't look like they *were* home; they looked like they'd been crammed through a time machine into some new hostile area of operations. They looked uneasy without their rifles.

Neil too was uneasy without the familiar weight of a CAR-15 under his right arm. If somebody opened up on him now he'd be fucked.

It was ten o'clock in the morning here, ten at night in Vietnam, give or take an hour; he couldn't figure out the time zones. He felt stupid in his khakis, wearing a green overseas cap that looked like an overturned boat on his head.

He planned to stay here at Travis long enough to pick up a decent tropical worsted uniform and get it tailored. He had a month to report to Ft. Bragg, and he hoped to see Juliana in New York.

Thirty days leave coming, and no notion of what to do with it other than to see Juliana. He'd visit his mother, of course, and turn into a child and a klutz again, until he could get out of there. But that was an obligation.

What he wanted was to spend the entire leave in bed with Juliana, except for brief excursions to spend money. But she'd only spent one night with him, under harrowing circumstances. It had been, sort of, well…epic, but what did that mean in the great scheme of things?

Moment of truth, old buddy. Drop a dime and find out… If she's home? He fumbled in his pocket for a dime of the five dollars in change he'd gotten when he turned in his military pay currency for U.S. dollars. Her phone number he had memorized, just as her eyes were memorized, and the freckles, and the way her ass moved when she threw her leg over a motorcycle.

He found a pay phone.

It wasn't a good time to catch somebody at home, but grad students kept weird hours and if he was going to have to keep trying, he might as well start now. He dropped a dime in the phone and dialed "O".

"Operator."

"Operator, I want to place a long-distance call to New York City. That's 212-591-8831."

"Thank you. Please deposit three dollars and fifty cents for the next three minutes."

Dutifully he dropped fourteen quarters into the phone and waited while it rang. Once…twice…three…four… He was starting to tense up, not sure how many times he could go through this and retain his composure…five…

"I'm sorry. No one seems to be at home now. If you'd like to place your call later…"

"Give it a couple more rings, operator. She might be in the shower."

The phone rang once more. "Hello."

The voice was breathless, as though she had just run up five flights of stairs to get to the phone. He gulped. "Juliana, it's Neil."

"Neil!" she squealed. "When are you coming to see me?"

"Right now! As soon as I can get a plane…unless you want to fly out here for a quick change of scene. It's beautiful here, and I'm loaded with money. I spent six months on a firebase while it just piled up in the bank."

There was a pause. "Oh, Neil, it sounds wonderful, but I can't. I've got classes, and my doctor says I shouldn't fly."

"You okay?"

There was a moment's hesitation. "Yes, I'm fine. But how are you?"

He laughed. "Got all my limbs, no grenade fragments. It took most of my tour to organize the platoon and get it operational. I only went out three times, and they were milk runs."

"Great! Now you've got one more milk run, to New York. How long can you stay?"

Grinning and jiggling, he said. "I can probably wear out my welcome. "I'll have to run down to DC to see my mom, and I want to see Doc McLeod. He's at Walter Reed. But I've got thirty days leave, and I'll spend as much time with you as you can stand."

He was consciously and deliberately holding back, because he knew how skittish she was, and how mistrustful, and why. He didn't know if it was possible to be reticent enough.

He only knew how she made him feel, as though he had entered a new kind of atmosphere, a gas lighter and sweeter than oxygen, a feeling beside which ordinary happiness was coarse and unappetizing. And yet, at the same time it hurt, from fear that it might be taken away.

"I can stand quite a bit of it," she laughed. "At least we can work up a good argument. Even the people I agree with here are full of shit. I can't stand it."

"Sounds right," he said jubilantly. "Argue about the war for a month. Then go down south and train kids to fight in it.

"Look, I'll be there tonight if I can get a flight."

* * *

On the plane he took a window seat. Neil loved take-offs and landings, loved to watch the land drop away and turn into a model, see the layout of different cities, and the countryside. He looked down at the sere golden tan hills around San Francisco and the row on row of old apartments, the buildings, the long translucent deep blue course of shimmering ocean. They climbed higher and the earth turned fuzzy brown.

There had been no time to get a decent uniform, so he was in civvies; loafers, jeans and a polo shirt. The businessman in the next seat eyed his G.I. haircut, but said nothing. Neil said nothing either. He fumbled in his hand baggage for the book he'd bought at the airport, a paperback copy of Richard Farina's *Been Down So Long It Looks Like Up To Me*.

It seemed strange to Neil that the only civilian thing he could relate to was the anti-war movement. If all he knew about the war was anti-war propaganda, he'd be against it too. There were plenty of parts of it he was against as it was.

He'd always been drawn to a Bohemian lifestyle, even before there were such things as hippies and LSD. Corporate America was like the worst part of being in the army, without any of the good stuff.

For that reason there were assignments he dreaded in his military career, the inevitable Pentagon tour, the staff job in a big headquarters. You had to do all that if you wanted to make a decent career.

Not that he was thinking about getting out of the army. With accelerated promotions due to the war he'd be making captain in less than a year and a half. He could go back to the Nam with his own "A" Team, or to command of a line company. He had a year of troop duty ahead of him, in the 82d, his father's old outfit. And before that he had a month with Juliana. He felt the old lust rising as he thought of her walking naked in her house in Buon Allay A, thought of her moving with him in that bed with the gauze mosquito netting, her tanned face pale in the moonlight, breasts flattened as she lay on her back, sweat pouring down his chest, running from his hair down his face, dripping off the end of his nose, into her face, making love to her all night long, weak from his wound, in pain and not caring, in ecstasy in her.

Down boy. He squirmed in his seat, there being few things less comfortable than an erection in jeans, held down by a seatbelt. He didn't want to assume, to presume, that just because they'd made love once that he could automatically jump her whenever he felt like it for the rest of his life. But that's what he wanted.

Below, clouds were banked solid under a clear blue sky, the sun burning down from the corner of his window, so bright it hurt his eyes. He thought about pulling down the shade, but he loved the brightness and the clearness of it, the spareness of it. It was a universe away from the firebase. He was beginning to relax a bit, and luxuriate in the knowledge that no one was likely to kill him today.

He picked up his book and tried to lose himself in it, but soon the stews in their Pucci costumes--you couldn't call them uniforms--filled the aisle with their drink cart, so he got a beer and a free bag of peanuts. He ripped the top off with his teeth, scattering a few peanuts on the floor and a few more in his crotch, which he dug out with an obscene pawing gesture.

Then the stews were back with lunch. The blonde with the not-so-great face ripped off the aluminum, and passed it over onto his little drop-down table. He could remember his mother and Hobart bitching about airline food, but this was the best meal he'd had in six months.

Best looking anyway. There was an odd tasteless quality to it, as though it was not real food, merely a model of food, to be eaten with one's arms held tightly to one's sides.

What he really wanted was a cheeseburger, fries, and a chocolate shake. He left half the plastic food in its little compartments. Only the salad disappeared completely, along with two bites of the "Beef Stroganoff". The "scalloped potatoes" went untouched. He dug his book back out.

Then, for some reason, he thought of Shoogie, and looked out the window. When he looked back his folding table was clean.

He went back to looking out the window, the book untouched in his lap. He wasn't really thinking. He was sort of zoned out, watching brilliant banks of clouds climb and drift below, thinking that the shifting of these vapors was like the geologic shifts of the surface of the earth, except that it took place in visible time. He pictured himself as a lighter than air creature, running on the cloudbanks, leaping from cloud to cloud like a kid jumping from pillow to pillow on a big bed.

He amused himself with these thoughts until he felt the shift in glide path that signaled descent. Slowly the aircraft dropped into the clouds. The mists rose to meet them, then tendrils of vapor, then the aircraft was immersed in gray and raindrops streaked across the outside of the window.

Then, just as suddenly, they were below the clouds, neat toy patterns of the Long Island countryside laid out below, blocks of houses, blocks of apartments, highways and railroad tracks, factories and golf courses, little blue swimming pools. He took all of it in, wondering if he loved America or was appalled by it, or if it was possible to be both simultaneously.

The airplane made a clean touchdown and he sat back to wait for the ride to the terminal. Then it struck him why he was here, and he felt that chill in his guts. Why had he gone back to Juliana in Vietnam when she had treated him the way she had? Because he knew why she was the way she was, and he wanted to be the guy who made it okay for her.

And what? She was the least likely army wife he'd ever met.

He got out the instructions she had given him. Take a bus to the Port Authority bus terminal, take the F train to Brooklyn, get off at Seventh Avenue. Sounded easy enough if he could just find it.

After a year and a half in an underdeveloped country the landscape on the ride in from Kennedy seemed unspeakably ugly. Vietnam was poor, but it was green and beautiful. Here was an entire cityscape of rust and filth, piled in a haphazard jumble. It occurred to him that all the true ugliness he had seen in Vietnam had been imported at great expense by the U.S. government. The Viets weren't particularly sanitary, but they were graceful.

But this, these rusting bridges, acres of junk cars, rude traffic, fat jostling people. This was a vision of Hell. Even the night sky had turned a hideous chemical bruise color that does not occur in nature.

Why am I risking my life for these people, he thought, when I like the people I've been killing so much better?

If he'd had his choice right then he'd have been on the first thing smokin' back to Pleiku, and fuck the United States, its decadent filth, its soft angry people. He had become a citizen of a new country, not Vietnam itself, but the war. I don't belong here, he thought, and I don't want to belong here. His longing for the people of Vietnam, for the smell and the heat of it, for the green, was a tangible thing.

At the terminal he dodged the crowds in confusion, until he found a cop who directed him to the subway.

"You a G.I.?"

"Yes sir."

The cop smiled. He was a young guy, about Neil's age. Neil didn't know how he knew, but the smell of the Nam was still on the guy.

"Marine?" the cop asked.

"Airborne."

"Drive on," said the cop.

"Semper Fi," Neil replied, lurching off toward the stairs to the subway, his heavy bag dragging him sideways.

The subway itself was a different kind of buzz. The cars were covered with graffiti, as though an army of Peter Maxes and San Francisco poster artists had wandered in drunk and gone crazy. He actually kind of liked the stuff, because it was wild and free. But when he got on the car he saw that, at least in the interior decoration, full West Coast flower power didn't play in the Big Apple. The graffiti inside the car was angry and angular, and all black.

A few black guys were crouched, smoking a joint down at the end of the car, and they weren't smiling.
He sat quietly in the almost empty car, watching his own dim reflection in the window across, the black tunnel roaring by behind the glass edged in the shadows. His face had aged at least ten years in the year he'd spent in Vietnam, and the black-backed glass, in the horror-movie subway lighting, added at least another ten, so that he looked like a middle-aged wino.

He scanned through the window over his shoulder at every stop; nervous that he might miss his own stop and have to negotiate his return in this filthy and complicated city.

Suddenly, and much to Neil's surprise, the subway started to rise and he was looking at a huge blackened granite pillar, an iron grating and a lot of trash. Then once again he was looking at the acid bruise of the sky, through bridge girders and stringers, and way down the river the graceful arch of the Brooklyn Bridge.

He had never seen it before, knew nothing about it other than that it was public property and that he shouldn't try to buy it from a street vendor. He was amazed at the old stone pilings, realized that it was very old, built like a cross between a castle and a suspension bridge. It was the first beautiful thing he had seen in New York. Jesus, he thought, this must be one of the first of those suckers they ever built.

And behind the bridge he could make out the torch of the Statue of Liberty. It didn't thrill him particularly. His people had come to this country long before the wave of immigrants the statue celebrated, probably as indentured servants or runaway horse thieves.

The train reached the top of its arc and picked up speed, roaring back into the tunnel. After some more blackness it came up on an elevated track and once again he was looking over the soot-blackened chaos of buildings and billboards, big pale moon, and gas pipes. It looked like decay, like death.

He looked at his instructions, scribbled on the back of an envelope, looking for the Seventh Avenue stop, when the three black guys, now the only other people in the car, got up to amble his way.

Their eyes were ready, and he immediately went into combat mode. He thought front-kick left, stiff-arm the one in the middle, side-kick to the knee of the one on the right. He rose, smiling a smile cold as death. The smile said, if this shit starts it won't stop until come person or combination of people is zipped into one or more bags.

They were not fools; they saw. The train stopped and the one in the lead said, "Yo!" and they got off.

One more stop. He got off, too lightly dressed for the crisp night air, and clattered down the stairs of the El. Trash skittered in the wind on the street, and a solitary jogger wearing black socks with his sneakers and a *yarmulke*, loped past.

Neil shouldered his bag and looked around for a street sign, found it, and headed down Seventh Avenue. It wasn't like any street he'd ever walked on before, nothing like the supermarkets and shopping malls of the America he knew, or like pictures he'd seen of Europe, or of the thronged streets of the Far East.

It was late and the streets were almost empty. The buildings were mostly dark brick or stone, darkened still further by decades of soot, but they were clean, at least compared to Manhattan or Saigon, and there was something sort of bluff and no nonsense about them. He liked that. In a way this street reminded him of the main street of a small town. Except that a small town wouldn't have a Puerto Rican grocery store next to an Italian restaurant.

Finally he came to President Street, where Juliana lived.

He was suddenly gripped by a mixture of anxiety and anticipation. She had made love to him and he still burned with the memory of it, had burned for six months, but she had never said she loved him, and although he thought he felt love from her, he did not trust his feelings.

What he feared most was that they would have a long earnest conversation which she would end by saying, "What we shared was beautiful, but can't we be friends?"

The hell of it was that he thought he *could* be her friend. He admired her intellect, her dedication, her courage: he even admired her anger.

He turned right and started up President Street toward her apartment. The street turned into solid rows of rundown, but elegantly constructed brownstones. They gave him claustrophobia, these densely packed rows of jammed apartments.

What am I doing here, he wondered? Here I am, an officer and a gentleman by my own rights, a barbarian by hers. Where can this go?

Three blocks. He found her address, found her name on the call box and pressed it. She buzzed him in to the dark narrow hallway, and he wound up three flights of stairs.

He paused outside the door, wondering what her greeting would be. Whatever, it would be good to see her, even just as friends. He knocked on the door and she opened it. She wore tan cords and a green turtleneck. Her red hair tumbled over her shoulders and the smell of marijuana rolled into the hallway.

"Hi!" he said, and she kissed him long and hard. When he came up for air she shoved a joint in his mouth and he sucked in the smoke, cheeks swelling like a blowfish. As soon as he whooshed out the smoke she kissed him again and they fell to the floor and tore each other's clothes off. She'd gained weight, and so what.

Juliana had no TV in her apartment, but she had a good stereo, and she was no audio purist. Her stereo had a changer that she could stack six albums on. Neil made love to her through *The White Album*, *After Bathing at Baxter's*, and Steve Miller's *Sailor*, before they made it to the bed.

Finally they lay back, passing a number back and forth between them, listening to Dylan's "Tombstone Blues." His leg was crossed over hers, and never in his life had he felt so happy, so relaxed, so full of joy. He was afraid to speak, afraid to hurry this perfect moment, or spoil it or crowd it with questions. For the moment the fact that she had loved him enough to love him was sufficient; he saw no reason to hurry something that was bound to end badly. He turned and snuggled against her, and by and by they were moving again.

When they finished the sheets were loose, bunched, and sweaty. He lay beside her and wiped his face with a corner of the sheet.

She smiled at him and said, "God, it's good to see you. I recognized your step in the hallway; you know that?"

He smiled. "No, I didn't know that. Didn't really know you cared for me."

She smiled. "No wonder."

He shrugged. "You were scared and you were pissed. I definitely know about scared and pissed."

She frowned. "It was only after I got back that I realized... The guys here are so...even when they agree with me they do it for the wrong reason. I respect what you guys do with the Montagnards, but I'm still not for the war."

He smiled. "Never thought you were."

"So, are you going to get out, or what?"

He shook his head. "I want to see it through." He stopped talking, unhappy with the turn the conversation had taken. "You still got that Supersession Blues Jam album?"

She smiled. "Do indeed. Why don't you make up the next stack while I roll another one."

Fair enough, only he'd noticed she only took about three hits off the first one, shallow hits at that.

He got up and padded naked to the corner of the room where about 300 albums and an off-brand Japanese stereo leaned against the wall. He figured six albums wouldn't overload the stereo, so he crouched and stacked the double album Paul Butterfield-Mike Bloomfield, side three of *Live Dead*, *Children's Children's Children*, *Revolver*, and Zeppelin II.

"You never did tell me why the doctor didn't want you to come to San Francisco," he said by way of conversation.

"Gunna have a baby," she said. She said it almost in a whisper.

He had the stack poised over the changer, but he dropped it, whirling fast enough to get rug burns on his ass. "Say what?"

"Gunna have a baby," she said again, a little louder this time, but still defensively, a bit of a shy smile lurking around the corners of her mouth.

He stopped, a bit stunned, picked up his stack of records and started them, running more or less on autopilot. What she meant was that *they* were going to have a baby. Then it occurred to him that it might not be his, might be Shoogie's. Didn't matter; he wouldn't want anybody else to raise either Juliana's or Shoogie's kid. Besides, how else could he ever get a woman like this to marry an army officer?

It was cold. The first record dropped and he dived back under the covers. "Jeez," he said, "why didn't you tell me this before?"

She snuggled against him, looking at him questioningly. "Didn't know how you'd take it," she replied. "It didn't go down so well the last time."

Somehow he hadn't made that connection. She'd lived with that asshole for three years, and when she got pregnant… He took a quick inventory of his own feelings. He was quietly happy, no, quietly ecstatic. He said, "I'm happy. I'm gonna be a daddy. I love you and I'm gonna be a daddy."

He looked at her, and at the way she looked at him. She loved him. She hadn't known before how she felt, but she loved him now, for this, for being there for her.

"It really is yours, you know," she said. "I expected to get laid the night of the party. It was the night before I left that was the surprise."

"I never doubted it for a minute," he lied.

She laughed.

Then it all poured out of him in a rush. "Look, we've never talked about this and I know you hate the army. If you don't want to marry me, I understand. The kid's mine, and it'll be my dependent. But if we get married it'll mean a lot more money, housing allowance, free medical and all that stuff."

Her look searched him. "You really want me, don't you?"

"Yeah!" The only thing I'm afraid of is that you're gonna hate the army, the peacetime army. It's boring as shit. I can't see you at a Wives' Club tea."

She made a face. "I'd really like to finish at NYU. But I can't raise a baby and do that too. I really want this baby."

All of a sudden what had been a party turned deadly serious. "You won't have to lay out more than a semester. I'm gonna be stationed at Bragg. Maybe you could commute to Chapel Hill. Help's cheap down there, so you can get someone to stay with the baby. You can get your Ph.D. and the University of Maryland has an extension program for G.I.s all over the world. You can still teach wherever we go. If we want to we can make it work."

She lay back on the bed and smiled. "A much different reaction than the last time I announced I was pregnant."

Neil didn't want to think about that. Didn't want to think about her ever being unwanted, beat up. He imagined that son of a bitch, whatever his name was, had really had the courage of his convictions, gone to Nam and fought for the other side. He imagined he was the white guy of the pair he and Shoogie had hit, imagined the motherfucker in his sights. He remembered Shoogie hosing down the white guy and smiled. Remembered Shoogie saying, "He said, 'Help me!' So I helped him. I emptied a full magazine into the son of a bitch."

"What are you thinking?" she asked.

"Nothing, really." He slid back down in the bed and took her in his arms again. "Wanta celebrate our engagement?"

"Again? You are horny."

He smiled. "I was thinking more in terms of a late dinner, little champagne. But now that you mention it… I'm a little depleted though. It would take a long, loooong time."

She slid down in the bed and kissed him. "Dinner sounds fine," she said. "Your haircut is a problem though. You're going to be hassled if you go out looking like that."

He arched an eyebrow. "Hassled, eh?"

She smiled warily. "You might enjoy a casual fistfight, but it would spoil my engagement dinner. We could go to Carroll Gardens. That's a Mafia neighborhood, and they support the war."

Briefly Neil's rage rose. Then he started to laugh. "You mean the only people who support our foreign policy are professional criminals?"

"That's about it."

"I fuckin' love it."

Chapter Eighteen

Neil's company stretched out for almost a hundred yards, marching at a route step, without cadence, in a split column on either side of the road, disappearing around a bend. Beside the road piney woods spread across flat sandy ground. Scattered along the road, in the woods, were the Ft. Dix firing ranges, and not, as he had hoped, the parachute drop zones of Ft. Bragg.

Neil had requested, and been granted, a transfer from one of the best assignments in the Infantry to one of the worst--basic training. He had done this so Juliana could finish at NYU.

Neil seethed with anger, which was how he spent most of his time in this place, anger at the way his troops were being trained, because he felt their chances for survival in Vietnam were being compromised.

Things weren't all that fucking wonderful at home either. Juliana hated army life, and he couldn't really blame her. Aside from Juliana, the wives in his regiment were all competing in the Miss Bouffant contest. They were friendly, and Juliana was superficially cordial, but there was no way. What was Juliana going to say to the Ray Coniff fans?

He turned and looked back at his Sad Sack trainees strung out along the road. The Drill Sergeants in his company had been together for a long time. Somewhere along the way they had developed the custom of walking at a breakneck pace. Probably they got it from SFC Arquette, who had been a walking racer in Rhode Island.

In one way he liked this gimmick. It was a good physical conditioner, and built *esprit*. What he didn't like was that his formation very quickly lost unit integrity; the weak got left behind, and the company turned into a ragged mob.

For that reason he mostly made the cadre march at a decent pace, and required them to patrol up and down the column, making sure the troops kept a proper interval and the column didn't accordion.

But all bets were off today. He let the sergeants have their head, and they were walking faster than most of the bastards could run.

His feet smoked on the macadam at this crippling pace. The trainee guidon bearer--the kid who carried the company flag--chuffed along at the head of the column, just behind the field first sergeant in his Smokey Bear hat, the kid's ugly new green fatigues black with sweat under the armpits and in the folds of his shirt and pants. He was a big fat kid. Huge droplets of sweat stood out on his forehead under his cocked-back helmet, and ran in rivulets into his red eyes. The kid was dirty and tired and miserable, and Bellows was walking him into the ground.

The thing which caused Neil such anger was that he had come to inspect his company, and found that the day before his final two firing orders, thirty-two troopers, had fired for qualification in total darkness. Ft. Dix was on an accelerated training schedule, and ranges that were designed for one company a day were firing two. The first started at first light and the second finished when they got through.

He was supposed to let his Drill Sergeants run the training, and stay out of sight. After being completely hands on with the Recon Platoon this made Neil crazy.

If not for the Drill Sergeant system he'd have been on the range all day yesterday and he'd have made half the company keep firing while the other half ate, and vice versa. As it was they'd got through an hour after the sun went down.

He was so pissed off that he sent his Operations Sergeant back in the jeep and walked in with the company.

He was angry with bureaucratic muleheadedness. He was angry that this army, run by the West Pointers who had expelled him for failing to turn in his roommate for cheating, were *teaching* these trainees to cheat. He was angry with himself for going along with it. But he just didn't want the hassle. If he protested he'd throw the timing of this entire cycle of trainees out of kilter, not only in his company, but for tens of thousands of trainees. He would also be flushing his military career over something fairly easily fixed. That morning he'd taken aside the drill sergeant of the platoon which had fired so late, thrown out yesterday's fake scores, and told him to double today's scores. Wasn't perfect, but it beat causing a huge megillah in the middle of a war.

But it still burned his ass.

Ahead he made out the corner of an ugly frame barracks. They were almost home. Behind him he heard his blimp trainee guidon bearer sigh in audible relief.

Neil whirled and walked backwards. His company was still strung out along the road, and even his Drill Sergeants looked a little ragged. Now they were all easing up because they only had about five hundred yards to go and they were home.

Normally Bellows would have slowed them down and closed them up, made them come into the company area walking tall, and looking proud. But as mean as he felt this day, that wasn't going to happen.

He pumped his right fist in the air as he bellowed, "Double-Tammmm, HORCH", turned and ran like a striped-assed gazelle toward the company area.

His guidon bearer gasped and fell to the pavement.

Neil turned to run backwards. The trainee platoon sergeant from the first platoon grabbed the guidon before it hit the ground. Good man.

All back down the road trainees were falling out. Neil turned and sprinted for the company area. He took the turn that lead to "O" Company, Outlaw Company. He entered the company area at the head of about half his men; the rest strung out halfway back to the ranges.

Bellows arranged them into formation and saluted. Bellows was an enormous wedge of a man in tightly tailored fatigues, which tailoring had been done when he had weighed thirty pounds less, and he wore a darker V of olive drab in the back of his pants to compensate. His Smokey Bear hat was perched just over his nose, slightly off center. In Neil's opinion Bellows was a pretty good troop, but he wouldn't have made it in Special Forces.

"Sergeant Bellows," he said, "give everybody in the company area the rest of the day off." It was 1800 hours, six in the evening. "Get 'em in to chow and let 'em go. Make 'em clean up if they leave the company area. The rest of these yay-hoo's, when they straggle in, form 'em up, feed 'em and tell' em to stand by for a full field inspection at 2100 hours. It's fine to walk fast, but we still need to move as a unit."

Bellows fanned his forehead in what was intended as a salute, but which more closely resembled a seal attempting to catch a frisbee.

Neil returned it, turned and mounted the Orderly Room steps. As he strode through the door his first sergeant sprang to attention, an action which raised him to a height roughly even with Neil's sternum, and bellowed, "TINCH-HUT!"

Neil had tried to break his first shirt of this habit except when senior officers were in the area. But the first sergeant said he preferred to be consistent, and they still did it when he arrived in the company area.

The little first sergeant was punctilious to a fault about military courtesy, and when he and Neil walked together to the messhall or one of the barracks he would always spring ahead and open the door so Neil could sweep through in a regal manner. All of this made Neil highly uneasy. He didn't see this ass kissing as a sign of respect, but as a sign of barely concealed contempt, an attempt to manipulate. He knew this little son of a bitch would jap him the first chance he got.

In fact he was pretty sure that the only thing which had prevented it so far was that Neil and Bellows got on, and Bellows and Snedden had been together since Korea.

"At ease," Neil said, and headed for his office.

"Sir," said First Sergeant Snedden, "Major Baines wants to see you at Battalion Headquarters."

Neil swept his GI baseball cap off and glared balefully at his first sergeant. "What the fuck does he want?"

Snedden picked up the cigarette he had been smoking when Neil entered. "Didn't say, sir. Just said you was to report."

"Okey dokie," Neil said. "Hit me."

Snedden pulled a box from his lower right hand desk drawer. Neil went behind the railing to the Top's desk. Snedden handed him a nylon stocking, and he carefully went over his boots. The stocking took the day's dust off without dulling the shine, and smoothed out any scuffs. Only the soles, and the creases around the eyelets stayed dusty. He flipped his belt loose and shined the buckle with Blitz cloth and a jeweler's rouge Shino rag, rebuckled and stomped his boots twice so his trousers bloused over his boot tops. He checked to see that his belt buckle and the fly on his trousers and flap of his shirt formed one continuous line. "Okay?" he asked.

"Lookin' good, sir."

"Bellows is gonna have the stragglers laid out for a full field at 2100. You wanta take it with me?"

Snedden looked pained. "Old lady's holdin' dinner 'til 1930, sir. If I'm later than that it's gonna cause problems. It's our anniversary or some such shit."

Neil grinned. "Methinks my old First Soldier's getting' pussywhipped in his dotage," he said.

"You oughta think about getting home at a reasonable hour some night yourself, sir. Don't your old lady ever get pissed off?"

Neil smiled. "Top, my old lady was born pissed off."

He put his baseball cap low on his nose in the approved wiseass manner and exited through the Orderly Room door, skipped down the steps, and set off at a brisk march toward the battalion headquarters, a tiny frame structure fronting on Range Road.

He couldn't imagine what old Baines wanted. In a training regiment the battalion headquarters was unnecessary, except as a warehouse for the inept. Major Baines was riding out his last years before retirement, when he would leave the army to swell the already swollen ranks of unsuccessful insurance and real estate salesmen. To give him something to do, the regimental headquarters let him handle minor personnel hassles involving the officers and NCOs in his battalion. As far as Neil knew neither he nor Juliana had bounced any checks. And their fights, while so frequent as to be almost continuous, were conducted in a low menacing tone, and did not disturb the neighbors.

He bounced up the steps of the battalion headquarters and strode in the door.

Baines' sergeant major, an embittered former captain, sat glowering at his desk, counting the days until he could retire at his highest rank, whiling his time in the interim by being surly and condescending to lieutenants.

"Evenin', Smaj," Neil said. "Major Baines in?"

The sergeant major responded with a nod toward the major's office.

Neil, who had become accustomed to a measure of respect, suppressed an urge to counsel the sergeant major on his attitude.

He rapped on Major Baines' door.

"Come in."

Neil entered, closed the door, halted at attention two paces from Baines' desk, and rendered a proper salute.

"At ease, Lieutenant."

At ease, but not take a seat. Neil moved his left boot a foot from the right and clasped his hands loosely behind his back.

"Thompson, I'll get straight to the p'int. Yore wife ain't j'ined the Wives Club, and she ain't been to no Teas."

It took Neil a full fifteen seconds to assimilate this absurdity, another fifteen to channel his rage. He had given up an assignment to the best division in the U.S. Army, his father's old unit, for this despised training post so Juliana could continue at NYU. He did not begrudge it, thought it only fair to her, but he didn't like it.

"Sir," he replied, as evenly as possible, "Juliana is in her second year of grad school, and she has a baby. That keeps her pretty busy."

The major gave him a look of puzzlement and disappointment. "It don't do yore career no good for her to be hangin' out with them hippies at that university."

"Sir," he said. "Juliana was working toward a Ph.D. in political science when we married. She's very good at it, and she could teach at a top-flight university. Married to me, she'll probably be teaching in junior colleges and the

University of Maryland extension program. She gave up a shot at the top of her profession to be my wife. I think it's a bit much to ask her to give it up altogether, just to go to fucking tea."

He saw no reason to acquaint the major with the argument they'd had over Juliana's wish to maintain her membership in the Students for a Democratic Society. The major would have considered both of them greater security risks than Xuan had been in the Project.

"Look," he'd said when she started filling out the membership application. "You're an American citizen. I'm under oath to defend your right to join the SDS if you want to, and I will. But if you do I'll lose my security clearance, and that will finish my military career. That's a given."

"That's just stupid," she had begun, and went on to detail the reasons, all of which he knew, and most of which he agreed with. But in the end she didn't fill out the application.

What Neil didn't tell her was that after a year at Ft. Dix he was pretty well fed up with the Stateside army. Growing up, he'd always thought of the Thompsons as this great military dynasty. But, neither his father nor his grandfather had lived long enough to have to put up with this shit.

"Well," said Major Baines, "I can't expect her to miss class. But she ort to join the club. She ain't even done that."

"How much?"

"Two bucks a month."

Neil pulled two dollars out of his wallet and laid them on the major's desk.

The major reached into his center drawer and took out an Officer's Wives Club membership card and handed it to Neil. Neil promptly zinged it into the major's wastebasket, aware that his efficiency report was sure to follow. He saluted and left.

* * *

To Neil the Officer's Lounge of the Third Training Regiment, Ft. Dix NJ, resembled, more than any Stateside bar, the Prayboy Crub at the 5th Special Forces Group headquarters in Vietnam, except, of course, that it was full of straightleg troopers, non-jumpers. Another difference was that you could stay at the Prayboy Crub as long as you wanted without pissing off the old lady.

The events of the day had not set well with Neil. Hell, nothing had set well with him since his leave ended. There is much to loathe in West Point careerism, but at least you had to be half-smart and show some initiative to get into the place. In Special Forces you could be a mean son of a bitch and make it, but you had to be smart and dedicated, and have brass balls.

But at Ft. Dix, if you were middlin' stupid, overweight and out of shape, unimaginative, undisciplined, a time-serving frightened little drone, you could still be in the upper fifty percent of your contemporaries. Neil wanted out of Dix.

And in the army of 1969 there was always an out if you wanted it. You could volunteer for Vietnam. But with a new baby and a wife he loved, even if things weren't really going that great, he had decided not to do that. The thing to do would be to tough out this assignment…then go back to Vietnam. By then he'd be a captain, commanding a real company, an infantry company.

For the first time in his life Neil was having doubts about his commitment to a military career. He had maintained his idealism through two military schools, rigorous training, and a tour in Vietnam. But he could see all the seams and holes in it now. It was obvious the U.S. had no intention of winning in Vietnam. Neil wasn't sure he wanted to make a career of leading good kids to die in a lost cause.

Even if he did get out, what would he do? Go back to school on the G.I. Bill, sure. But what the hell would he major in?

He signaled for another beer.

He really should be getting on home, but he knew Juliana would be in a shitty mood, and he just didn't want to put up with it after such a shitty day. This attitude was self defeating, because the longer he was out the more shitty her mood would be, but he had hopes that if he took awhile longer, between the shitty day and the shitty evening, in this brief period of numbness, he would heal enough to make it to reveille without breaking something.

He had a brief vision of himself in a tiger suit, nose pressed into the fecund jungle floor, AK-47 bullets snapping through the sound barrier over his head. In his mind Shoogie was up first and returning fire…then it faded and he was filled with sadness because he doubted he would ever be that happy again. He wasn't sure happy was exactly the word. It certainly didn't seem right, but he thought of himself then, free and loose, not like now, weighed down by troubles and responsibilities, hectored by mediocrities. A phrase from Faulkner came to him, 'half in love with easeful death'. He couldn't remember for sure where it came from, *Sanctuary*, he thought, but he wasn't sure. What the fuck was he doing in this place?

* * *

It was late, late when he rolled into his driveway. He sat down on the concrete step under his carport, unlaced his boots so he wouldn't wake Juliana, and looked out under his carport at a low hanging moon. He was not very drunk, he'd just been passing time, but the longing for freedom was strong in him.

He hadn't stopped and looked at the moon since that night about a month before he left the brigade. He and

Pappy Flagg had sat on the top of the TOC bunker, smoking cigarettes, talking about Apted's team.

Theoretically he should have the same sense of mission about teaching basic, but he'd had a pretty free rein in Vietnam. Here he was just a cog in a big machine, and in his view a malfunctioning machine. McLeod had taught him that the key to success in guerrilla warfare was support of the people, and when he'd got to Dix his sergeants had been teaching "If it moves, shoot it." Neil had learned that the first defensive principle of revolutionary warfare was to never set a pattern. And at Dix he'd found that the conventional units were geared to establish a pattern and follow it to the letter.

Why was he thinking about this shit now? It was 0100 hours, and he was sitting on the step of a government-built tract duplex in New Jersey, dreaming of being a man in a society that did not value manhood. Sometimes he didn't know if he really wanted to fight for a country that had meant everything to him as a boy, but now made him a little sick to his stomach.

Shit, he thought, I've got to be up in three hours and forty-five minutes, and I'm out here looking at the moon and thinking about philosophy. He unlaced his boots and pulled them off, tiptoeing in on his cushionsole G.I. socks. He set his boots down, walked into the baby's room, and stood looking at his daughter, sleeping in the moonlight. He felt his heart turn over, and was overwhelmed by regret that he rarely ever saw her, and probably wouldn't as long as he worked for Sam. He went back into his and Juliana's bedroom, stripped off his uniform, and slipped into bed.

The sleeping form beside him stirred. "Hate to say it, old boy," she whispered, "but you smell like a brewery."

"Yeah," he said, "I feel like one."

"I was worried about you."

"No need. It was just a late Officer's Call, and I fell into drunken brooding about our lives."

"We don't have much of a life, do we?"

"Shit! We don't have any life at all. We never see each other; I never see the baby, and I got no respect for what I'm doing. I never thought I'd say it, but if I could get out of the fuckin' army I would.

She stirred against him. "Early day tomorrow?" she asked.

"Yeah, and I smell like a brewery."

"You could brush your teeth."

"Yeah, I could. We're not gonna get any sleep anyway."

"No, we're not."

Chapter Nineteen

Counting the cadre two hundred and seventy-three pairs of combat boot clad feet slapped against the asphalt as Mighty "O" double-timed the last half-mile to the company area. They looked a lot better than they had three weeks before. The company formation was tight. There were no stragglers, and the formation did not accordion.

"Ah'm gonna beee an eh-bawn rainjaw!" boomed Sergeant Bellows, the only paratrooper in the company besides Neil.

"I'M GONNA BE AN AIRBORNE RANGER!" the company chanted back.

"Leeeead a laff of blood and dainjah!" he continued.

"LEAD A LIFE OF BLOOD AND DANGER!" the chorus continued.

"Jus' two thangs that Ah cain't stan'!"

The company dutifully repeated his words.

"A boooooowlegged woman and a straightleg man."

This too was bellowed loud enough to rattle the windows in adjoining barracks, even though the trainees were all themselves "straightleg men" at this point in their enlistment, and they hadn't seen a woman in so long that they would be pleased to encounter one with bowlegs, knock-knees, or almost any other configuration.

"Quick tamm!" Bellows shouted.

"Quick time," the other cadre echoed, so everyone got the word.

"HORTCH!"

In two steps the company went from 180 steps a minute to 120. Neil spun and marched backwards, hawk-eyed under his baseball cap, checking his cadre more than the troops, to see that they were on the recruits, as the idiom so colorfully put it, "like flies on shit", correcting their step, the squareness of their shoulders, head and eyes straight to the front.

"Hawn-toop-thrip-fawp!" Bellows chanted. "Take the count on your heels, gents. *Don't* dawg-eye me, 'croot…toop-thrip-fawp."

They were looking okay, not good yet, but okay. They were learning, at least, to obey orders swiftly and with some precision. Now, if some of them were lucky enough to wind up under a commander who could figure out which orders to give, they might survive their year in the Nam.

Bellows gave them a column right and they swung off Range Road and into the regimental area. Neil halted in front of the PT platform in the company area and stood at attention as two platoons marched past. Bellows halted the company and Neil took his salute.

"They did good today, Sergeant Bellows," Neil said. "Just feed 'em and put 'em to bed with a minimum of harassment and bullshit."

Bellows saluted and Neil returned it, then wheeled and headed for the Orderly Room. Behind him Bellows was screaming, "You hear that? The Old Man musta seen something I didn't see, because he said you done good. That means you assholes…"

The Orderly Room door slammed shut behind him.

"TINCH-HUT!" The first sergeant and company clerk sprang to attention.

"At ease," he said, and they sank back into their seats.

"You had a phone call from the Pentagon, sir," said First Sergeant Snedden. "Some colonel from DCSOPS."

Snedden had a kind of smarmy expression on his face. Calls from the Pentagon were seldom good news.

A freak grin broke across Neil's face. "McLeod?"

"Yessir, that's the name."

Neil got the number, went into his office, shut the door and dialed the Pentagon. He kicked back and put his feet on his desk. He hadn't felt this relaxed in months. He picked up the phone and dialed. "Special Warfare, Sp4 Warner speaking sir," said a cheery female voice.

"Colonel McLeod, please."

"One moment please." There was a long pause on the line and then a voice snapped. "McLeod!"

"Neil Thompson, sir. What can I do for you?"

"Ah, Thompson, you want a job?"

Neil smiled. He felt a chill that raced up his spine and burst in his cortex. But whatever else happened he knew that at least once more during his life he was going to be free and at peace with himself. "Yessir, but just to be on the safe side, you mind telling me what I'm volunteering for before I do it?"

There was a chuckle on the other end of the line. "Christ, what a pushy kid you've become! Pretty much the same thing as last time, only this time you're the Operations Officer, and we're working for the 'Studies and Observations Group'." You could hear the quotes when he said it. SOG had changed it's name from Special Operations Group to 'Studies and Observations Group' for "security." Like nobody would figure it out. "I'm taking over an operation at Ban Me Thuot. It's the old Omega, but now it's called Command and Control South."

"Same mission, but, like, over the fence."

"In a manner of speaking."

"I'm your boy."

"Okay, you'll get your orders in about three weeks.

Chapter Twenty

"You're going to what?" She should have known there was something wrong. He was home before eight o'clock. He had stopped and picked up a pizza and a bottle of burgundy, and a big salad. But she was tired and wasn't thinking. Then he hit her with it."

"McLeod called today."

"She looked up. Happy that the baby was asleep. Tired, but doing well in her classes, barely hanging on, but coping, and enjoying the wine and the pizza. "Yeah, what did McLeod want?"

He was grinning, and it went all fiendish in the candlelight. In that moment she knew it all, knew what McLeod wanted, knew what Neil's answer had been, what the result would be, knew in that moment how much she loved him, in spite of the fact that he was a fool, maybe because he was a fool. Twisted as it was, he had something worth dying for, and that made him the most alive person she had ever known.

"I'm going back. McLeod got a new project, and he wants me to be his operations officer. It's a captain's slot and he wants me to take it as a junior first lieutenant. Senior captains would kill for this job. Hell, majors would take it for the experience."

Something turned in her. She loved him, but she was going to have to close herself off from it to survive, and she wasn't sure it would ever kick in again. "So," she said coldly, "you've been married less than a year and you're the father of a new baby. But McLeod called, and without even talking it over with me you put my life and Lauren's life and your life in jeopardy. Just like that.

"A few weeks ago you were talking about getting out of the army."

There was anxiety in his face. He was trying to explain carefully. He wanted so badly for her to understand, and she never would. It was like a rejection of everything that was right or made any sense. It was not as though he had nothing else to live for. She loved him; he loved her and the baby. It was not as though the fate of the nation was at stake and the whole country was behind him.

"It's not what you think," he said. "We're miserable here. I hate this job and the hours. You're killing yourself commuting. It'll be a desk job. My life won't be as much at risk as it is on the grenade range here at Dix. I'll be able to get out right after I get back, and at least I'll live long enough to do something neither my father nor grandfather did. I'll make captain."

She was…she felt eviscerated, outraged. "You'll make captain…you'll be in a desk job…and then you'll get out. Neil, you're such a fool if you believe that. And a bigger fool if you think I believe it. You'll be on the ground in the jungle a week after you're back in Vietnam, one way or the other."

He slapped the table and his face clouded over with anger. "The ops officer doesn't do that," he said. "At the most I'll be up over it with McLeod in his C&C ship."

She started to cry, hot tears welling up from nowhere, because she knew she would raise her baby without a father, as she had been raised mostly without a father, and Neil had been. It occurred to her that if the Bible was right and the sins of the fathers were visited on the sons, yea and unto the sixth generation, then this curse had three more generations to run in Neil's family. She was glad her baby was a girl and couldn't go to West Point or fight a war.

She bit off, "How many times did you tell me McLeod flew into the shit to pull you and Shoogie out of a hot LZ?"

This time he really did look stupid. "Once or twice," he muttered sheepishly.

"And you were one of twelve teams. That's some desk job."

He shrugged. "Yeah, well, I owe him I wouldn't do this for anyone else."

"You owe him, but I think you owe Lauren and me more."

She had never seen him look so sad, just beat down and whipped. "Yeah, you're right," he said. "Okay, I'll call him tomorrow and back out of the deal."

Angrily she said, "And hate me for the rest of your life. No, if you want to do it that badly, go ahead and do it." When she said it she was pleading in her mind, Dear God, just this once let him, just this once, think of his family first, and not himself or the army, or his buddies. He couldn't be going to Vietnam to be with his buddies. Most of his buddies were already dead.

His face lit up and shone; he grinned like a boy caught with his hand in the cookie jar, and then told to have as many as he wanted, the big oatmeal jobbers with the chocolate chips. "You mean it? Christ, baby, that's terrific. I knew you'd understand."

A solid iron gate closed in Juliana's heart.

Chapter Twenty-One

Kicked back on the rear two legs of his folding chair, greenbacked G.I. memo book braced on his knee, Neil watched the briefing officer, his assistant. He thought about his insistence that he would come home after a year in a nice safe desk job, and Juliana's insistence that, as McLeod's Ops officer, he would spend half his life flying dangerous helicopter missions.

So far they'd both been right. He'd been spending ten or twelve hours a day in the TOC and four or five in the air. He'd averaged a new cluster on his air medal every two or three weeks. He probably hadn't gotten more than five consecutive hours of sleep in the eight months he'd been here, except for the R and R in Hawaii…and there he hadn't been able to sleep either.

He and Juliana had had some fun, but she'd seemed distant. Hell, he knew why; she'd written him off.

He wasn't worried about it. If he lived through this he'd win her back. He could finish college and grad school on the G.I. Bill. It was hard for Neil to visualize himself as a civilian, but after Ft. Dix he couldn't see himself in the peacetime army either. He was going to have to find or make a place for himself in the world.

Neil's mind wandered as the lieutenant laid out the plan. He was thoroughly familiar with it. It was his plan. The only difference was that Mike Loden, who had been slotted to lead the task force, had been shot down on an aerial recon the day before, and there was only one captain left qualified to lead the mission—Neil Thompson.

That was why he was sitting here in a tiger suit, taking notes, rather than standing up front in a crisp suit of faded green jungle fatigues, tapping the map with a pointer, and trying to sound like he knew what he was talking about.

Within the preceding twenty-four hours, RT Jackhammer had been pinned down by an NVA company they had stumbled upon. The NVA were guarding a truck park. Jackhammer managed to break contact, but they hadn't been able to hold an LZ and they were on the run with two indige KIA and one American wounded.

McLeod had quickly scrambled an extraction team of five choppers, plus his own C&C ship. Neil had seen it many times now, sitting in the left door of McLeod's C&C when the new STABO rigs, replacement for the old McGuire's, pulled a team out of the hole. If Shoogie'd had a STABO he would have been solidly locked in the rig and still had his hands free to fire. Neil smiled mirthlessly. Shoogie would have still bled to death from the severed artery in his leg, but they would have got the body back. Such a comfort for his mother, if he'd had one.

But they got the team out, and the One-Zero offered to lead them back into the truck park. McLeod accepted.

Neil quickly assembled a Hatchet team of 34 Indige and six Americans, built around three augmented recon teams, led by the Intelligence Officer, a captain. The captain had flown over the area and been blown out of the sky by a 12.7 mm Soviet anti-aircraft machinegun, and Neil stepped in over McLeod's objections to lead the force.

The object of the game was to go in, hit the truck park, blow the trucks, whack as many Gooks as possible, and get the fuck out.

Colonel McLeod sat to Neil's right, sucking in every word of the lieutenant's briefing. He was less than thrilled to have his Ops Officer leading an assault force, and had flatly refused Neil permission to command the force when the subject was first broached.

"Sir, goddammit," Neil said, "look at what's here. Major Thoreson's forty years old and hasn't been on the ground since '62. He fought VC in IV Corps, and that's no preparation for this. The One and the Four are admin officers; they don't know shit about ground combat. You send any of those officers and you'll lose men that will live through this op if I take it."

"Maybe so," McLeod mused, "but what about the people I'll lose in the next four months if I lose my Three and have to break in a new one."

"Sir," Neil insisted, "A, I don't intend to get zapped this trip, and B, you're the tactical genius here. If you have to break in a new Three, you'll have to put in some longer hours, but you won't lose any more bodies."

McLeod gave Neil a long, thoughtful examination. "You're right that you're the best man for this job. You're not right about my tactical wonderfulness. I need you here, and you'd be very hard to replace. But okay, you have the command."

They both knew that if this mission went well Neil would get another Silver Star, and if it went very well he'd get a DSC. Barring any subsequent major fuckups that would almost assure that Neil would retire a full colonel if he chose to stay in.

But he'd just about decided to get out of the army after this tour. He'd lived to make captain, and that sort of made up for the disgrace of being thrown out of West Point. He'd even lived to see the West Pointers themselves disgraced in the eyes of most of their countrymen, just for being in this war. The peacetime army was out, so why had he come back to Vietnam, and why did he want to run this raid?

Simple enough, he thought. Just to crank the adrenaline up to a high keening shriek and ride it. If you died at such a moment it meant nothing, because everything after this would be an anti-climax anyway.

But why spoil a perfect moment by worrying that it wouldn't last forever.

When Shoogie whistled in from three hundred feet, still fighting, something had turned in Neil. He had been good before, technically good, but now he was better, because now he cared only for the mission. It didn't matter if the mission was a bummer in a losing war. The mission was all, Zen satori, the way that could not be named, above and beyond. In the mission was a state of grace.

He looked at the men who were going in with him, six Americans, two with each element of the patrol. The three senior were old line Special Forces NCOs, two of them on their third tour in Vietnam. The other, Les Nelson, had been in Laos with White Star, then spent '67-'68 chasing Che in Bolivia. They were the world's best warriors, bright and hardheaded, totally one-pointed in their dedication to the mission, scathing in their contempt for anyone whose dedication was less than their own.

Neil thought that, for the most part, the officers of Special Forces were pretty good, way above average, but the NCOs, particularly the older ones, were magnificent.

His admiration was slightly tempered by the fact that they agreed with him so totally.

They sat crisp and clean in this late morning briefing before infil. They wore clean, worn tiger fatigues, the trouser legs not bloused, as they would be if they were staying in camp, shirts not tucked in either. They sat on G.I. folding chairs, scribbling call signs and coordinates in their green issue memo books, making grease pencil marks on the plastic bags wrapped around their maps, faces intent. The lieutenant finished his spiel and it was Neil's turn.

He got up, all eyes on him.

"Once more over the concept, gents," he said. "Last light infil at three separate LZs, so Charlie thinks it's three recon teams, or one and two decoys. Link up on the ground in the morning, move eight klicks, blow the trucks, kill all the Charlies we can, leave a beacon so the Air Force can blow the shit out of anything we don't. As always, if you can take a prisoner, do it. Any questions?"

Les Nelson's hand went up and Neil nodded. "Sir, any last minute intel on the defenses on this truck park."

Neil shook his head. "Nope, the unit here is the 312B Division, which has an estimated strength of about four thousand troops spread out over a ten-klick grid square. That's why we're moving on a compass azimuth. We don't want any contact before we hit the park. We anticipate anywhere from three to twelve trucks in the park, with their crews, guarded by probably a company. Hundred enemy max, probably no more than sixty."

Les nodded. "And thirty-six of us."

Neil nodded. "We have the element of surprise," he said. "And if they're not surprised, wave your beret at them. They'll be demoralized."

That got a laugh, a nervous guffaw. Everyone here knew the odds, knew that in a conventional operation it takes a battalion, three companies, to successfully knock one company off a hill. They were attacking with the ratio reversed, and without the objective being prepped by artillery or air. What they had going for them was, as Neil had said, surprise. The enemy were deep in their own territory, and in a place even the bombers couldn't find. It was a rare unit that could maintain a continuous state of alertness for month after month with no significant enemy activity save the occasional recon team one or two ridgelines over.

Neil glanced at his watch. "Okay gents. I now mark 1402 minus fifteen seconds…ten seconds…five seconds…hack. We'll rendezvous at the pad for final equipment check at sixteen hundred. Colonel McLeod would like to say a few words.

McLeod stood up in the back of the room and strode, limping slightly, his mangled leg in a dropfoot brace, to the podium. Neil was struck by how much the little colonel had aged since their first tour together almost three years before. He still had a tight springy body, the body of a man of thirty, and the face of a man of sixty. His true age was forty-eight. This job put the miles on you. One of Juliana's classmates had guessed Neil's age as thirty-three about two weeks after his twenty-fourth birthday.

McLeod stepped in front of the podium. He faced them and stood with his hands on his hips, clean and starched in green jungle fatigues, high and tight white sidewall haircut a couple of inches long on top, like a WWI German general, neatly trimmed moustache on an old face with pop eyes. McLeod wasn't hitting the juice this trip like he had last time, and his eyes had cleared, but as they'd cleared they'd become sad, with deep purple rings under them, and something else in the eyes themselves. They were the eyes of someone who knew and accepted the full range of beauty and horror in the human condition.

"All right, gentlemen," he said. "You have a difficult mission, but the plan is sound and you're the best people to carry it out. I don't want any heroes. Follow the plan and watch your ass. You're more valuable to us than that truck park is to them, so we don't want to lose anybody. Be careful, do your job, accomplish the mission, and get back. That's all."

They rose and filed out to make their last minute equipment checks and make sure their Montagnards were up to speed on the plan. As they left McLeod gestured Neil over.

"Yessir?"

Neil looked into McLeod's eyes, at the permanent grief that lived there. The colonel clapped Neil on the shoulder. "Good luck, m'boy."

"Thank you, sir."

Neil was puzzled. McLeod looked like he'd wanted to say more, volumes more, but he'd closed with this banality.

* * *

There was no barrier on the ground marking the boundary between Vietnam and Cambodia. It didn't matter very much because no Vietnamese or Cambodian civilians lived there, at least not on the border of Darlac Province, Vietnam, and Mondul Kiri, Cambodia. What Neil saw was a rolling tangle of green. But there was no question which country their objective was in. It was, by the most conservative estimate, thirty klicks inside Cambodia.

Neil sat in the door of the chopper; his cravat tied in a headband, its tails whipping in the rotor wash. He was concerned because he wasn't afraid. He'd been on enough of these missions to know how he should feel. The old adrenaline should be raging in his system so strongly that he'd barely be able to keep a lid on it. He should be sitting here wondering how he'd ever been conned into this. But that wasn't happening. He sat calmly, hands in his lap, as he watched the jungle below. He could feel a stirring of excitement, but not the raw raging fear of the old days with Shoogie, nor even the deadly calm that had come with command.

His map was open in his lap and he effortlessly followed the progress of their flight, river on the right, peak to the front, LZ to the left front, Intruder One's LZ to the direct front.

"Intruder Two breaking off, zero five out from Lima Zulu."

"Roger, Intruder Two," his own pilot replied. He too was a captain, flight leader, the other two choppers flown by warrant officers. The LZ for Intruder Three was ahead, but much closer than Intruder Two's. They should all be on the ground within two minutes of each other, disappear into the bush, and link up in the morning.

"Lima Zulu looks clear, goin' in," said Intruder Two. There was nothing on the radio for a moment, then, "Okay, the team is out, and we're taking ......heavy fire."

Quickly Neil got to his knees and leaned forward, just in time to see the chopper keel over on its side and burst into flames, down in the little hole in the trees that made up the LZ. He shoved the earpiece off his left ear and grabbed the handset on his PRC-25 backpack radio from Nolan, who held it behind him. "Ax one-zero, this is Electric Six. How you? Over." Henderson's voice came back dead calm. "Taking heavy fire from the treeline, Six. Got one 'Yard KIA, two WIA. Over."

"Can we get this chopper in to reinforce? Over."

"Dicey. Over."

"Fuck dicey. Is it possible? Over."

"It's possible. Over."

"On the way. Break, break. Screwdriver one-zero, this is Electric Six. How copy? Over?"

"Got you loud and clear, Six. Over."

"Roger. I'm goin' in after Ax. Get Covey and get some jets in here, *macht schnell*. Over."

"Roger, Six, Screwdriver out. Break, break. Covey, this is Screwdriver one-zero..."

Neil handed the handset back to Nolan, put the headphone back over his ear and keyed the intercom mike. "I'm goin' in after Ax. Take us into Lima Zulu Two. Over."

The pilot turned, gave Neil a hard look, then said, "I'll come in just over the trees on this heading, drop you off between Two and the fire, and back the fuck out. Got it?"

"Roger that," said Neil. "You're a brave and noble airman."

"I'm as big a fucking idiot as you are," said the pilot, and dropped straight down for the jungle like a WWII dive-bomber. He flared about a hundred meters from the LZ and about two feet over the treetops. Neil heard limbs hit the skids as the chopper skimmed in.

The pilot flared again, none too gently, behind the wreck of his burning buddy, and Neil dropped to the ground. Heat from the burning wreck was scorching. Neil ran across the charred smoking grass, catching a quick glimpse of the melted co-pilot in the left seat as he passed. His men fanned out around and behind him as their helicopter pulled pitch and bolted out of the hole, momentarily taking all the incoming with it.

Neil flopped behind a pile of brush and reached for the handset. "Ax, Electric Six. We're on the ground; where are you? Over?"

A different voice came over the radio, a bit shaky, but holding it together. "Ax One-one. Three zero degrees from the LZ, five-zero meters in the brush. One-zero's down. Taking heavy fire. Get here quick if you're gonna do any good. Over."

"On the way. Out."

Neil was up and running, barely conscious of the rounds impacting around him. He heard a cry from behind, and one of the 'Yards went down. Two of the others grabbed the casualty and dragged him along as they ran into the brush. Neil entered the jungle, running and dodging, suddenly crouched because now he could see the incoming from the way the foliage was snapping. He skidded in beside Ax One-one, a young sergeant named Redmond. "They're all around, right?"

"Yessir."

Ax One-zero, who had been a one-one on the old Theta project when Neil was, lay on the ground with a pressure bandage on his head, no color in his face. Neil figured he had about an hour to get him out or he was gone. "Bring your people in tight," he told Redmond. "I'm gonna put air in all around here. Clear?"

"Yessir," Redmond said, as he started moving at a crouch to get his people in as tight as he dared. Meanwhile the recon team with Neil fanned out a bit and began pouring fire into the jungle, attempting to put a curtain of jacketed lead between them and the enemy. Neil reached for the handset again. "Covey, Covey, this is Electric Six. How long on that air? Over"

"Six, Covey. I estimate zero-four, I say again, zero four minutes. Can you hold out? Over."

"As opposed to what?" Neil snapped. "Yeah, we'll still be here, one way or the other. Over."

"Roger that. Out."

Nothing to do but hunker down and shoot back. Neil whipped his CAR-15 over his head, untied the cravat he'd used as a sling on infil, and started scanning the trees for targets. Very quickly he spotted the abrupt snapping of the foliage that told him where the bullets were coming from.

His people were good, and they were in a tight perimeter, so Neil didn't have much directing to do. Every time he spotted where some firing was coming from to his immediate front he poured a short burst toward it.

Christ, they were close. He fired a burst of two at a wicker helmet not fifty feet from him. Jesus, where was the air?

"Electric Six, this is Driver One-zero. Do you want us to reinforce? Over."

He picked up the handset. "Driver, this Six. Lemme check with Covey. Over."

"Roger, out."

"Covey, this is Electric Six. How long on the air? Over."

"Six, one minute. Over."

"Roger, Covey." He paused to pour a burst into the trees. "Wave Screwdriver off. They're close and all around, so I'll pop smoke when the fast movers are on station. Just lay it to within fifty meters all around. Acknowledge. Over."

"Roger Six. I copy fifty meters all around. Over."

A dull roar broke over the horizon, followed by a flight of giant killer darts the size of railroad engines. Neil's heart lifted as the air was filled with power. American power. He reached for the grenade on his harness and pulled the pin. "Popping smoke, Covey."

"Roger, Six. I see six smokes. What color? Over."

"Purple. Over."

"I see two purples. Over."

The firing had risen to a crescendo.

He grabbed another grenade and threw. "Popping another smoke. What color you see? Over."

"I see one yellow and one red. Over."

"We're the red. Put your ordnance all around the purple and the red. Over."

"Roger. Out"

Neil dropped the mike and changed magazines. Auto fire snapped over his head and B-40 rockets fell behind him. His upper left arm was bleeding. He'd felt nothing and had no idea how bad the wound was, but it wasn't gushing and he had no time to check it. He noticed that Hansen, the radio operator, had picked up some more shrap too. His right arm and face were peppered with it. A couple of the guys around him in tiger suits were lying still. One of them was missing half his face.

Neil felt a sharp slap on his right shoulder and looked to see a charred and ragged hole in the sleeve of his tiger shirt. There was some blood, but not enough to worry about. He tested the arm by firing a burst and now he didn't even bother to aim, because he was as likely to hit something as not.

The high roaring shriek of the jets changed pitch as the flight began its ordnance run. The roar was all around and Neil saw the fins deploy as high-drag 500 pounders dropped into the jungle around them. True to his instructions the Air Force put them in close. Neil buried his head behind the brush as the explosions burst and his ears hurt and rang with the impact. He felt a burning on his leg and looked to see a jagged piece of smoking steel buried in a fold of his trousers.

Neil had no idea how long the air attack lasted. Looking at his watch never crossed his mind in that maelstrom of explosions and shrieking steel. Brave leader, he cowered with the rest, and lay still amid falling and smoking metal that had mostly landed, he hoped, in Mr. Charlie's neighborhood.

The smell of cordite that hung in the grainy white smoke drifting across their perimeter was overridden by oily black smoke, reeking of gasoline, and the temperature rose another twenty-five degrees. Neil didn't care. He was alive and they weren't.

Suddenly it was still. The temperature slowly fell back to its normal maybe 105. The smoke settled a bit. There was no firing and the jets had gone. Slowly Neil stood and looked at the jungle, the matted, fecund, growing jungle. Somewhere a monkey whooped.

"Sir! Sir?"

Neil came back to real time. He held out his hand for the handset, at the same time making a quick visual check of the perimeter. He counted three Montagnard dead and one American. He didn't see anybody who wasn't wounded to one degree or another. "Intruder, Intruder, this is Electric Six. You better get us the fuck out of here before Charles comes back. Over."

"Roger, Six. Intruder on the way. How mark Lima Zulu? Over."

"Panels and smoke," Neil replied.

"Roger, I understand panels and smoke."

Neil flipped the panels out of his pack and walked to the clearing to set them up. Men all around were moving with him, most carrying dead and wounded.

"Electric, we have your panels. Over."

"Roger," said Neil into the mike. "Popping smoke." He threw the grenade and bilious yellow smoke streamed into the clearing.

"I have yellow smoke."

"Roger that. Bring 'em in."

The first chopper flared and settled over the panels.

"Saddle up, Goddammit!" Neil bellowed. Almost everyone moving toward the choppers carried someone either wounded or dead on his shoulders.

"Wounded on the first chopper. Dead on the last," Neil hollered. Nolan nodded.

"You take the first bunch out, Nolan. I'll bring up the rear."

"Sir..."

"Sir's ass. Get on the fucking chopper."

The last of the wounded were on the first chopper, and it lifted off just before the second settled in. Neil was left with a pile of six dead and one guy, Staff Sergeant Ackerman, to load them with, plus the chopper crew chief who jumped out and joined them. He picked up the first stiff and it came apart in his hands. Firing broke out again on the perimeter and there was nobody manning the perimeter to return it. Therefore, very soon, hordes of khaki-clad motherfuckers would come pouring out of the woodline and it would behoove them to be elsewhere when that happened. Neil grabbed an arm and flung half a dead Montagnard on the chopper. Fuck the other half. He piled in two more stiffs and helped his sergeant load the heavier dead American. He paused briefly to zing a burst at the first wide-eyed dickhead to emerge in the clearing. He bellowed, "Let's Go!" and hitched his ass onto the chopper just as it lifted off.

Firing picked up from the perimeter as Neil and his one sergeant poured fire into the treeline, as did the two doorgunners. The door gunners fired long bursts, and rounds impacted all around Neil. This appeared to be his charmed moment because none of them hit him. Then the engine started smoking and the tail rotor lost power. The ship began counterrotating, away from the spin of the main rotor. Neil watched as the chopper slowly spun and the trees rose. Then the Huey went in, tilted, and crashed down through the top branches. Neil pushed off and grabbed a branch that fell about twenty feet, where he lost it and grabbed for another. Slowing his fall like that he almost managed to make it down uninjured, but his last slip threw him against a right-angled root and pulled his back.

First he tested to see if he could move at all. Then he slowly picked himself up and moved a bit. He was in pain, but not unbearable pain.

Meanwhile the chopper had moved, screeching and jerking, breaking up as it slid into a break in the trees to the ground about fifty meters away, in a little bare patch that was almost a clearing. Slowly and painfully he limped toward the helicopter. Flames licked the back of the fuselage.

Approaching, he could see his sergeant sitting to the side of the helicopter, his left leg bent at a bad angle.

The fire on the chopper wasn't large, but it was spreading. And as he approached he saw the pilot in the left seat move and heard a groan. Neil tried to pick up his pace and pain shot through his lower back. But the flames were spreading and if he was going to do anything for the pilot he was going to have to get there. "Fuck a bunch of pain," he thought, and forced himself, grimacing as he lurched forward. He pulled open the pilot's door and saw a young face, saw that the kid was bleeding from gunshot wounds in the chest and side, saw the panic in the boy's eyes, saw that his legs were pinned under the control panel, the metal bent. Maybe two or three guys in good shape, with plenty of time and a couple of jacks, could unbend it.

"Sir! Sir!" the boy said, his eyes pleading.

"Look!" Neil exclaimed, and pointed at the right door, over the dead pilot. Desperately the boy turned his head and Neil shattered his helmet and stopped his brain with a two-round burst.

Strange to do what you knew was right, and know you'd never be able to live with it.

For the second time that day Neil almost lost it. If he had not had a man he could possibly save he might have wandered off in the jungle until the NVA found and killed him. After killing that kid he would probably never get another decent nights sleep again, and his dreams were filled with enough rent flesh as it was.

He hauled himself over to the man with the broken leg. "How bad is it, Babe?"

Ackerman looked up at him and grimaced. "Wouldn't be no big deal if we was anyplace else. What you oughta do is leave me and get the fuck out. I won't let 'em take me, but I can sure take a bunch with me."

"No," Neil said. "I've lost all I'm losing today. We either make it together or we don't make it. You got any morphine. I got no time to splint that leg."

Ackerman winced and fumbled in a spare ammo pouch for a morphine syrette. He jammed the needle straight into his leg and squeezed the tube dry, hooking the needle into his pants so if he ever did see a medic it would be clear he'd had morphine.

It would take a while for the drug to take hold, and Neil had no time to wait. He quickly rigged a sling for his CAR-

15 with his cravat and hung it across his chest. Then he bent to pick Ackerman up. Ackerman screamed as the ends of his legs grated together and Neil screamed as his wrenched back cramped all the harder. Ackerman moaned and laughed a harsh grating laugh. "Ain't this a bitch," he said.

Neil didn't reply. He hurt like seventy-five motherfuckers; he was near to fainting. He busied himself making sure he had a fresh magazine in his weapon and three grenades where he could get them quickly. Round in the chamber, selector on full auto. "Brace yourself, Don. We're going for a walk," he muttered. Ackerman whimpered as he took his first step. Neil was trying to walk as gently as he could, but he was hurting and the terrain was rough. He concentrated on not stumbling, but he also had to scan the jungle for the NVA he knew would be coming. Ackerman was right, this was a bitch. Neil calculated the odds against them living another ten minutes as about fifteen to one.

Ackerman slowly settled down as the morphine hit him. Neil wondered if it would have been better if he had taken a shot too, but, bad as the pain was, he was okay as long as he had something else to think about, and right now there was plenty of that. He saw flickers in the bush. He should drop to the ground, but he'd be ruined if he had to pick Ackerman up again.

Pith helmet, and the doofus little shit hadn't spotted him yet. He seemed to be alone, and Neil wished he had Shoogie's old silenced K. He took the Gook out with a two-round burst and thought about dropping Ackerman and splinting his leg with the kid's carbine, but he was up and moving and he better stay that way.

More of them would be coming soon. He quit walking the trail and started moving from one thick tree to another.

Not exactly stealthy woodcraft. Not exactly Natty Bumppo there, old son, he thought, and became aware that his thought processes were not honed to a diamond point. He was drifting. Think about Gooks. Think about sight alignment, sight picture, breathing and trigger squeeze. He did exactly that and killed two more, as they rounded a curve in the trail. He would not have been surprised if they had simply spun 180 degrees and started marching back the other way, like the bear in the shooting gallery with the glass lens in his arm that you had to hit with a beam of light from your rifle. But they didn't do that. They fell to earth and died.

Gotta get away from this trail, he thought.

Drifting, drifting from tree to tree, Ackerman bobbing on his shoulder, barely conscious now, from shock and morphine. Under the weight it felt like somebody had put a white-hot anvil in his lower back.

How was he doing this? He wasn't running on empty here; he didn't know what he was running on. Maybe pride, maybe instinct, maybe just training.

He paused beside a tree. The clearing was ahead now, and choppers still orbited.

The Gooks were thicker near the LZ. One of them should get lucky and kill him, but it wasn't happening and he continued his march toward the LZ.

As he got closer the light became brighter as the trees thinned, and oddly enough the firing fell off. Then he realized why as he heard a long br-r-r-r-p from a minigun, and recognized the sound of a Cobra overhead, mixed with the sound of the circling Hueys. Looks like all he had to do was get himself and Ackerman out on the LZ without being turned into hamburger by friendly fire. He let his CAR-15 dangle from its improvised sling and held his strobe aloft, walking out into the LZ.

Some little gerbil with an RPD started bullets toward him, but the Cobra took him out with a belch of fire from a minigun.

He had one smoke grenade left, a yellow one, so he popped that and lobbed it into the clearing, standing there with his dozing sergeant draped over his back like a cape.

Suddenly no one was shooting. Except for the clack of rotors it was quiet, then the Huey broke over the trees, flared and settled, door gunners opening up on the treeline. Neil walked forward, not even ducking under the blades this time, not hurrying. Unbidden, a feeling of elation started to rise. Not yet, he thought. We're not home yet.

The crew chief grabbed Ackerman off his shoulders. The pain in his back faded to something almost bearable, a dull throbbing ache, and he turned to hitch over the door of the chopper. The crew chief screamed, "We've got to get out of here!" grabbed him under the armpit and dragged him into the chopper. He was barely on board when the ship lifted. The feeling of elation became a strange mixture of exhaustion, resignation, and exaltation. The air seemed suffused with it, a soft golden glow. The ground dropped away and became a green tangle.

A stream of green tracers arced out of the jungle toward the ship. He leaned back and watched, seeing at the last moment that they were headed straight for him.

A freight train hit him and he fell back into the chopper. He felt cold; he was looking through a small opening down a long deep-red tunnel into a world on the other side, sea green and unimaginably wild and stormy. They were all waiting for him there.

Epilogue

Doc McLeod awoke in pain, and in unfamiliar surroundings. The pain was nothing new. He'd been in pain, or stupid from drugs for much of the past twenty-two years. The unfamiliar surroundings were his room at West Point's Thayer Hotel, a bit Spartan, but comfortable.

Gingerly McLeod eased himself from his bed. Don't whine, old boy, he thought. Get up, get dressed, get something on your stomach. Then you can take *three* of your lovely white pills and feel like Samuel Taylor bleeding Coleridge.

His prescription painkillers eased his pain, but they also turned him into an idiot. Today, though, he had nothing to do but watch a parade and shake hands. Today was the day Lauren Thompson graduated from West Point.

Lauren had invited him, and on her advice he'd booked the room over a year before. He wondered if he didn't perhaps know the girl better than her mother did. Juliana had not been so forewarned, or at least had not heeded the warning, nor had Thalia, her grandmother, the Madame Secretary.

The pain in his leg was fierce this morning, probably because he'd spent all day yesterday in airports and on airplanes. When he was teaching, military history and political science at the Military College of South Carolina, the Citadel, he had to accept a certain amount of pain to stay sharp enough to think on his feet. But not today.

He worked himself off the bed and grabbed a cane, ignoring the leg brace until after his shower. He limped, wincing, into the bathroom, highstepping to keep his bad foot from dragging. Hooking his cane over the basin, he examined himself in the mirror. After thirty years in a crewcut he now had a nice head of curly brown locks, just a little gray at the temples, and a neat professorial beard with a lot of gray in it.

With razor and scissors he shaped and trimmed his beard. Cane and the pain pills aside, he worked to keep himself fit. Hatha Yoga exercises, which he called "stretchers" to his cronies, kept his body supple. He'd been off the booze for twenty years. At sixty-two, pain and all, he looked younger than he had when he retired from the army thirteen years before.

He showered quickly, wishing for a continental breakfast in the room, not because he was hungry, but because the pills tore his guts if he took them on an empty stomach. He limped back into the room, eager to get his brace on and quit limping. He pulled a pair of jockey shorts over the long pucker of scar on his leg, a pair of tan, pleatless slacks over that, brown oxfords and the brace.

He selected a blue buttondown shirt and a Special Forces regimental tie, which went hideously with it, put a small enameled replica of the Distinguished Service Cross ribbon in his lapel, and slipped the blazer on. Pretty sharp for an old fart, he thought, checking himself in the mirror.

Looking good, but hurting, McLeod headed down to the coffeeshop to lay a base for his codeine.

After some toast, a boiled egg, and three of his little white lifesavers, he sat over another cup of coffee and the paper, feeling his mood improve and his I.Q. drop. He was waiting for Juliana, who liked him in spite of political disagreements, and Thalia, who he suspected held him responsible for her son's death.

He supposed he could wait out front in the lobby. After all, Thalia…Jesus, the things that had happened to Thalia since Neil bought it. She'd married Hobart. As far as he knew Thalia was still supporting Hobart's ex in the sanitarium. Then Hobart died and she inherited his seat in Congress, then won another term, then been appointed Secretary of Housing and Urban Development, and a goddam good thing for him it hadn't been Education. Well, the woman had wanted a career, and she had one; a career, a condo, a limo, and three cats.

Thalia and Juliana had stayed the night in New York, Thalia at the Plaza, Juliana--despite Thalia's invitation to join her--at a small, inexpensive, but quite nice little place, at least as she had described it, called the Gorham. But she had accepted Thalia's offer to ride in the Secretary's limo, and he had accepted their offer to pick him up at the Thayer.

He was trying to read the *Times*, but his thoughts weren't on the news. He had kept track of Neil Thompson's family through Juliana, through correspondence, and their professional association. They were both professors of political science, and met once or twice a year at conferences.

When women were admitted to the Academy he made sure Juliana knew that the children of Medal of Honor winners were entitled to an automatic appointment. He had no children of his own, and took an interest in Lauren's upbringing, counseling by correspondence, recommending books.

But he hadn't actually met Lauren until the previous summer. He'd been doing research in the Ft. Benning Library when Lauren's class went through jump school. He had wondered about the propriety of horning in on what he assumed would be a family occasion.

But, as it turned out, neither Juliana nor Thalia had realized the significance of this particular three-week course, and had not attended. So McLeod had done it up brown, shaved off the beard and gotten a regulation haircut so he could wear the uniform, worn all his decorations, and pinned Neil's wings on her in formation.

Blood wings, your first wings, are a treasured talisman, seldom worn, kept separate. For her to have her father's blood wings for her own was extraordinary.

He'd taken her to the Club for a celebratory drink. “The wings were Neil's," he said. "Thalia tossed all his father's army stuff out, and Neil was afraid Juliana would do the same. He wanted you to have his blood wings, and asked me to keep them for you. But he couldn't have known you would actually wear them. The army didn't have women parachutists then."

"Do you think he'd be proud?" she asked eagerly. She was a freshfaced kid, peaches and steel. "Or was he a chauvinist? I guess they all were in those days."

McLeod laughed. "He'd be proud. If I ever knew a guy with an affinity for strong women, it was your dad."

Returning from his reverie, he folded the paper under his arm and rose, a pugnacious, scholarly man with a wry twist to his mouth and the limpid eyes of a mystic. He went into the lobby and gave the desk clerk the paper to put in his box for later, then gimped upstairs to the men's room to wash the newsprint off his hands.

Juliana entered the lobby from the street just as he came back down.

Very nice, he thought. Juliana had never taken care to be beautiful, she just was. She wore pretty much the female version of his costume, blue skirt, tweed jacket, plain blouse with a bow, highly polished oxford loafers. Her hair was still long, but she had it piled up in an artful way, not so tight as to appear severe, not so loose as to appear...loose. Easy to tab as a college professor; not so easy to tab as someone who had taken LSD, or had crabs. "Howdy, Doctor," he said.

"Hello yourself, Colonel...Doctor. Which do you prefer?"

"Your worship will do nicely," he replied. "I've become a Bishop of the Universal Life Church. When Lauren gets married I'm going to officiate." He returned her hug and bussed her cheek. He thought back for a second to the pissed-off feisty kid she'd been when he first saw her through an alcoholic haze. He had liked her then and he liked her now.

"Big day, huh?" he said.

A pained look crossed Juliana's face. "A *highly* ambiguous day," she replied.

McLeod laughed. "Her rebellion. She chose a perfectly respectable career that her mother can't abide."

She gripped her purse tightly. "I keep thinking that if Neil hadn't...had lived, she wouldn't romanticize the military. If she'd grown up on army posts she wouldn't want to have anything to do with it."

McLeod was fairly sure that Neil would have gotten out. The peacetime army wasn't for him. And he was equally certain that if Neil had stayed in, Juliana would have left him. Juliana was her own woman, and her world was the university. Life on an army post would have killed the thing in her that Neil loved. "I wouldn't be too worried about it," he said. "She'll probably finish her obligation and get out. I don't see much future in the army for a bright kid like her these days."

"Right now," said Juliana, "she wants to fly helicopters."

McLeod got a quick chill; the girl wasn't fooling around. But he shrugged. "Narrow career field. Just reinforces my opinion that she'll get out."

Juliana looked worried. Aside from style she was the same person she had been when they met, except for a few crows feet around the eyes when she smiled, and brow wrinkles where she frowned, as she was now.

"She owes them five years, Colonel. In five years of flying helicopters for the army she'll be an instructor. She'll fly the border in Germany, and, my God, that could still go up. She could fly combat troops on drug raids in Peru, or get blown up by some terrorist in an officer's club. She could get killed in some unimaginable war in the Mideast. This is my baby we're talking about."

McLeod grimaced. "Equal opportunity," he said.

She gave him a disgusted look. "She doesn't need to prove she's as good as any man. I want her to do something sane, and prove she's better."

They exited the front door of the hotel. Waiting in front was a limo, the driver dressed in a dark suit.

McLeod escorted Juliana into their car and painfully angled himself in after her. Thalia Norton Thompson Crane sat back in the corner, in a pink suit that reminded him of the one Jackie Kennedy had worn the day JFK got shot. It was different, but he didn't have the vocabulary to describe the difference.

"Good day, Mrs. Crane," he said. He would never be at ease around this woman, or any woman like her. To his mind they were the knuckle-rapping nuns of his childhood.

"Colonel," she said, and extended her hand.

He shook it, and there was a long silence that would have been awkward if he had expected more.

"Colonel McLeod is of the opinion we should be proud Lauren has struck a blow for feminism," Juliana said.

Thalia snorted. "Really," she replied. "I would be more proud if she had struck it in another venue."

"This would have pleased Neil, I think," McLeod mumbled. He sat hunkered on the pull-down seat across from Juliana and Thalia, watching the emerald lawns and gray stone fortress buildings of the Academy go by outside, backwards.

Pleased, he thought, Neil would have been ecstatic. Lauren's graduation was a vindication of his life.

The limo pulled to a curb adjacent to the parade ground. The chauffeur came round and opened the door for Thalia. She alighted briskly and surveyed the scene before her with obvious hostility. Without question she hated the military, its trappings and procedures, and anybody who had anything to do with it. He hoped she would chill that when they talked to Lauren after the parade. Juliana scrambled after her, and blinked warily at the great expanse of the Plain, the crowd gathered at the edge.

McLeod painfully dragged himself out after them, into the light. The throbbing in his leg told him to boost the dosage. He leaned his cane against his leg, reached in his pants pocket and took a couple of pills from their little plastic bottle, worked up some saliva and swallowed. The taste was foul, but soon his leg would stop hurting and his mood would improve.

The crowd was middle-aged and middle class. There were the middle American couples who'd encouraged their children to go to West Point for the scholarship, hoping the kid would get out after five years and come home. There were career lieutenant colonels and their wives, who'd pushed their sons, so the next generation would be part of the army elite and have a shot at some stars.

McLeod fell in beside a short, whipcord sergeant major from the 82d, in full uniform, with bloused jump boots and a cocky maroon beret. "Big day, Smaj," he said.

The little man eyed him suspiciously, then smiled a hard and twisty smile. "Too right, sir," he said, and McLeod returned the smile; the man had tabbed him as a retired SF light colonel with one glance.

"McLeod, right?" the sergeant major asked.

"All day."

"Thought so. I seen you in Saigon once when you was with Theta. I run the message center at Camp Goodman."

McLeod searched his face to see if he could connect this hardened veteran of Vietnam and Grenada with the kid clerk he must have been then, but there was no way.

"My kid's gonna graduate from this place this afternoon, and I'm gonna be the first NCO to salute him."

McLeod grinned. "What are you doing with the money?" He referred to the custom that army second lieutenants give the first man to salute them a dollar.

"I'm gonna frame that motherfucker and hang it higher than all the rest of my shit."

McLeod turned just in time to see General Frenier heaving down on them. "Ah, McLeod," he said. "Good to see you."

McLeod was astonished. He actually did seem glad to see him.

Frenier was thin and a trifle stooped. He wore a plaid jacket that fit his neck loosely. He wore a DSC ribbon in his lapel, like McLeod's, and underneath that a tiny enameled replica of his brigade's patch. McLeod thought wearing more than one pin on one's lapel was tacky, but some old soldiers just couldn't keep themselves from pinning badges to their clothes.

McLeod had to admit though that he had a helluva tan.

"Sir," he said, extending his hand. "It's good to see you also." And in some funny way it was. Bereft of power Frenier was a monument to the Peter Principle, but one for whom one had a residual respect.

McLeod remembered him as a colonel, that he had been a considerable success. He was firm, but reasonably fair. He did his work efficiently. He looked right and talked right. It was only when he got stars and a command, had to improvise, that he started making big mistakes.

What the hell, he thought. Us beat-up old farts have to stick together. Who else do we have? And for that matter, who else would have us?

"How's the leg?" Frenier asked.

McLeod smiled. "I haven't won any marathons lately, but I get around."

Frenier smiled back. "I read your book on the Ia Drang campaign. Solid piece of scholarship."

"Thanks," McLeod said. He'd worked for four years on that book, and so far it had sold 2,318 copies, but it had boosted his academic reputation. He'd been working for six years on a book about SOG that he hoped would do better.

"What brings you to this, sir? Anybody graduating?"

Frenier shook his head. "No, a bunch from my class get together every five years at graduation. I lost my boy at Khe Sanh. Thought you knew that."

"No sir."

"He went to the Naval Academy. Didn't want to ride on the old man's coattails. I was proud of him for that."

"Yes sir." McLeod noticed for the first time that the old man's eyes were rheumy; either that or he had teared up at the mention of his son. Maybe both, but in any case it was time to change the subject. "Where are you living, sir? You didn't't' get that tan up north."

General Frenier shook his head. "San Antonio," he said. "I moved out there after Deborah died."

Oh fuck, McLeod thought. There isn't anything right to say to this guy.

"There wasn't a goddam thing for me in Minnesota after she died, and I ached all over in the cold, so I moved to San Antonio. Plenty of retired generals to play golf with. We're like that goddam brigadier in Beetle Bailey."

McLeod smiled at the image of a quartet of General Halftracks in plus fours and little plaid caps with fluffy balls on top, creaking around nine holes before they headed for the bar.

"Been thinking of writing my memoirs," said General Frenier. "Maybe we could get together on that."

McLeod's heart sank, as it did every time some former hero or master strategist made that same suggestion. You can't tell them you don't want to do it, that you have topics until hell freezes, because they'll take it personally. Time for a diversion. "Sir, there's a couple of people here I'd like you to meet." He would have used the sergeant major, but he had moved away to chat up a buddy from XVIII Airborne Corps. Very quickly McLeod shuffled General Frenier over to Thalia and Juliana. "Neil Thompson's mother and widow, sir," he muttered under his breath as they walked.

"Thompson? Thompson?"

"He set up your recon platoon."

"Ah, Lieutenant Thompson. Disgrace as a cadet, but he did a good job for me in the brigade."

"Captain Thompson, sir. He won the Medal in '70. He was my Three."

"Won the Medal! Very good."

"Posthumously. His daughter's graduating here today."

"Daughter?" The general's eyes shot up. "God help us!"

He led General Frenier over to Thalia and Juliana, who stood primly in their suits, clutching their bags, watching the alien culture unfold before them. They were chatting amiably enough now. He thought he heard Thalia say,"…seen so much polyester…" but then he lost it.

Ladies," said McLeod, "I would like to introduce General Frenier, the man who gave Neil his commission. General, may I present Neil's mother, Mrs. Thalia Crane, the Secretary of Housing and Urban Development, and Dr. Juliana Kos, Neil's widow."

Frenier shook both of their hands, and smiled a charming rictus. "Doctor" he said. "At my age it's a pleasure to meet someone who can give free medical advice. And Mrs. Crane, did I understand that you're a secretary?"

Thalia gave him a look that would have melted steel, but it went right past Frenier.

"I'm afraid I'm not that kind of doctor," Juliana said. "I'm a professor of political science. Colonel McLeod and I are colleagues."

"They say it's my prostate," Frenier went on, "but I'm going to get a second opinion. Too serious not to."

Juliana looked helplessly at McLeod. He was saved by a rhythmic tapping sound.

The band marched out to drumsticks tapping on rims. They were a band of army enlisted men, led by a warrant officer. They didn't wear the cadet uniform, or the regular army uniform, but a kind of hybrid, regular army blue cut like a cadet uniform, with white trousers. The crowd hushed as things started happening.

The cadet brigade staff marched out, seven upright young people in white pants, gray tunics with brass buttons and shakos. They marched with drawn sabers, and light flashed off them as their arms swung in unison. The cadet brigade staff marched to their position in front of the reviewing stand, down to the right about a hundred feet from where the four of them stood.

The brigade marched out and took its place on the field. The cadet adjutant marched from his place beside the brigade, marched in the tightassed rapid strut prescribed for adjutants, and barked his stream of incomprehensible orders. Then the adjutant quickstepped to his position with the staff. The First Captain of Cadets bellowed, "PASS IN REVIEW!" or possibly, "Piss in your shoes!" a variation generations of adolescent cadets had found terribly funny.

They marched by, and they looked good, lines straight, nobody out of step. Not the best he'd ever seen, but really good.

The cadets marched off the field and McLeod and the ladies stood awkwardly, until Frenier excused himself to go talk to some of his retired general cronies.

Since Lauren was a cadet captain, they didn't have to wait for her to put up her rifle. She would march her company to the barracks, dismiss them, sheath her saber, and meet them where they stood for a few minutes before her next activity, whatever it was.

They stood making awkward conversation. Over half the crowd drifted away after the parade, people who were in no way related to the graduating cadets. What was left, sitting in the bleachers, or standing by the bleachers, were little knots of expectant middleaged people, some accompanied by teenagers, all waiting for their young man, or young woman, to show.

And then they came from around the far barracks, so straight that even the short ones looked tall. The sun gleamed on the brassoed rows of buttons running up either side of their tunics, and the brims of their shakos rode so low on their noses that from a distance shadows hung over their eyes. They were not in formation, but where they walked in groups they walked in step, an arms length apart, the legs of their white trousers scything in unison, *hawn-tup-thrip-fawp*. The light from their scabbards caught the sun and left afterimages like exclamation points in McLeod's eyes.

The cadets broke out of their informal formation and headed for the little knots of waiting parents.

For a second McLeod had the feeling that Lauren was Neil, advancing toward them at 120 steps per minute, ramrod straight. He clearly remembered Neil as a cadet, same open trusting face with a hint of larceny at the corner of the mouth.

She stopped in front of them, looking boyish, female at the hips and bust, with the girl cadet's Dorothy Hamil haircut. She halted directly in front of McLeod and rendered him a perfect saber salute, the guard just in front of her lips, blade extended skyward, shining. The only decoration she wore was Neil's blood wings.

Technically, in civvies, he didn't rate a salute, nor should he render a salute. He nodded and said, "Congratulations, Lieutenant, welcome to your father's world."

BRENTWOOD PUBLIC LIBRARY